THEIRS TO MASTER

MIAMI MASTERS BOOK SIX

BJ WANE

BLUSHING BOOKS

Published by Blushing Books®,
a subsidiary of

ABCD Graphics and Design
977 Seminole Trail #233
Charlottesville, VA 22901
The trademark Blushing Books®
is registered in the US Patent and Trademark Office.

BJ Wane
Theirs to Master

EBook ISBN: 978-1-61258-833-9
Print ISBN: 978-1-61258-901-5
Cover Art by ABCD Graphics & Design
v1

CHAPTER 1

"*S*lide two more down here, Paige."

Paige Wilcox lifted her hand to the two cops sitting at the other end of the bar. "Coming your way, guys." Sticking a frosted glass under the beer spigot, she pulled the lever, drawing their refills one at a time. Old-fashioned rock-and-roll resonated amid the chatter of personnel from Fort Lauderdale's cop shops and the courthouse. Here at The Precinct, their favorite hangout, officers unwound with their counter city law enforcement employees from the D.A. office, and she loved the camaraderie and good-natured teasing of the Friday night crowd.

"Heads-up," she called before sliding first one then the other glass down the shiny mahogany bar top. The guys caught their drinks with appreciative grins, one sending her a two-fingered salute she returned with a smile.

She'd picked up the part time evening job bar tending in the club a year ago and loved every minute she spent mixing drinks and shooting the breeze with the city's finest. After her rebellious teen years, her grandmother would have never believed Paige would one day be on friendly, first-name terms with a good number of cops and district attorneys. A stab of longing pierced her heart. She would give anything if both her mother and grand-mother were still with her. Even though she had as yet to do something noteworthy with her life, she would have liked them to know she'd outgrown the trouble she'd been so fond of getting into.

Fighting back a yawn, Paige wiped down the bar and tossed the damp cloth into a Rubbermaid box under the counter before squatting to do a quick liquor count. As Mel, the owner and other bartender often said, it wouldn't do to run short. She'd been up since 5:30 a.m. taking care of the two dogs she was pet sitting before heading out to clean the first of two houses. While she enjoyed not answering to anyone but herself and her clients running a cleaning business, the monotony of doing the same, tedious chores day in and day out, and working six days a week was starting to get to her. It was time for another change, something she'd gotten good at in the last thirteen years. As with men, she'd grow bored and the urge to try something new would creep up on her, leaving her powerless to resist. Unlike her twin sister, Penny, Paige couldn't be bothered with going to college, and she'd never find satisfaction with an eight to five job, stuck in an office with a demanding boss.

"You want to pop up and get our usuals, sugar?"

Paige jerked, banging her head under the counter. *"Tiddle twat!"* she muttered, rubbing her crown as she pushed slowly to her feet. The amusement in that familiar voice curled her toes, and her body reacted with the same warm flush she experienced every time she heard it. Before turning around, she tried to guess which Carlson brother this time had her fired up on all cylinders with just a few words. Her libido never failed to jump-start when either man spoke to her, or assessed her with those dark brown eyes, or brushed his fingers against hers when she handed over a drink. The fact she experienced the same quick reaction to both men always left her flustered, and just a touch annoyed.

Pivoting, she aimed a smile at Troy and Trevor seated at the bar, her heart tripping at the sight of the two hottest city employees it'd been her pleasure to serve. *Man candy. Hunk on a stick. Drool worthy. Panty melting. Hunk a hunk a burning... lust.* Every one of those euphemisms described the brothers who were so far out of her league they may as well be on the moon. Unlike a few other regular patrons, neither man had ever made a pass at her, never even hinted one might be interested in rolling around on her bed for a few nights of hot, sweaty sex, but that hadn't kept the fantasies from giving her more than one sleepless night.

"Tiddle twat? I must have really startled you." Trevor, the one with the sexy face scruff and a twinkle in his eyes cocked his head and winked.

"You did. I didn't hear you come up." Glancing at Troy, she nodded, stretching her smile. "Detective. You two haven't been by in a while." Setting two glasses on the bar, she reached underneath and grabbed the whiskey. She knew her customers.

"Too many bad guys to track down. How have you been, Paige?" Troy asked, his low, deep voice sending a delightful shiver down her spine. If she didn't know better, she'd think he wanted an honest answer and would care about her reply instead of delivering polite platitudes. Both men possessed that way about them, talking to you as if you mattered, as if they really wanted to hear what you had to say. Maybe that accounted for her continued, uncharacteristic responses to the brothers whenever they came in.

"I'm good, thanks." Adding sour mix to the whiskey, she dropped in a slender straw and slid the drinks over. "At least we're not being plagued with a serial killer, or some other such cretin. And spring break is still weeks away, so you don't have those headaches to deal with yet." A shadow crossed both men's faces, Troy's jaw clenching when she joked about a serial killer. "Have I missed something in the news?"

"No, nothing you need to worry about," Trevor soothed. Of the two, he seemed to be the easygoing one. He often expressed more of a sense of humor than his brother. "No openings for us on your schedule yet?"

3

They'd asked her to put both of them on her waiting list for cleaning services a few months ago, but so far Paige hadn't been able to squeeze them in her busy schedule. She may flit from job to job, but with every position she'd held, she'd given her all, ensuring the only complaint when she moved on would be over her leaving.

"Not yet." She shrugged. "What can I say? My clients stick with me, I'm that good." She drawled the double innuendo on purpose, just to tease. Both men carried a hard edge vibe that went against her independent nature regardless of the attraction she couldn't seem to control, but that never stopped her from wanting to get under their skin the way they had hers.

"You don't say." Troy glanced askance at his brother. "It looks like we'll have to keep waiting, bro."

"By the time she squeezes us in, our places will be a mess. Might take extra effort on her part to... please us." Paige's face warmed from Trevor's wink. She could swear there was a hidden meaning in their innocent remarks, but their expressions remained bland and just a touch too innocent.

To settle one craving, she plucked her half-eaten candy bar off the shelf and bit into the nutty chocolate, enjoying the pleasant wave of awareness their presence and chummy banter always produced. If she couldn't have one in her bed, she could damn well enjoy their company.

"I see you haven't given up your penchant for junk food." Troy eyed the candy with an amused tilt of his lips.

She yanked her arm back with a mock frown. "Mine."

"You should try sharing sometime, sugar. You may like it." Reaching across the bar, Trevor chucked under her chin before the two of them slid off the stools and strode through the crowd to join a table of three others.

Damn, those two have nice butts. Paige gave herself a moment to enjoy Trevor's lingering touch and the flutter of her now damp pussy as she watched them walk away without a backward glance. It wasn't just her they showed little personal interest in. The brothers had a way of politely rebuffing the blatant attentiveness and obvious advances of the clinging women who frequented the bar. Troy adeptly sidestepped one woman's groping hand as they waded through the crowd, but Trevor winked at her with that amused curl to his lips. Yeah, Paige acknowledged with a sigh, there was good reason the cop groupies refused to give up on getting one —or both—men's personal attention.

With a sneer toward the woman, she got back to work. The crowd dwindled around 10:00 only to pick up again close to 11:00, clock-out time for the second shifters. Some nights she could swear every cop in the city stopped by The Precinct on their way home. By the time 1:00 am rolled around and Mel announced last call, she was more than ready to get off her feet and head home.

"Fill 'er up, baby." A glass slammed on the bar and Paige shifted down to pick it up, avoiding direct eye contact with the one guy she couldn't stomach to be around.

Her teeth snapped together to control her irritation at the way Detective Mike Evans called her baby with a snide connotation and insolent look in his inebriated blue eyes. Everyone knew the twenty-five-year veteran Vice cop drank too much, and of the trouble it caused him on the job. But thus far, no cops showed an inclination to cross the ever-present blue line, not even for a reckless, rude screw-up like Evans.

"Mike, I think you've had enough. Hitch a ride home with someone or I can call you a cab." Mel intercepted her reach and snatched the glass off the counter.

"Fuck you, old man. I'll say when I've had enough. Besides, I was talking to this sweet piece of flesh, not you," Mike leered, drawing several scowls from those close enough to hear him.

Before Paige could let loose with a scathing reply, Mel held up his hand and Mike's partner, Aaron Devri, strolled up. "Let's go, man. I'm beat and my old lady will have my hide if I don't get home." Gently taking Mike's arm, Aaron steadied him before Mike shrugged him off with a belligerent glare.

"I've been telling you you need to get that broad under control. No man should kowtow to a fucking cunt." Mike switched his glare back to Paige. "That includes you, Wilcox."

Paige's red-head temper rose to the surface, and she leaned her hands on the bar top, leveling the jerk with a steely eyed glare. "No woman would be dumb enough to have you, so if you think—"

An ominous low voice cut off her irate retort. "Apologize to the lady. Now."

Paige shuddered at the underlying menace in Troy Carlson's tone and piercing cold look he leveled on the other cop. Trevor, the usually affable District Attorney, stood behind his brother portraying the same incensed expression. She didn't need either man coming to her defense, but surprise kept her from saying anything—that and, okay, the touch of pleasure from the macho interference on her behalf. What woman wouldn't be thrilled when two hunks came to her defense?

"Fuck you, Carlson. I don't need this shit. I'm outta here." Shrugging off his partner's reaching hand, Mike stormed toward the door.

"Sorry, Paige," Aaron said, his eyes as apologetic as his voice as he flipped her a quick look before following his partner.

"He needs to quit babying the guy," Trevor growled before his face softened as he addressed Paige. "I don't blame you for snarling at him, sugar, but don't bait him. That man's been a ticking time bomb for far too long."

Now, why was it a generic endearment coming from him could give her a warm fuzzy, yet hearing something similar from an asshole made her itch to send his balls up into his throat? And that was *before* Evan's crude comment.

"No one talks to me that way, but thanks for stepping up." Turning to Mel, she added, "You too, boss."

Mel squeezed her shoulder. "You're a good girl, Paige." He delivered a scathing sweep of the few people still lingering. "You all know I support law enforcement a hundred percent, but I'll ban

Evans the next time he gets out of line. Now, clear out, I'm shutting down."

Paige breathed a sigh of relief when everyone filed out without complaint, the Carlsons the last to go with a final nod to her. "Well, wasn't that fun?" Reaching under the counter for her purse, she slung it over her shoulder and lifted a hand to Mel. "See you tomorrow night."

"You take care, girl."

She didn't let him see her small smile as she went out the back door leading to the rear employee parking spaces. A cross between a father figure and boss, Mel always protected her back. It was the way Troy and Trevor had jumped to her defense that rattled her. They weren't steady weekend customers like some others. According to Mel, they usually stopped in during the week. In the year she'd been bar tending, she doubted they'd come in on a Friday or Saturday night—the only nights she worked at The Precinct—more than a dozen times. But their rare appearances didn't negate her response. In fact, it always surprised her how quick her happy places sat up and drooled when the two of them walked in after she hadn't seen them in weeks.

Sliding into her beloved, 1960's renovated Jeep, Paige tried shoving aside the conflicting emotions of irritation at her continued absorption with the two men and pleasure from the way they'd interfered on her behalf. She swore at the way those two kept her waffling on tenterhooks of pulsing awareness while never exhibiting an ounce of interest in her other than as a casual acquaintance. Her unrequited fascination with the brothers had grown slowly since meeting them shortly after starting the bar tending job, escalating in recent months until it had become her sole source of pleasure, and frustration. Experience reminded her it wouldn't do to read more into the way they'd come to her defense other than as men who weren't afraid to stick up for what's right.

Driving home, she thought back over the past few months, and could pinpoint the exact time frame she'd begun itching for something new to break up the tedium of her life. Hitting thirty hadn't fazed her as that milestone birthday did some people, but thirty-one? That birthday four months ago sent her into the dumps so deep, she'd failed to pull out of the discontent riding her. *Over thirty* sounded so much worse than simply *thirty*, and seemed to emphasize the fast track to nowhere she'd been on during her twenties, something Rick, her last boyfriend, enjoyed pointing out to her. Splitting with him eight months ago had been the highlight of the past year.

Paige turned into the driveway of the small Cape Cod house that was the only inheritance she and Penny would ever receive. Funny, she mused as she parked and slid out with an exhausted sigh, she could think of nothing she could desire more than the small home she'd grown up in with her sister, mother and grandmother. Although she'd felt for Penny when her sibling had returned to the house one morning with a swollen black eye that ended her three-year relationship with a controlling man Paige never could tolerate, she relished the time they'd been living together again. Because of her sister's insistence, Paige reined in her anger on Penny's behalf and agreed not to enlist her cop friends' help in pressing charges against the jerk. But, damn, that had grated.

Tiptoeing past Penny's room so as not to wake her, Paige took a moment to greet the two greyhounds she enjoyed pet sitting before stripping out of her jeans and tee bearing the bar's logo on the way to the bathroom. A few minutes later, she slid into her double bed and succumbed to exhaustion, two pairs of dark brown eyes following her into sleep.

～

"Let it go, bro," Trevor advised.

Troy slid Trevor an askance look before returning his gaze to the road, eyeing the streets with a cop's scrutiny as he drove the two of them back to their twin townhomes in the Pensacola Lake condo complex. "You were just as pissed as me when Evans spouted off."

"Sure, but sitting over there simmering won't help. I doubt Mike is long for the force, especially if he keeps drinking. Let him do himself in. I did enjoy seeing Red's temper flare. The girl doesn't have a reputation for backing down."

Interest colored his brother's voice and Troy sent him a sharp glance with a snort. "Forget it, Trev. Paige would skewer you with those silver eyes alone if you tried anything with her." But Troy had to admit, he'd fantasized more than once about stringing up the pretty bartender and keeping her at their mercy for a few hours. Indulging in ménages with Trevor and a willing submissive was his favorite recreational sport, but one neither of them attempted to play with a vanilla partner. He enjoyed bantering with Paige's feisty, independent nature, but preferred a meeker bed partner to ease the stress of his job as a cop.

"Think of how much fun it would be to tame her," Trevor replied with a grin that hinted at the image in his head.

"Work, not fun. Unlike you lawyers, cops get down and dirty on the streets to bring you the bad guys. I need a tamer diversion during my time off."

"Admit it, Troy. You've wondered what it would be like to have her sandwiched between us," his brother prodded in his usual, affable way. "The girl's got legs up to her delicate neck and can mix a damn fine martini. What's there not to like?"

"I didn't say I don't like her," he returned as he pulled into their complex. The two-story condos circled a one-acre lake that was home to a slew of Canada geese the residents enjoyed feeding. "Or that she isn't attractive."

"Or you haven't indulged in a few fantasies of your own? You forget how well I know you."

Troy forgot nothing, notably the close bond he shared not only with his older-by-a-year brother, but with five other guys. After pummeling on each other the first few days spent at a summer camp for juvenile delinquents, their small group discovered they'd all come from troubled childhoods. Even though their circumstances were as varied as their personalities, they'd formed a bond that still held tight today, twenty-three years later, and had expanded to include a shared interest in BDSM proclivities.

Parking in the drive adjacent to Trevor's, he cut the engine of his Tahoe and grabbed the door handle. "Last I checked, I've still got a dick, so, of course I've thought of her. Now, get out of my vehicle, moron." Trevor's deep chuckle echoed in the quiet dark, and Troy smiled at his only sibling over the hood. "Get your mind off Paige and onto Crystal. She's free for the afternoon tomorrow and wants to meet us at the marina." The BDSM decked out mega yacht their multi-millionaire friend, Zachary Allen-Vancuren had surprised each of them with a deed to guaranteed bondage fun galore to satisfy their needs and their privacy.

"Good. That way we can stick around afterward and drum up a game—that is, if any of the others can pull themselves away from their girls," Trevor returned.

Trevor, Troy knew, found their friends' recent decline into commitment a good thing, but he was still on the fence about the recent changes within their group. Not that he didn't adore their women, he did. They complemented each of the guys to a tee, but regardless of their obvious happiness, neither he nor Trevor were inclined to follow suit. He worried those newly formed relationships would soon result in splintering the tight circle the seven of them had formed together.

Troy nodded. "With any luck, they'll wear them out and the girls will be only too happy to leave us to a few hands of poker while they recuperate. I'm heading in. Catch you tomorrow, Trev."

"Later, bro." Trevor lifted his hand as he strode next door to his identical house.

CHAPTER 2

"*R*ough night?" Penny asked as Paige stumbled into the kitchen the next morning. "I let the dogs out and fed them already." Pouring a cup of coffee, she dumped a healthy dose of rich creamer into the cup and wrapped a napkin around a chocolate-glazed donut. Carrying them over to the small table nestled under a window that offered a view of the backyard, she set the sugar feast before Paige, saying, "You look like you can use this."

Paige expelled a lusty sigh of appreciation before sipping the piping hot brew. "God, thanks, sis. You know me so well." What she didn't know was the reason Paige slept until almost 10:00 a.m. had been due more to the erotic dreams plaguing her sleep than the long night at the bar. She really needed to get her mind out of the gutter and off the Carlson brothers.

Penny took a seat opposite from her and Paige looked up to see her worrying her lower lip. "Uh, oh. What's up?"

"You know me so well," she mimicked with a smile that didn't reach her gray-green eyes. Taking a deep breath, Penny blurted, "I'm going to the club tonight."

Setting the cup down, Paige regarded her sister with a solemn gaze and worry gnawing at her insides. Penny's split with Jim

Bates, whom she'd met at a BDSM club, had come just a few weeks after Paige had ended her affair, and the two of them had been celibate together ever since. It wasn't that Penny was ready to end the long months of self-denial that bothered her; heck, Paige was more than primed to relieve her own sexual frustration with a man instead of a vibrator. But she'd never understood what attracted a woman to turn herself over to a man's sexual, dominant control, or the need Penny claimed to possess for the lifestyle.

"After the abuse you suffered from Jim, the asshole, I'm surprised you want to seek another similar relationship. I don't like it, Penny, but you knew I'd say that."

"Yes, and I love you for caring so much, but Paige, don't put me down just because it's not your thing, or because you think I'm being careless. Most Dom/sub relationships are very fulfilling, and most Doms don't cross over into abuse the way Jim did. If you'll recall, I left as soon as he did, and have refused all his overtures since." A visible, delicate shudder shook Penny's slim frame. "I'd never go back to him or put up with such domestic abuse."

Paige often suspected there'd been more to Jim's actions than a fist to Penny's face during an argument where he'd accused her of cheating on him. No matter how much she prodded, her sister continued to insist her black eye had been the extent of it, but her doubts continued to unsettle her.

Casting her gaze out the window, she watched the dogs play as she admitted, "I know that. You're one of the smart ones." She flipped her twin a cheeky grin. "I taught you well."

Penny rolled her eyes, returning her teasing smile. "You may be only a few minutes older, but you've always been overprotective." Her look turned sly. "You could always come with me."

Paige's hand jerked at the incongruous suggestion. Setting down the cup, she grabbed a napkin and wiped up the small spill, saying, "Very funny. Can you picture me saying, 'yes, sir,' or kneeling at a guy's feet?"

It pleased her to hear Penny laugh. Unlike Paige, who had

walked away from her six-month affair with Rick without a backward glance or an ounce of regret, Penny had been in a depressed funk over her breakup. Not because she missed the asshole, Paige knew, but because she missed having her needs as a sexual submissive met. She may not understand her sibling's desires and responses to a controlling man, but Paige understood the discontent of going day after day without an intimate connection to someone special. Still, worry over Penny's safety and wellbeing wouldn't release its painful claws from digging into her abdomen, and she couldn't keep from trying one more time to dissuade her from going back to a club and seeking the same type of man.

Playing a trump card she knew was wrong, Paige blurted, "Nana would roll over in her grave if she knew what you planned to do, especially after what happened with Jim."

"Damn it," Penny exploded, her rare temper rising to the surface as guilt suffused her face. "Don't go there with me, Paige. I wasn't the wild child after Mom died, or the one who refused to settle down, go for further education after high school and do something worthwhile for a change."

Pushing back from the table, Paige let her worry-based anger get the better of her even though everything Penny threw in her face was true. "Fine. If you're so perfect, then don't come crying to me if you meet up with another asshole at that place."

Storming outside, she ignored Penny all afternoon, stewing over her own stupidity in bringing their beloved grandmother up, the woman they'd both cherished and would have done anything for until her death five years ago. They both still missed Geraldine, or Nana Gerry as they had called her. Despite her grief over the death of her only child, and her advanced age, Nana hadn't hesitated to keep her two preteen granddaughters with her following their mother's death in a car accident. It had been just the four of them since Paige, Penny and their mom moved in with Geraldine after their father's death in a military accident when they'd been just toddlers, and the void Nana's passing had left continued to press down on them.

Penny left for the afternoon and it was after five when she returned and found Paige sweeping out the garage. She looked up as her sister got out of her car and strolled toward her, a rueful grin tugging at her lips. She always left it up to Penny to apologize first, something else to feel bad about, Paige thought with a burst of irritation.

"If you have time before work, I'll spring for tacos," Penny offered.

"Sneaky, sis. You know my weaknesses and how to use them against me." Paige loved junk food and anything Mexican.

"And you know mine. Nana may not have approved, but I can't change who I am any more than you can. Sanctuary is a reputable club, and I know, or used to know, almost all the members. I'll be fine," she assured her.

"At least you know why I was an ass and tossed Nana in your face. Are you sure Jim is no longer in the city? What if you're wrong?" According to their mutual friends at the club Penny and Jim frequented, he'd hightailed it out of the city after the club banned him for abuse.

Penny shook her head. "I checked with Sanctuary's owner and head Master again. He hasn't seen or heard from Jim since he accepted the offer to open an office in Savannah a month after we broke up. He also assured me Jim wouldn't be welcome at any club in Florida."

Paige refrained, barely, from rolling her eyes at Penny's title of Master. "Okay, I'll trust you know what you're doing, and what you want." Dropping the broom, she threw her arms around Penny and squeezed tight. "I want you to be happy, and safe. You know that."

After returning the hug, Penny stepped back, her eyes misty as she replied, "Same goes, sis. Aren't *you* getting horny yet?"

A relieved laugh burst from her, and she shook her head in amusement. If only Penny knew how she lusted after not one, but two men. Talk about kinky. "I'm holding out for the one who can do a better job getting me off than I can. Until then, I'll continue taking care of my own needs, thank you very much. Give me ten minutes to clean up and you're on. I don't have to be at The Precinct until eight."

"A vibrator can't compare to the real thing," Penny called after her, laughing.

"Maybe not," Paige quipped without turning around. "But it also doesn't order me around."

"STRIP." Trevor crossed his arms and watched as Crystal, a favorite sub of his, slid the thin straps of her sundress down her arms, her blue eyes gleaming with anticipation.

Reaching out to wrap a hand around her upper arm to steady her against the slow rocking of the luxury yacht on the open water, he took a moment to admire her denuded labia when the dress dropped to her feet and she stepped out of both her sheath and panties. The mouthwatering aroma of grilled burgers wafted down from the upper deck where he knew Sean and Jackson were manning the grill. The slight ocean breeze was enough to keep the late February temperature more on the cooler side, but he didn't fret over Crystal getting chilled. He and Troy would warm her up soon.

He wasn't sure when their occasional desire to indulge in a ménage had changed to a steady preference. Not that either of them minded. There was nothing like watching a woman writhing in the throes of ecstasy under their hands, mouths and cocks. If you added in the vulnerability of her bound state, the other sounds of BDSM play resonating around them and the pleasure of sailing on a pleasant afternoon, the gratification couldn't be matched.

Trevor cupped his palm over the soft, plump folds and felt the telltale dampness at her slit. Crystal's nipples puckered, and she released another spate of cream when her gaze shifted behind him to where Zach and his wife, Sandie, still sat behind the helm. "The rest of the gang are upstairs, where we're headed in a minute. You'll like parading around naked in front of them, won't you, sugar?"

Her eyes brightened at the offhand endearment, and he couldn't help remembering the annoyed snap in a pair of dove-gray eyes when he'd called Paige the same pet name. Unlike his brother, Trevor wouldn't mind taking a stab at dominating the feisty bartender. He loved a challenge. Shoving aside the image of that woman, he returned his concentration to the one before him. Releasing Crystal's arm, he yanked hard on her light brown hair. "Answer me."

She bobbed her head in agreement. "Oh, yes, Sir."

"We'll head up then, but you have a long wait before we get to this." With a slow insertion of his middle finger, he teased her clit just enough to leave her frustrated before he tugged her up the spiral stairs leading to the third tier.

The steady drone of the yacht's motor dwindled to a stop as they reached the upper level, which meant Zach and Sandie would join them soon, followed by dinner served on the tables nestled under the covered outdoor kitchen. Towing Crystal toward the center dining area, Trevor spotted Miles already seated with a heaping plate, Hope perched on his lap.

"Damn, are we already too late?" Trevor's reference to the former Martial Arts champion's bottomless eating habit was met with chuckles from the group gathered around the aft of the boat.

"You snooze, you lose," Jackson called out from his stance at the grill. Shoveling a burger onto a bun, he held the plate out to Trevor. "Here. Sean and I wouldn't be dumb enough not to ensure everyone got fed."

"So back off," Miles rumbled, flicking a black, mean-eyed glare Trevor's way.

"You'd think you would be used to our ribbing by now." Troy thumped Miles on the back as he walked by the table to join Trevor and Crystal at the grill. "I see my brother has you ready for us," he said to Crystal before gripping her nape and drawing her mouth up to his for a hard, probing kiss.

She leaned into him with a soft moan until he released her. "Yes, but he's being mean and making me wait for my fun." The brunette reached out and curled her hand over his crotch. "You'll be nicer, won't you, Master Troy?"

Sean, a much more hardcore Dom than the Carlsons, cocked his head, his steely eyes conveying his displeasure with the forward sub, the look belying his mild tone when he commented, "If you were mine, you wouldn't sit comfortably for a week."

"Then it's a good thing I'm not with you," she shot back, her impatient nature spewing forth.

"Enough." Trevor snatched a rubber spatula sitting on the grill sideboard and landed one blistering swat on Crystal's right cheek and then tossed the implement into a bin holding dirty dishes. Reaching for a plate, he handed it to her, instructing in the same cool tone, "Go sit down next to Alessa and see if you can behave with as much respect as our newbie."

Crystal had played with him often enough she knew when he used his rigid Dom voice, he meant business. Turning in a huff, she padded over to the table and plopped down next to Sean's new girl. The pretty strawberry-blonde had been friends for months with the other girls already enjoying committed relationships with his friends. Alessa and Sean's recent pairing after discovering they were just right for each other left Trevor and Troy the last of the gang of seven still playing the field.

"Maybe you better hang on to the spatula," Sean said, his cold countenance thawing when he looked at Alessa. Her lush curves spilled out of the skimpy, bright floral bikini with a thong bottom. No matter how many times Sean had bared her in front of the group, she still found it difficult to expose her round body to people she also socialized with.

"Good idea. Trevor was too lenient." Troy snatched it out of the bin and picked up his plate. "Thanks, Jackson. Are you sticking around when we dock for a game or two?"

"No, Julie and I need to get back. We're driving up to see her parents tomorrow, and you know I have to be well-rested to remain cordial to my future in-laws," Jackson answered with a frown.

"You need to let the past go, bro. You two will be much happier," Sean advised. As a psychologist, he enjoyed mothering them, and dishing out unasked for advice whenever he felt a situation warranted it. They either ribbed him about it or ignored him.

"You stepped into that one, Jackson," Trevor stated without sympathy. He lifted the thick cheeseburger to his mouth and took a huge bite. "*Mmm*, good. Thanks." Saluting him with the burger, he strolled over to join Troy and Crystal.

Can't get better than this, Trevor mused when Zach and Dax and their wives joined them topside and rounded out their group. The banter circling the table volleyed back and forth between friendly gabbing and ribald remarks. He couldn't ask for a finer way to end the week than by enjoying a pleasant afternoon cruise with the best friends a person could ask for, food aplenty to appease one appetite and a naked, willing sub pressed against him, waiting and willing to sate another. He was just swallowing his last scoop of potato salad when Dax had the gall to bring up the one topic sure to sour his mood.

"We haven't heard from our resident abuser in several weeks. Do you still have people stationed in the clubs along the coast, Troy?" The heart surgeon tightened his arm around Krista's waist, pinning her on his lap. She wore his collar along with his ring, and the pleasure she received from their strict, twenty-four/seven, Dom/sub lifestyle always shone in her vivid, blue-eyed gaze when she looked at her husband.

"There are only a few extras planted in the nearby clubs now since people don't have unlimited time to travel on the weekends. All the club owners were warned to be diligent about admitting new members, and advised about his talent with disguises and coming up with verifiable false IDs. One or two have taken it seriously enough to put a hold on new memberships until we nab the son-of-a-bitch." Troy shrugged, but anger toward the man who had been infiltrating BDSM clubs up and down the state and leaving abused, traumatized submissives behind, darkened his eyes.

"Not enough," Miles growled, his jaw tightening with the frustration reflected on all the men's faces.

Three documented victims of the unknown violator had come forward, but everyone suspected there were those who refused to report an assault fearing condemnation for being at such a place. The first case had landed on Troy's desk as lead detective in the Assault Department, and for the past several months, Trevor's frustration had matched his brother's, and the rest of the gang's, over the lack of leads to follow. Whoever he was, he knew what he was doing as, along with the effective disguises and altered IDs, the culprit had managed to keep his back to the security cameras when he'd lured the unsuspecting girls away from a club before showing his true colors. It didn't help he'd scoped out different clubs each time.

"All we can do is hope he'll make a mistake before someone else gets hurt," Trevor sighed before glancing down at Crystal and squeezing her thigh. "Come on, sugar. Let's get our minds on a more entertaining topic." He looked over her head toward Troy.

Troy nodded. "I'm with you. Let's make good use of a lounge."

Crystal followed them over to a chaise that faced the shuffleboard and skeet shooting activities and then sprawled on the padded cushion with a blatant lift of her hips in invitation. The low murmurs of the others dispersing reached Trevor, but he didn't pay attention to where everyone else was heading to play. Neither Dax nor Sean would appreciate Crystal's silent demand for them to get on with pleasing her, but he wasn't as strict as either of them or his brother when it came to the degree of his guest's submission. As long as she was okay with bondage and got off on a touch of erotic pain, he could ignore her greedy, self-absorbed shenanigans.

"Not yet," he chided, moving to the head of the chaise. "Raise your arms."

"Spread your legs while you're at it," Troy instructed from the foot, his frown telling her he wasn't happy with her pout and exaggerated sigh. "Knock off the theatrics if you want us to allow you to climax."

Crystal complied by lifting her arms above her head and shifting her long legs apart so they could bind her wrists and thighs, but never did know when to keep her mouth shut. "You know I'm not into orgasm denial," she snapped out.

"Tell me again why we invited her," Troy groused, this time leveling his scowl toward Trevor.

"She was available."

Troy answered Trevor's simple reply with a tight jaw and a sharp slap on the inside of Crystal's thigh. "I'd be more than happy to bend you over and let each of my friends deliver a few smacks on your ass," he threatened.

Peeking down at her flushed face, Trevor noted the gleam of excitement in her eyes and had to work at holding back from smirking at Troy. They'd both played with Crystal enough times his brother should know she wouldn't find that punishment a hardship. After checking to ensure the cuffs he'd wrapped around her wrists weren't too tight, he pulled off his polo shirt and ran his palms down her arms and over her breasts before grasping both nipples in a pinch.

"Or, I can retrieve a cane from downstairs." The sudden tautness of her muscles and adamant shake of her head revealed her dislike of that particular instrument.

"No, I'll behave. Sorry, Sirs," Crystal answered with as much contrition as she was capable of.

Troy nodded in approval. "Better."

As Trevor began alternating between kneading the plump fullness of her breasts and tugging on her puckered nipples, Troy delved between her labia and pumped two fingers in and out of her pussy, setting up a steady rhythm. Frustrated groans pushed past her compressed lips as they drove her to the brink of orgasm over and over, but stopped short of letting her topple over the final hurdle into a climax.

"Shit!" she exclaimed the third time they pulled back the moment her body strained toward release. "I swear, if you two don't let me come, I'll never join you again."

A smirk curled Troy's mouth as he pinched her puffy, red clit. She screeched at the sharp pain, her perspiration slick body quivering from the need they'd built inside her. "Do something about her mouth, would you?"

The polite way his brother phrased the request didn't fool Trevor. He suspected this would be the last time Troy would agree to inviting this sub to join them.

"Hey, you can't blame me because... *oh!*" she gasped when he shucked his shorts and straddled her chest with his erection clasped in his fist.

Trevor slowly stroked his cock while grasping a handful of hair from behind Crystal's head and bringing her face forward. "Open your mouth, Crystal." He knew he didn't have to issue the order; he already enjoyed firsthand knowledge of her talent in fellatio. But it never hurt to reiterate who was the boss with a sub who had trouble setting aside her independent nature during a scene. He liked a woman who could give as well as take what he dished out, except during sex. Then, he preferred her to take, desired the relationship on his terms—or his and Troy's.

Soft lips and a warm tongue wrapped around his girth, sending a shiver of lust straight down to his balls. He felt her hips shifting under him, her low moan of frustration vibrating down his shaft, forcing him to tighten his grip where he still held on at the base of his cock. Troy's deep chuckle hinted at the torment he continued to heap upon her, the telltale sound of his fingers pumping with the aid of her copious juices giving away her enjoyment of his attention.

Trevor gazed down at Crystal's flushed face, her cheeks hollowing as she pulled up with a tight suction, and another face flashed into his head. Instead of light brown, sun-streaked hair, an image of short, wavy, deep red hair filled his vision, dark lashes closed over sultry silver eyes. The curl of Crystal's tongue under his cap sent a wave of heat gushing through his veins, returning Trevor's full attention to the woman servicing him. He would wonder later why Paige Wilcox's face kept intruding on his fun time.

"That's it, sugar," he crooned, executing short jabs into her mouth. The friction pushed his orgasm up from his balls with small contractions of pleasure, and he braced for the relief of an impending release. "Suck hard now, yes, just... like... that." His hands tightened in her hair and at his base as his climax spewed forth and pleasure spiraled through his body in a torrential deluge of ecstasy.

"About fucking time."

Trevor barely caught Troy's mutter as he pulled with savoring reluctance from Crystal's clinging mouth, his breath still coming in shortened puffs. "Enough," he demanded. "That is if you want your turn."

"Oh, I want," she purred as he swung off the lounge and Troy shifted over her body with his sheathed cock at the ready.

Reaching for his shorts, Trevor watched as his brother thrust into her welcoming pussy and set up a rigorous, pounding tempo that shook the lounge. Yeah, he liked sharing with Troy, whether it was taking a woman in tandem or, like now, relishing the sight of his sibling enjoying the same woman who'd just pleasured him. What more could he ask for than an enjoyable cruise on a pleasant day with the best friends a man could boast having and a woman willing to indulge both him and Troy in their ménage fetish?

CHAPTER 3

C lub Sanctuary

The familiar sound of edgy metal rock reached Penny's ears when she entered the foyer of Sanctuary. Taking a deep breath, she ran clammy hands down the sides of her leather mini skirt before showing her membership card to the receptionist she didn't recognize and signing in. "Thanks," was all she said to the young girl with a pierced eyebrow before placing her purse and shoes in a locker then opening the door into the spacious playroom. Her nipples puckered with the high-pitched cry that greeted her entrance, and it was as if she'd never stayed away these many months. The heavy scent of leather mixed with the pungent aroma of sex tickled her nostrils, the telltale sound of slapping against bare skin overriding the music and murmured voices. God, she'd missed this place, and what she could find here.

Penny hated fighting with her sister, and knew Paige would never understand her sexual, submissive needs. That second part was okay, as long as she didn't throw it in her face as she'd done when she brought up their beloved Nana. It had been easy to forgive her when she remembered how Paige had jumped to her defense, threatening fast retaliation after Jim had made good on his

23

recent threats and taken his fist to her. To her credit, she'd refrained from saying 'I told you so' to Penny following that disastrous night.

Weaving through the crowd, Penny nodded to people she knew or recognized but didn't stop to talk until she reached the bar. Sliding onto a stool, she ordered a Manhattan, something sweet and strong to pump up her nerve. None of the apparatus spread around the room that she could see from her perch were new, and neither was the charged, sexual activity taking place. She used to enjoy spending the first hour or so at the club just watching and socializing, but tonight her stretched, taut nerves kept her from wanting to waste time idling. She craved the snap of leather searing her skin as much as the control of an experienced Dom bringing her to orgasm. A part of her worried the memory of that last night with Jim would return to haunt her, but she refused to allow that possibility to keep her from indulging in the lifestyle she loved.

"Good to see you again, Penny," Master Connor, the bartender, said as he set her glass in front of her. "It's about fucking time you got your sweet ass back in here." The fierce look in his eyes revealed he knew what had happened with Jim.

"Thank you, Sir. It's nice to be back." She took a sip, the blend of whiskey and sweet vermouth sliding smoothly down her throat with a taste of cherry. "No one makes a Manhattan like you, Sir."

"And don't you forget it." He looked behind her and smiled. "Master Damien, look who's returned to brighten the place."

"Penny, welcome back."

Penny closed her eyes as that deep voice washed away her insecurities and replaced them with a wave of pulsating longing. No one possessed a voice like Master Damien. After indulging in one more fortifying sip of alcohol, she braced herself for the full impact of the one Master who had always been out of her reach.

Swiveling on the stool, she looked up, way up, and offered the black-haired, blue-eyed Dom a tentative smile. "It's nice to be here again, Master Damien. I've missed the place."

"Then you shouldn't have let that fucking asswipe keep you away so long." To her utter shock, he held out his hand, a silent invitation to join him in a scene.

Penny had lusted after the owner of Sanctuary since she'd first visited the club as a newbie two years ago, falling in line behind every other sub in the place. Before she'd hooked up with Jim—she refused to gift her ex with the title of Master—Master Damien had maintained a cordial friendship with her, one that hadn't included a drop of personal interest other than seeing to her welfare as a new member of his establishment. After she'd committed to Jim, he'd maintained an even more staid distance.

She wasn't about to turn down such an offer, especially tonight, when she needed an experienced, hard-edged Dom to put her through her paces with no expectations. If given too much time to sit around and think, she feared bad memories would interfere with her goals tonight. Sliding her shaking fingers into his hand, she exhaled when he tightened his grip and tugged her up to follow him without another word. She didn't need a lot of dialog tonight, just someone to take her over until she could put that last night with Jim away for good.

Winding through the crowd, Master Damien led her to a new addition to his array of equipment she'd missed on her quick scan of the room. Penny's heart tripped with nervous excitement as she eyed the Sybian and the large, condom-covered, double penetrating dildo centered on the undulating, padded apparatus. She'd known she needed someone to take her over, but wasn't sure if she could handle such intense sensations after such a long dry spell.

Lifting her face up to his, it took effort to swallow past the lump lodged in her throat before she could admit, "Sir, this might be… a little too much. It's been… a while."

Damien nodded. "Since the asswipe took his fist to you, I imagine. You came here because you know who you can trust, and that includes me. I'm sure you recall the club's safeword: red. Now, strip." Releasing her hand, he folded his arms across his chest, his thick muscles bulging under the tight sleeves of his black silk shirt. The perpetual shadow covering his jaw darkened his already swarthy complexion and highlighted his bright blue gaze.

With her mouth dry and her pussy already damp, Penny slid the thin straps of her simple sheath down her arms and wiggled out of the dress. Left standing in front of him wearing nothing but a silky thong, it only took one heated look from his cobalt eyes to tighten her nipples into even more prominent pinpoints and increase the shaking of her fingers as she lowered the panties. He'd always been a man of few words and a master at getting his point across with a look, which benefitted her tonight. Without giving her a chance to think, or fret, Master Damien clasped her waist and hoisted her onto the apparatus that resembled a gymnastic vault.

"Hold on and I'll assist you. Watch with me."

Grateful for his insight, Penny nonetheless blushed when she grasped the small handle in front of her spread thighs and glanced down. She sucked in a deep breath as he tightened his hands on her waist, lifted and then lowered her onto the phallus one slow inch at a time. A low moan slid past her lips as the lubed, fake cocks inched into her tight orifices, stretching long unused muscles and teasing dormant, sensitive nerve endings back to life. He was careful to ease her down, both of their gazes glued to her crotch, watching as the vibrators disappeared inside her and the way her labia folded around the ridged toy in a welcoming clasp. A shudder rippled through her body when they became fully embedded, her pussy and anus throbbing around the toys, her entire body waiting for his next command.

Master Damien reached up and kneaded her breasts, flicking her nipples with his thumbnails, the small scratches heightening her simmering arousal. "Oh, God... please, Sir..." Her sheath spasmed and gushed, and Penny breathed a sigh of relief when she found herself on the precipice of an orgasm just from his steady, penetrating eyes and hands on her breasts.

"Not yet." Removing his hands, he unclipped the long, thin crop at his waist, his jaw tightening as he ran the flexible, square end over her puckered nipples. "As I recall, you used to enjoy a small amount of pain with your pleasure. Ride the dildos, Penny."

The direct order accompanied a flick of the Sybian's side switch and another searing look as he tapped one nipple, the pinprick of pain and sudden vibrations from the dildos sending a wave of combustible heat straight down to her core. On a gasp, Penny lifted and lowered, each rise bringing on a light stroke of the crop—one across her buttock, the next snapping a nipple, followed by a prickling swat on her inner thigh. Her copious juices caused an embarrassing slurping sound as her gyrations increased. This was what she'd needed, why she'd come here tonight—for someone to drive her to the brink of forgetfulness, someone who wouldn't let her fall into the abyss of painful memories. Funny how being the sole focus of Master Damien's concentration and gaze could accomplish both goals.

Biting her lip against the onslaught, she struggled to remain focused on his stern face while maneuvering up and down, the pulsating ridges of the silicone cocks rubbing along her inner walls, setting fire to dormant nerve endings. A sharp cry spilled from her lips when he tapped her bare folds where they wrapped around the vibrators. The sharp pain ricocheted up her vagina and the small contractions heralding a climax clutched at the invading objects. Her rectum tightened around that phallus, the discomfort of the double penetration giving way to escalating pleasure.

"Now, Penny. Come for me." Master Damien swatted her buttocks again, then again, and again, his hard look and command leaving her no choice but to obey.

Tears rolled unheeded down her face as her body gyrated and exploded with such intense pleasure her vision blurred. Through it all, she managed to keep her eyes on his, his single-minded focus her only anchor to reality as she lost herself in the mindless ecstasy. She didn't remember being lifted off the vault, hardly noticed the soft blanket Master Damien wrapped around her as he settled her on his lap in a comforting embrace. She didn't rouse to complete awareness until he shifted her off his lap with a regretful sigh and whispered, "I'll be right back."

By the time Penny got herself under control enough to get dressed, she knew she needed to leave before she made a fool of herself and begged him for more. Master Damien wasn't a Dom known to scene more than once with a sub, and women found themselves lucky if they were one among his chosen. He'd known what she needed and had given it to her; time to go home and regroup, decide where she wanted to go from here.

~

THE PRECINCT

Paige leaned on her elbows on the bar top and gazed around The Precinct, the crowd small tonight compared to last night. She couldn't pinpoint the reason for her discontent this evening, which added to her annoyance over her uneasy mood. Restlessness didn't bother her if something specific preyed on her mind. But when she couldn't come up with a concrete reason for the disquiet plaguing her, she grew irritable. How could she deal with it then set it aside when she didn't know what 'it' was?

Over dinner with Penny, she'd managed to hide her continued displeasure with her sister's decision to return to the alternative lifestyle that had led to so much grief for her before. The year Penny and Jim were together had been fraught with arguments which escalated after Penny moved in with him during their last two months together. Paige had warned her about his increasing jealousy, begged her to at least move back home and put some breathing room between them. But Jim had been the first man to take Penny under his dominant control and he'd latched on to her so fast, with such effective manipulation, her sister couldn't see past the relief of having her needs met for the first time.

That admittance hadn't surprised Paige as much as when Penny had revealed her craving for the alternative sexual practices brought out into the open with the success of *Shades of Grey*. For the life of her, Paige would never understand how a grown woman could allow a man to control her, not even for sex, or when she'd noticed the undeniable change in her sister after Penny visited the club. Within the first few visits, her mood swings ceased, her general attitude had improved, and she'd seemed so much happier and content. The effects of whatever she'd been doing on weekends were profound, in such a glowing, positive way that Paige, if she were honest, had envied.

Before Jim had revealed his true nature, the worst part of their relationship had been how much Paige missed Penny after she'd moved in with him. They'd lived together their whole lives, and the loneliness of their childhood home had been unbearable at times. She'd never lived with anyone else, never wanted to.

"Oh, tiddly winks," she muttered under her breath, straightening as two regulars sidled up to the bar. Okay, so maybe her relationship with Rick hadn't been as satisfying as Penny's kinky hookups had appeared to be. That just meant he wasn't the right one for her, that's all. Neither was Jake, Wyatt, Asher or Theo who'd come before him. But just because she found more satisfaction with her bedside buddy than with any of the men she'd slept with didn't mean there wasn't someone out there who could rock her world and leave her eager for more. Unbidden, the memory of her body's response whenever the Carlson brothers were within viewing range popped into her head. "No, no, no. Go away," she grumbled while reaching under the counter for a bottle of brandy. The last thing she needed tonight was those two plaguing her thoughts. She had enough with fretting over Penny's decision to foul her mood, thank you very much.

"A couple of Between the Sheets, Paige," Detective Calhoun ordered with his usual, teasing grin as he and his Vice partner, Marshall, stepped up to the bar.

Setting the bottle of brandy on the counter, she turned to lift the triple sec off the mirrored shelf behind the bar, tossing over her shoulder, "As if I didn't know. I've already got you covered." She whisked out two glasses then mixed the detectives' favorite drink comprised of an ounce of brandy, and a half ounce each of light rum and triple sec stirred together with sweet and sour mix. "How are my fave customers tonight?" Both in their late fifties, the veteran cops were among both Mel and Paige's most liked patrons.

"We're good, kiddo. I'd be better if I thought I was really your favorite," Detective Marshall returned as he picked up his glass. "Everyone knows you say that to all your regulars."

"Not *all* of them. I've never told Evans he was my favorite," she admitted with a shrug. "But that doesn't mean I'm not sincere when I do say it."

Detective Calhoun stood up for the other cop. "Mike's been a damn good cop until recently. You know his wife left him. He gets out of line when he's had too much to drink, but otherwise, he's an okay guy."

It didn't surprise or upset Paige that they made excuses for the troubled detective. As a whole, the men and women in blue were a tight-knit group, regardless of personality flaws. Only a few, like the Carlsons, possessed the integrity to speak against a fellow cop when he crossed a line. Another plus in their favor, damn it. It was bad enough to have the hots for two men when neither showed an interest in switching from friendly banter with a bartender into a more personal relationship; she didn't need the reminder of what honorable guys they were.

"If you say so." She wasn't so put out with Evan's remarks last night she would risk alienating her best tippers. "Holler when you're ready for a refill."

"Will do." Marshall lifted his glass in a 'catch you later' gesture before the two of them joined a group in the far corner.

Despite the evening turning busy, the customers keeping her on her toes with orders and refills as well as idle chatter, Paige couldn't shake the uneasiness troubling her. A mild headache developed around 10:30, backed by an increase in her nervous agitation. By 11:00, the pain had blossomed into a deep throbbing that encompassed her whole head. Rubbing her temples, she started to call to Mel she needed to leave early when her phone buzzed and the caller ID lit up with the hospital's name. Dread set off a wave of vicious nausea churning in her stomach as she answered with a catch in her voice.

"Hello."

"Ms. Wilcox, the is the emergency room at Cyprus General. Your sister... assaulted, beaten... severe concussion..."

Stunned, Paige couldn't comprehend the nurse's words, her mind a jumble of disbelief and fear, her throat clogging with the bile that rose from her abdomen. *Not Penny, please God, not my sister.* "I'm on my way," she choked out before stumbling in blind distress against Mel's sudden appearance at her side. He reached out a hand to steady her with a grip on her arm, which helped to ground her and regain her focus.

"What's wrong?" he asked, sharp concern etched on his craggy face.

"I have to go. My sister..."

"Let me get someone to drive you," he insisted without hesitation.

"No, I have to go now. I don't know how bad..." The need to get to Penny overwhelmed Paige, threatened her composure and almost sent her to her knees. The blinding pain in her head added to the overwhelming sense of disbelief and despair.

Mel barked out something and the next thing she knew, several cops were offering to get her to the hospital as fast as their sirens could clear the way. She nodded her acceptance to Calhoun and Marshall, who were the first to reach the bar, and as she settled in the back seat of their non-descript sedan and heard the wail of the siren, her gratitude for the speed with which they got her to the hospital knew no bounds. Her entire body shook with fear for

Penny, her mind jumbled with too many questions and the multitude of abysmal possibilities.

Paige flung open the back door before they rolled to a complete stop at the ER entrance and flicked the two cops a quick look of appreciation. "Thank you. I have to go."

"No thanks necessary. Go." Calhoun waved her on.

Nodding, she raced into the hospital without a backward glance, her heart in her throat as she dashed up to the desk and demanded to see Penny.

The receptionist remained calm in the face of her distress. "Take a seat and I'll let her doctor know you're here."

The compassion reflected on her face and in her tone came close to undoing Paige. "Thank you." Spinning about, she shuffled to the far end of the busy Saturday night emergency room visitors and paced in nervous agitation. The need to see Penny clawed at her abdomen, her fear for her sister a tight, painful vise squeezing her chest. A sense of panic threatened her composure a few minutes later when a nurse led her into a small private room and stated the doctor would be right with her, fearing the delay could mean bad news. When the forty-something doctor entered with the same expression of sympathy the girl at the desk had shown her, Paige sank down onto a chair and braced for the worst.

"I'm Dr. Matthews, Ms. Wilcox. First, your sister is alive, but critical," he hastened to assure her as he took a seat across from Paige. Her vision blurred and her head swam in dizzying circles as relief washed through her trembling body. *Thank God.* "Put your head between your knees if you need to," he encouraged, reaching out to give her hand a comforting squeeze.

"No, I'm fine. Please, tell me what happened." Paige forced the lightheadedness back, along with the nausea that came with it. She needed answers now she knew Penny was alive.

"As I said, she's critical from an assault. You can get the details of that from the police as I don't have that information. Her brain is swelling from several hard blows; I can't tell you whether she hit her head against the building or ground, or if her assailant is responsible, but I can tell you there are no signs of significant brain damage. Her reflexes and eye responses are normal, and she was awake and knew her name, and gave us your name when she came in, which is the good news."

She refused to look away from the doctor's eyes as she choked out, "That means there's bad news."

Running a hand over his chin, he replied, "I've put her in a medically-induced coma until the swelling goes down. We'll closely monitor her over the next few days, and she might need surgery if her brain continues to swell. We need to count on her suffering physical difficulties when she wakes, maybe even memory lapses. But she's young, and appears healthy in every other way, so my prognosis is guarded, but positive. I'm sorry I can't give you more than that."

That was enough, and Paige would be there for Penny every step of her recovery. "You've kept her alive so you've given me everything, doctor. When can I see her?"

"They're settling her in a room now, but as long as I have her under, you can't touch her or speak to her. Her brain needs to rest to heal, and any type of communication would engage a mental response, which could do more damage. Sit quietly with her for a few minutes, then go home and rest. She's in good hands."

Dr. Matthews' assurances went a long way in helping Paige hold it together when she entered Penny's private room and saw her head swathed in bandages, tubes hooked up everywhere, and the beginnings of bruises forming on her face and arms. The steady beep of the heart monitor aided in confirming she was still breathing; without it, her stillness would have terrified Paige. Sinking onto a chair next to the bed, she lowered her head into her hands and let the dam burst, unable to hold back the tears of anguish, terror and rage any longer.

CHAPTER 4

"*A* winning streak's one thing, but this is ridiculous." Zach tossed in his hand with a glare toward Troy.

"No one else is complaining." Troy scooped up his winnings with a smirk.

Once they'd reached the marina, Jackson and Julie had headed back to his rescue shelter and veterinary clinic forty miles out of Miami. Crystal, who lived in Miami, had also taken off, leaving Sandie, Krista, Hope and Alessa to hang out together topside while the guys played a few rounds of poker in the gathering room. Just like the outside decks, the spacious, enclosed playroom with its arched walls and plush, teal carpeting boasted a plethora of apparatus for various BDSM indulgences. After dealing with Crystal's pouts and demands all afternoon, Troy was more than happy to take his friends' money. That girl was a pleasure to fuck, but she could be tiring.

"No, we're just plotting to get even," Dax put in as he gathered the cards and started shuffling. "Revenge can be just as fun."

"Careful, Doc. Our good cop can be a hard-ass," Miles warned, reaching for a handful of nuts.

Trevor grinned at Miles. "Takes one to know one, bro. You should be more like me, easygoing, charming…"

Troy rolled his eyes then bit back a curse when his phone buzzed and he pulled it out to see his precinct's number. He wasn't on call, so the dispatcher shouldn't be contacting him. Unless… He answered then cursed. "Son-of-a-bitch!" Snapping his phone shut, he pushed back from the pop-up table in front of the sofa that curved along the back wall. Rising, he looked around the table and growled, "We've got another club victim."

Their teasing mood vanished in the blink of an eye, all six men as frustrated and angry as Troy over the failure to nab this assailant who'd been plaguing clubs around the state under different disguises and IDs. He'd first struck last fall, and there had been three victims brave enough—or desperate and hurt enough—to report the attack. God only knew how many hadn't come forward and what kind of trauma he'd put them through.

The victims were all fairly new to the lifestyle which, Troy believed, was how the culprit could lure them outside of the clubs without setting up any signals a more experienced sub would heed. These women had only enough time to jump one hurdle in admitting to their submissive needs, and another by seeking a venue to get those needs met before they'd suffered an assault. The degrading abuses this perpetrator heaped upon them had done a number on their self-esteem, not to mention filled them with so much fear, the three he'd interviewed had, as yet, refused to return to the lifestyle.

"Hospital?" Sean asked, his gray eyes flinty. Earlier in the month, Sean had spotted Alessa at two different clubs and hadn't hesitated to step in and offer to tutor her in alternative sexual practices in a much safer way than club hopping. He was the fifth of the gang of seven to commit to one woman and looked damned happy about it.

"Cyprus General. The fucking bastard is back in our town, right where he started. Security found her outside of Sanctuary," Troy answered before turning to Trevor who had already stood. "Ready?"

Nodding, Trevor said with a rare thread of fury lacing his voice, "He broke from the pattern, otherwise we could've nailed him."

Troy shook his head. "Or the pattern we thought he was taking was wrong. Let's go."

"Text us, no matter how late," Zach called after them. Troy lifted a hand in acknowledgement but didn't slow his stride as he dashed out to his unmarked, police-issued SUV and jumped behind the wheel. "Hold on," he warned Trevor when his brother slid in the passenger side. "We're flyin'."

"Just go."

Thirty minutes later, their frustration and anger increased as they listened to Penny Wilcox's doctor describe her injuries before telling them she would remain in a medically induced coma until the swelling in her brain went down. "You can see her, but, as I told her sister, you can't touch her or speak to her at this time. I'm sorry, but my patient comes before your investigation." Without giving them time to respond, Dr. Matthews spun on his heels and returned to work.

"Let's stop by her room anyway," Trevor suggested, moving toward the elevator. "Maybe her sister will know something."

"Wilcox. That name sounds familiar." Troy jabbed the elevator button, chomping at the bit with the need to act. Problem was, there were still no clues to follow up on and no suspects to investigate.

"Paige's last name is Wilcox. You don't think..." The elevator door swooshed open, offering a direct line of vision into the room across from the nurse's station, answering Trevor's question.

"It looks like it," Troy responded. There was no mistaking that bright red hair, or the way the thick waves framed Paige's arresting face and curved under her jaw. As they approached the room, she looked up and his rage rose yet another notch at the devastation reflected in her pewter eyes. He was used to seeing those eyes glitter with teasing flirtation or snapping with annoyance, and his cock's instant reaction to her. His muscles went taut and the tight coil forming in his abdomen reminded him of the surprising rush of anger he had experienced when he'd heard Evans disparage Paige at the bar. The sudden urge now to pound on something or someone on her behalf, mimicked the same reaction he'd felt last night.

She stood and joined them in the hall, the grief etched on her face replaced by fierce determination. "Do you have Penny's case?" she demanded of Troy in a low voice. "What happened? Who did this? I need…"

Her voice broke, and she looked away while Troy rushed to give her the only reassurance he could at that point. "We don't know, but I promise we'll find him." Clasping her elbow, he guided her away from the open door, Trevor remaining quiet and letting him take the lead. His brother was better at giving comfort to distraught women as a general rule, but Troy's recent involvement dealing with the previous victims of this abuser, as well as being in charge of the case, put the responsibility in his hands this time. "Tell me about her, anything you can, like how long has she been going to Sanctuary, and do you know if anyone's been harassing her?"

Paige shook her head and stepped back from them to lean against the wall and fold her arms over her waist. "No. She split from her ex months ago and he isn't around anymore, he's not even in the state. Last night was her first time in that club since they broke up."

Troy pulled a small note book from his back pocket. "I'll need his name, regardless. Were you there with her?"

Her soft lips curled in derision. "Not my thing, Detective. And now look where it's gotten Penny." She gave him the ex's name before adding, "Everyone loves my sister. This can't be someone she knows."

Everyone says that about their loved ones. Troy didn't have the heart to point out the obvious, that this man didn't love her sister,

37

or any other woman. "No, it's not. She's the fourth victim of this guy, that we know of. He's smart, has enough resources to disguise himself and come up with impressive fake IDs, and seems to target vulnerable submissives, or those new to the lifestyle."

"We're just lucky he hasn't killed anyone, at least not yet," Trevor commented, rubbing a hand over his bearded jaw. "Shit, but I want to get this guy. I'd make sure he didn't see freedom until he was one step from the grave."

"You and me both."

Sidling around them, Troy watched Paige's eyes turn as flinty as her glare. "If you haven't been able to stop him in months then I can't count on you to find him now. The more people out looking for him, the better."

"Hold up," Troy snapped, a frisson of alarm raising goosebumps on his arms. Snatching her elbow again, he turned her back around to face him. "You stay out of this. This guy is dangerous, likely unhinged. I don't need another victim on my hands."

"Penny didn't know about him, that I'm sure of. She's not stupid, or reckless. She wouldn't have returned to the club if she'd heard this man was targeting women at those places. And I'm not stupid or reckless either, or uninformed. Find him." Her scathing glance included them both. "Or I'll do whatever I have to to see my sister's avenged."

Troy started to reach for her again when she pulled away and stomped off, but Trevor stopped him with a simple, "Let her go."

"Fuck that, Trev. We don't need a novice butting in, and you know it."

"She's grieving, and angry. She admitted, with that curl to her mouth I want to straighten with mine, that she's not into the lifestyle. Odds are, whatever she might do won't put her in jeopardy or catch this guy's eye. If I'm guessing correctly, the two are more than sisters. They look to be twins."

After glancing back at Penny, he knew Trevor was right. They may not be identical, but as close as they could get. Troy watched

Paige step onto the elevator, her gaze stony when she looked their way while punching the button. Neither of them knew her well, but enough to know she possessed a backbone of steel. It was obvious she was close to her sister, and he could sympathize with her need to act on Penny's behalf. That was what worried him.

"Let's hope you're right." The elevator pinged open again before they reached it. They both recognized Damien Masters, the owner of Sanctuary, striding toward them with rage swirling in his cobalt blue eyes.

"How is she?" Damien demanded. "I just now got through closing down so I could get here."

Troy followed Damien's eyes as they shifted to the glass partition separating them from Penny's room and saw his throat work at the sight of her lying so still and pale, hooked up to multiple machines. His own anger rushed to the surface again at seeing the bruises forming on her face. Oblivious to his friend's distress, he swung on Damien and got in his face, unleashing a wave of impotent bitterness on him.

"Where the fuck were you? I warned you about this guy." He poked him in the shoulder, a taunting gesture that darkened Damien's eyes. "Where was your fucking security?"

"Troy..." Trevor cautioned, laying a hand on his shoulder.

"No, it's all right, Trevor. I deserve his anger. My security was out there, but he can only be in one place at a time. I checked the cameras, and this guy knew the exact location of each one and how to avoid letting his full face come into view. He moved fast, and she'd be in worse condition if my guy hadn't spotted them less than a minute after he attacked."

"We saw it too, Damien, and you're right. After that, your man did the only thing he could by getting Penny help instead of going after the guy." Trevor looked at Troy. "Chill, bro. We're all on the same side."

Troy blew out a frustrated breath and offered Damien an apologetic look, just now noticing the guilt swirling in his eyes and the pinched set to his mouth. "Sorry, Damien. It fucking pisses me off we can't get a handle on this ass."

"You weren't off base, Carlson. I should've walked her out after our scene instead of leaving her bundled in a blanket to deal with an altercation. By the time I returned, it was to hear all the commotion from security. I want this fucker as bad as you do."

"Then let's get him. She won't be awake until the swelling goes down, which could take days, if not longer. I'll be back when she is. Are you coming?" Troy asked Damien as he and Trevor pivoted toward the elevator.

Damien's gaze rested on the young woman, his expression turning bleak with his reply. "No, not yet. I'll sit with her for a spell."

"I wonder if there's something there besides guilt," Trevor murmured as they entered the elevator with a wave to the club owner.

"For God's sake, don't go playing matchmaker. It's bad enough we're the last of the gang to still enjoy playing the field," Troy growled.

An amused smile tilted the corners of Trevor's mouth. "So, you're not worried our turn's up next?"

"Not in the fucking least. Not going there, no way, no how." He glared at his brother when Trevor laughed. The moron never did take anything seriously.

BY TUESDAY, the swelling in Penny's brain had gone down significantly and the doctors started the slow process of bringing her out of the coma. Paige sat outside Penny's room that afternoon, watching through the large window with bated breath as the doctor reduced the medications going through the IV for the last time. Penny had already begun to stir, her fingers moving, her legs shifting with restlessness. Her doctor turned and beckoned

Paige inside and she dashed through the door praying for good news.

"All of her vitals are still good, and more importantly, normal. You can sit with her now, talk to her, touch her. Let her know you're here, and that she's safe and in good hands. The nurses will monitor her for full consciousness and notify me when that happens." Reaching out, Dr. Matthews squeezed her shoulder before he and his team left Paige alone with her twin.

Pulling up a chair next to the bed, Paige sat down and gripped Penny's hand. "Way to go, sis. Your first night back in the saddle and you manage to land yourself in trouble. You're going to be fine." She choked back a sob. "Do you think I'd allow you to be otherwise? Wake up whenever you're ready. I'll be here. In the meantime, want to hear about the hot detective and his DA brother who are on your case?"

Paige leaned her head on her bent arm resting on the armrest while relating what she knew about the Carlson brothers, admitting in a hushed voice to her secret lusting after the two men these past months. She may have been pleased to discover Troy was assigned to Penny's case, but she didn't hold back when she relayed how the cops hadn't been able to catch this guy in months, and how she found that inexcusable without mentioning her intention to see what she could do to aid in his arrest. There was no sense stressing Penny out, and the plan brewing in Paige's head may not happen or yield any results.

If the only way to draw out the bastard meant pretending to be something she wasn't for a few nights at a kink club, then so be it. How difficult could it be? She may not get off on letting some guy tie her up and spank her butt a few times, but she could fake it as good as any other thirty-one-year-old woman who'd been enjoying orgasms for over ten years. Her most intense, pleasurable climaxes had come from her own hand, so she was used to minimal responses when with a man, and could call on those memories to get her through while baiting this guy to approach her. Armed with foreknowledge and several years of kickboxing classes, she'd be ready for him if she caught his attention.

An hour later, Penny's eyelids fluttered and slowly blinked open to reveal her hazy, confused gray-green eyes. "What... where..."

Her hand jerked in Paige's grip and she rushed to reassure her. "I'm here, sis, and you're okay. You're in the hospital, Cyprus General."

Two nurses dashed into the room and Paige rose to make way for them. Moving to the corner, it took every ounce of patience she could muster to wait in silence while the doctors entered next and went through a barrage of tests and questions. From what she heard, Penny had seen no one come at her as she left the club, she only remembered being slammed against the building followed by horrendous head pain before everything went black. That left little for Paige to look for if she went through with her plans, but she couldn't sit back and do nothing, not after the nightmare of the past few days and how close she'd come to losing her only family. Someone had to pay for her sister's suffering.

Troy and Trevor arrived a short time later, and much to Paige's annoyance, another quick, warm response to seeing the brothers again spread throughout her body. For the life of her, she couldn't understand the draw she felt in equal proportions to two polar opposite guys. Their blood relation aside, the brothers differed in personality as much as they did in their clothing. Trevor's tie in varying shades of maroon and charcoal complemented his gray dress slacks and deep red silk shirt, the attire befitting his position as a District Attorney. His short, scruffy beard and wavy brown hair left long enough to cup his nape and curl around his ears went against the professional image.

Next to him, Troy was just as eye-catching wearing his standard dress code of denim paired with a dress shirt and jacket, and with his neat, shorter hair and clean-shaven face. Both men's tall, muscular frames, tanned, rugged features and golden-brown eyes had drawn the attention of every woman who'd entered The

Precinct, but they'd gifted very few with more than a friendly greeting. They'd given Paige the most time, and that had been pitifully little compared to how often they'd slipped into her fantasies.

Fiddle faddle body, she groaned, facing them head on. She may desire the two men more than she'd ever lusted after another man, but that didn't mean she'd let them browbeat Penny for information.

"She didn't see the guy, so she can't give you a description," she stated, hoping to cut them off before they could pounce on Penny.

"Hello to you, too," Trevor returned with his usual half smile. Undeterred by her glare, he stepped up to her and ran one finger down her bare arm in a light caress Paige felt all the way to her toes. "Relax, sugar. Believe it or not, we know what we're doing, and we're on her side."

Troy spared her a quick glance with one elevated brow before taking the chair Paige vacated and leaning toward the bed, bracing his forearms on his thighs. With a concerned look and soft tone, he told Penny, "I'm Detective Carlson, Ms. Wilcox, and I'm in charge of your assault case. I've spoken with your doctor and you are very lucky. Other than a concussion and bruising, you'll make a full recovery. I need any help you can give me to stop this guy from hurting someone else. You aren't his first."

Penny's eyes widened and Paige dashed to her other side, flinging Troy an angry glare. Resting her hand on Penny's arm, she said, "Apparently the club owner knew of this guy and his security saw to you instead of chasing him. Don't worry, we'll get him, sis."

Troy blasted her with a glacial look. "There's no *we*, Paige. You stay out of it."

That rough demand and cool gaze shot off tingles of sexual awareness to zip around under her skin. For someone who didn't take orders kindly that reaction alarmed her on several levels she didn't care for. "Of course, Detective," she replied in her sweetest voice to counterbalance the urge to lash out.

Trevor chuckled, drawing her scowl. "Save it, Paige. We know you well enough to know you're not meek and biddable."

Penny's perplexed frown cleared, and she smiled at Paige. "That's what you get for working in a cop bar." Turning to Troy, she said in a whispery tone, "I'm sorry. I didn't see him. I remember his voice, definitely male, and the names he called me before I passed out, but that's all I have." Her face paled when she reached up a shaky hand and brushed her bandaged head. "I've been in here three days?"

"Yes, but you've already given us more than we had before." Trevor moved to the side of the bed, next to Troy's chair. "How's your memory from that night? Can you recall if anyone paid extra attention to you, watched you for long periods of time? Anyone you turned down a scene with?"

Paige knew Penny was uncomfortable about something when she averted her eyes before answering. "No, nothing like that. Master Damien, he's the owner, approached me right after I got there. I hadn't even finished my drink yet." A light blush stained her white, bruised face, cementing Paige's suspicion there was some-thing there, maybe between Penny and this Master Damien, her sister didn't want to discuss.

Coming to her aid, she stated, "That's enough. Come back tomorrow if you have to, but she needs to rest now."

"Paige…" Penny groaned and shook her head, a small wry smile lighting her eyes. "You said it yourself; I'll be fine. No need to hover." She held up the arm sporting the IV. "Besides, I feel like I'm floating on a cloud, no pain or discomfort. There must be some good stuff pumping into my body."

Paige's tense shoulders relaxed for the first time since she'd heard the news of Penny's attack. Seeing the teasing sparkle in her eyes and hearing the soft chiding behind her words went a long way in reinforcing what the doctor had told her. "Hey, as the oldest, it's my job to look out for you." And she'd never failed to such a degree before. Guilt sliced through her with razor-sharp pain. She always knew when Penny was determined to go through with something, like her return to alternative sex, which had led to Paige backing off from arguing with her about it. Too bad knowing the futility of an endeavor didn't negate feelings of impotent, guilt-ridden rage.

"By two minutes." Penny looked back at Troy. "Do you have any more questions, Detective?"

He nodded. "A few, if you're up to it."

"I am," she insisted, switching her gaze back to Paige. "I love you, now go away. I'll see you tomorrow."

"Fine," Paige conceded with a grumble. "I'll be by after work."

She was reaching for her purse sitting on the chair behind her when Trevor surprised her by saying, "I'll walk you out."

"Why?" Whirling, she clutched her purse against her chest, as if the faux leather bag could protect her from another searing touch if he reached for her. Her arm still tingled from the simple glide of his finger earlier. "I'm perfectly capable of getting to my car without mishap. It's still daylight, and I'm parked in the outside, public lot."

"But I insist." Grasping her elbow, Trevor steered her to the door, tossing over his shoulder, "Be right back, Troy."

"*Addlepated dim doodle,*" Paige groused under her breath as they walked to the elevator.

"Tsk, such language will earn you five strokes with my belt. You'd do well to remember that," Trevor returned with humor.

Her eyes flicked down to his waist, her mouth going dry at imagining the one-inch, braided black leather strap licking her skin. This time when she shivered, she knew it wasn't from lust. "I'm not my sister, Trevor. *You* would do well to remember *that,*" she emphasized.

"Oh, I'm well aware of that, sugar," he drawled. He didn't relinquish his hold on her arm on the ride down, or as they strolled out into the balmy evening air. His amiable demeanor and amused tilt to his mouth remained in place as he guided her straight to her car. "But when it comes to ensuring you stay out of the investigation into Penny's attack, you *will* abide by our dictates."

Ignoring that statement, she pulled from his hold and grasped the door handle. "How did you know this was my car?"

"We asked Mel to point it out to us months ago so we could be sure you always parked near the back exit, under the street light. Never can be too careful." Slipping one hand under her hair to cup the base of her skull, he brought her body flush against his by applying pressure with his other against her lower back. Paige wanted to stiffen against him but her body, the traitorous bitch, possessed other ideas. Going soft and wet all at once, she braced her hands on his thick pectorals to keep from giving herself away with the feel of her throbbing nipples against his chest. The steady beat of his heart under her palm did nothing to lessen her heightened sensitivity to his nearness, an effect impacted by his admission he and his brother had been looking out for her. Turning serious, he stated, "We want this bastard as much as you do, Paige. Let us do our job and stay out of the way. Please."

Please? Okay, asking nicely wasn't playing fair. Not that it would change her mind. "Find him." With a light shove, he backed off, and she slid into her car.

CHAPTER 5

*P*enny watched her sister walk out with the good-looking DA, wondering what was going on between Paige and the Carlson brothers. She knew her twin well, and Paige didn't get flustered around men, and only grew irritable when she was uncomfortable with a person or situation. She'd never been more appreciative of Paige as when she'd awoken in a state of groggy disorientation with pulsating waves of discomfort surrounding her head and seen her there by her side. It had taken most of the day, but the drug-induced fuzziness blurring her mind had finally cleared. A dull throbbing still encompassed her entire skull, and she ached from head to toe, but as she said earlier, she imagined the drugs pumping through the IV in her arm were numbing the worst of her pain. Her sibling's presence had helped tamp down the fear and panic when flashes of remembered shock and pain from the attack filtered through her mind.

She couldn't begin to understand how she could get off on the snap of leather against her bare skin when just recalling the man's fists pummeling her drew beads of cold sweat along her brow. *That* excruciating agony was so different from the erotic sting of leather or a rough, calloused hand slapping her buttocks.

"Are you sure no one stood out, no one caught your attention, for any reason? Sometimes a small thing will lead to something bigger," Detective Carlson asked again.

Only one face popped into her head, one man who had snared her attention, and her. After she'd taken Master Damien's hand, Penny's awareness of everyone else had slipped away. Shaking her head, she replied, "I'm sorry, but no. I wish I could be of more help."

"How about away from the club? Problems with anyone at work? Have you seen anyone suspicious around your neighborhood?" Trevor knew the questions were long shots, but had to be asked.

"No." Penny shrugged in apology. "I'm sorry."

"Well, if you think of anything else, call me." He stood and laid his card on the bedside tray. "I'll let you rest now."

Looking up, she figured he was an inch or two over six foot, an imposing, muscular man just like his brother. "You look familiar," she remarked, unable to pinpoint where she'd seen both him and Trevor before.

Troy cocked his head. "How long have you been a member of Sanctuary?"

"Over two years, but I hadn't been back in almost eight months." Not since the first time she'd been a victim of a man's rage. Thank God Jim had moved out of state and left her alone a few weeks following their split.

"Trevor and I used to be regular members. Other than an occasional visit, we don't frequent it as often as we used to. You may have seen us there. Your doctor said you'll be in here a while yet, at least another week. I'll be back to check on you. In the meantime, if you remember anything, or need anything..."

"She'll have me."

Penny's gaze flew to the door and the one man she'd been trying not to think about. Master Damien was just as big, hard and intimidating outside of Sanctuary as he appeared immersed in that sexually charged atmosphere. With his blue eyes riveted on her bruised

48

face, he sauntered into the room, and she had no trouble remembering the feel of his wide palms and long fingers kneading her breasts, or the way he'd commanded her attention and submission with just a few words.

"I… what are you doing here?" Heat enveloped her face from her rude outburst, but his sudden presence caught her off guard.

"Checking up on you." The inflection in his tone hinted that should be obvious. Turning to Troy, he questioned bluntly, "Anything new?"

"No, not yet. I'll keep you informed. Take care, Penny."

She nodded as the detective turned to leave. Lifting the sheet up to her chest, Penny squirmed in uncomfortable awareness of the way she must look. Master Damien had a way of looking at a person, especially a sub, that compelled her to either drop to her knees in front of him or run and hide. Right now, the latter sounded good. "It's nice of you to stop by, Sir, but…"

"I'm sorry, Penny." He stepped next to the bed, leaned down and covered her mouth with his, taking her breath as he pushed past her lips and stroked over her tongue.

Shaken, aroused and confused, her lips trembled against the pressure of his and her heart stuttered with his nearness. She feared this man, but in a different way than she had her ex. For someone who'd exhibited scant awareness of her in the past, she found his sudden interest and possessiveness both exciting and worrisome. For the life of her, she couldn't figure out what he wanted from her.

He released her mouth with a sharp nip on her lower lip that caused her sheath to clench. Lifting her fingers to the throb, she looked at his face still so close to hers. "What are you sorry for?"

"The other night. You were my responsibility, and I let you down. That was my fault. That and my security wasn't as adequate as I thought. Why didn't you come find me before you left?"

The slight accusation behind his words sent a frisson of guilt through Penny, but she couldn't tell him she'd fled because of him, because he'd taken her higher, faster than any other Dom, and she'd known it was a onetime thing. Hadn't he just admitted she'd been his 'responsibility', nothing more?

"I'm sorry. I was a bit overwhelmed after it being so long since I'd been with someone. And you were busy."

Damien sat back in the chair Troy had vacated and folded his arms across his chest, his black brows lowered in a frown, his mouth set in a stern line. Penny's palms turned sweaty from his silent, probing gaze, and she held her breath, wondering what he was thinking.

"Get one thing through your head, little one. From here on out, I'll never be too busy to see to your needs, no matter what they are."

The nurse entered just then, distracting Penny from that startling disclosure. Wasn't the roaring in her head enough to cope with? Why did the one man who'd always been able to fluster her have to add to her woes right now with that succinct remark?

"I'm sorry, you need to leave now. The staff is under strict orders to limit Ms. Wilcox's visitors to short stays," the nurse told Damien as she checked the IV bag.

He looked as if he wanted to argue, but instead rose and said, "I'm leaving. Penny, I'll check back with you soon."

Penny released a relieved sigh when he walked out, wondering how her life had gotten so complicated all of a sudden. Thank God for Paige. At least her sister wouldn't add to her headaches or give her something else to fret over.

PAIGE CHECKED the time again while drawing two beers. Uncharacteristic nervousness had kept her on edge since reporting early for her Saturday evening shift at the bar. After Mel agreed to let her off by eight, she'd started to second guess her decision to check out Penny's club as a new guest. Her online research into her sister's sexual lifestyle had uncovered eye-opening facts she'd never imagined. Whoever knew there were so many aspects to kinky sex, or so many outlets to indulge in your preferences? She had no idea how far Penny had gone during her months with Jim, or what she'd done last week before she'd been attacked. And, she didn't want to know, did she?

Honesty forced Paige to admit some of the information and pictures had caused flutters of arousal to tickle her girly parts, but that just meant she was a normal, thirty-one-year-old woman with a healthy sex drive, didn't it? "Okay, enough with questioning myself," she scolded under her breath as she slid the brews down the bar toward two customers. With a wave, the female paralegals from the DA's office caught their glasses and moved to a table. Tonight, all she planned to do was scope out the place and, if she was lucky and Penny's attacker returned to the scene of his crime, maybe catch his attention. Troy had revealed this guy appeared to target either new subs or those vulnerable enough to let their guard down. Since Penny wouldn't have come across as a newbie, she must've displayed a certain amount of vulnerability that snagged his attention. Which just went to prove she'd been right and her twin shouldn't have returned to that lifestyle.

Cursing the futility of indulging in hindsight, Paige signaled to Mel, who was making the rounds between tables. If she intended to do this, she needed to get going before she lost her nerve. Every day this past week she'd debated with herself over her determination to draw out the person who'd hurt Penny, but all it took was a visit with her sister in the hospital to shore up her resolve. While Penny wasn't in danger now of losing her life or of brain damage, the lingering swelling still brought on bouts of dizziness and vicious headaches that added to the aches and pains of her bruised body. Once physical therapy got her up, the weakness on her left side had become more pronounced, and Paige hated seeing her so distressed.

The only time Penny appeared calm enough to rest undisturbed was when Paige's visit followed on the heels of this Master she'd spoken of, the one Penny admitted to being with that night. Paige tried not to think about what that meant. She'd yet to meet the man, or even learn his name due to her sister's refusal to share much about him. Paige supposed that worked in her favor given she was about to enter the same club he frequented for the sole purpose of catching the eye of an assaulter. She didn't want anyone to know about this endeavor.

"Go ahead, Paige. My nephew just pulled in to help out for a few hours," Mel told her when he came around behind the bar.

"Thanks, boss." She hadn't given him a reason when she'd requested to come in early so she could clock out early. What she was planning was no one's business but hers. Penny would only try to talk her out of it, and so would Mel. As for the Carlsons and their warning not to interfere, well, what they didn't know wouldn't hurt them, right?

Fifteen minutes later, Paige pulled into the parking lot of the converted warehouse down by the wharfs. Running clammy hands down the sides of her short denim skirt, she sat a moment to get the rapid beat of her heart under control. It wasn't the people inside who were causing jitters to dance in her stomach, but her possible reaction to what they were doing inside that building. If she'd gotten hot and bothered from just reading and looking at pictures, how would she react when face to face with sexually charged scenes she'd always sworn held no appeal for her? She didn't yearn for a man to call the shots during sex and still didn't understand the appeal of being tied up or smacked with a paddle. None of that had turned her on before, yet when she'd imagined one of the Carlsons in the descriptions she'd read or in the pictures with her instead of the models, there'd been no denying the instant surge of lust rushing through her body.

"Okay, enough procrastinating." Hopping out of her Jeep, she dashed inside, determined not to think about the two men who'd been hijacking her thoughts all week.

A young, twenty-something receptionist greeted Paige from

behind a small counter as she entered a large foyer. "Welcome to guest night at the Sanctuary. Do you have your approved application form?"

"Right here." She'd been careful to use her mother's maiden name instead of Wilcox when filling out the online application so no one would know of her relationship to Penny. There was no telling what all this perpetrator knew about his victims, but he would likely be smart enough to stay away from a relative of one.

"Looks good," the girl said after checking the papers Paige handed her, including a copy of her last physical. She hadn't expected that requirement. "You can store your belongings in a locker, including your shoes. When you enter the main room, someone will escort you to the seating area for guests, where you'll wait for one of the Doms to give you a tour." She handed Paige what looked like a sign-up form. "Since you marked you aren't new to the lifestyle, you're eligible to partake in our annual charity auction tomorrow. There's still time to sign up if you get that form filed by midnight. The club's not open on Sundays, but for this event, the boss makes an exception. All proceeds go to the Children's Miracle Network."

Good grief, an auction? It appeared there was more to this stuff than what she'd read thus far. "I'll give it some thought," she replied, folding the sheet and putting it in her purse, refusing to feel guilty over lying about her experience.

"Either way, have a good time tonight."

"Thanks." Paige didn't have a plan, but she knew she wasn't here to have a good time. If she didn't get lucky enough to draw the assailant's attention tonight, if he was even here, maybe she would at least satisfy her curiosity about her sister's sexual preferences. The auction could give her a second, more visible opportunity. Maybe, if she could muster the courage to take part in such a thing. *If, if, if.* That word annoyed her.

As promised, a tall, burly man with a friendly smile led her to the center of the room and the circle of sofas where at least twelve new guests already sat and conversed. Settling in the only vacant spot open at the end of one plush couch, she tried smiling with confidence at the other girls, but the goings on around her were too distracting. *Wow.* Internet research couldn't compare, or prepare anyone enough for the real thing.

The bondage equipment lining the back walls appeared to resemble the pictures she'd seen, but eyeing someone strapped face down on a spanking bench, her buttocks bright red from the vigorous hand spanking a man was taking great pleasure in administering, was enough to have her questioning the wisdom of this endeavor. Would she be required to submit to a stranger in such a way? Paige hadn't planned on participating, just socializing enough to make herself a target. A shudder of distaste ran through her at the thought of being bound on the St. Andrew Cross while a man did whatever he pleased to her body in front of all these people. She wasn't a prude by any means, but the possibility of jumping right into exhibitionism with a stranger left her cold.

A strong drink would work wonders right about now, but since guests weren't allowed alcohol, that option to loosen her taut muscles was out. Shifting her eyes away from the sexually charged scenes, Paige watched the dancing on the opposite side of the cavernous room, itching to join them. Yeah, there looked to be a few eager hands exposing and exploring naked flesh, but it had been ages since she'd let her hair down on the dance floor, and just sitting here, waiting on the whimsy of some man, was starting to chafe. Several of the girls already biding their time when she'd arrived were off exploring with a Dom, but she didn't feel like wasting any more time remaining idle.

Standing on shaking legs, Paige wound her way through the crowd toward the dance floor until her path was barred by a nice-looking man wearing tight jeans and a t-shirt that matched the vivid green of his eyes.

Cocking his head, he gave her a once over and approval lit his gaze. "You don't want to dance alone, do you, sweetie?" His appreciative eyes rested on her cleavage above the stretchy tube top that left her midriff, shoulders and upper chest bare.

Paige shook her head with a smile. "No, I honestly don't."

Grasping her hand, he tugged her into the center of gyrating bodies, the song switching to a fast, hard beat that stirred up her excitement over cutting loose and ridding herself of the stress from the past week. Within moments, she lost herself in the wild tempo and movement around her. Her partner bent his head, whispered, "I'm Master Jason," then stepped back to whirl her around. He stayed with her through two more songs, making her lose track of time until someone tapped on Jason's shoulder and he turned to reveal one of the last people Paige wanted to see.

"Mind if I cut in, Jason?" Troy Carlson asked, his dark brown eyes pinning her in place. With all the speed and flare of a shooting star, her pulse skyrocketed and her body grew flushed. What the hell was it about him and his brother that could turn her inside out with a look or a few words?

Jason glanced from Troy back to her. "I was just going to ask if she'd like to take this to the back."

Both men waited for her decision, which Paige made without having to think about it. Better the man she knew than the stranger. "I'd like to keep dancing, but, thank you."

Nonplussed, Jason nodded and strolled away, Troy stepping forward to take his place. Pulling her against his large frame, he kept her in place with one hand pressed against her lower back and the other shackling her right wrist to hold between their chests.

"What the fuck are you doing here, Paige?" he growled, his low, guttural tone conveying suspicious displeasure as much as his rigid jaw.

"I was dancing with a very nice man. Are you going to make me regret choosing you to continue with?" Her head may be unhappy with the detective's sudden presence, but her body sang his praises, notably where their groins were grinding together in tune with another fast beat. The blatant press of his semi-erection left no doubt of his size; the angry glint in his eyes revealed he wouldn't be beyond using sexual control to intimidate her into backing away from taunting the guy he was after.

Troy bent his head until he spoke right above her mouth. "I'll make you regret coming here tonight if your purpose is to catch this culprit's attention. Or, do you want to play, baby?"

Another tall, rock hard body pressed against Paige's back at that moment, and she didn't have to guess to know who'd joined them. Trevor's amused voice whispered in her ear, "Before you answer my brother, remember there are rules, and consequences if broken, to our play."

Oh, she wanted to play, she admitted under the dual assault of Trevor tonguing her ear and Troy nipping at her lower lip. Paige just wasn't sure she would abide by their rules. Now, with the hard shape of two cocks rubbing against her mound and butt, and Trevor's hands clasping her hips to move her in sync with their pelvis rotations, she couldn't think straight. Awash with the heated rush sizzling through her veins, she struggled with a reply.

"What's wrong, sugar? Weren't expecting a proposition in a BDSM club? You *are* green around the edges." She lifted her head up and around until her eyes landed on Trevor's curved lips. Her sheath contracted with damp need and a sudden ache to feel that mouth possessing hers.

Other than enjoying his dance skills, she'd remained neutral to Jason as they'd danced. Why these two? And which one would she choose if it came down to relieving the ache they were both responsible for?

"She disobeyed by leaving the guest area without a Dom's permission," Troy put in without missing a coordinated beat with his brother. "At a minimum, a lesson is in order."

"What are you talking about?" Paige found it damn near impossible to concentrate sandwiched between them, her mind conjuring up all kinds of images that left her breathless and increased the cream already oozing to soak her panties.

"Weren't you told to remain in the center seating area until a Dom offered to show you around?" Trevor asked before sinking his teeth into her earlobe and sending a delightful shiver down her swaying body.

"I was bored." Okay, she'd read enough to know that excuse wouldn't cut it, but it was the truth. Thinking a change of subject was in order, she tightened her hand on Troy's shoulder and turned the questioning around. "What are you doing here? You don't have a description, and you didn't mention this guy targeting men."

"We're members, so we can visit whenever we want. Since you haven't answered my question, I'll assume you ignored our warning and are here trying to get on our assailant's radar. Two infractions you need to answer for." Troy kept his gaze on her face as he released her wrist and ran one finger over the top of her breasts before dipping inside the tube top.

Reeling from Troy's announcement they were members, Paige sucked in a deep breath and held it, waiting to see how far he'd go right there on the dance floor. She'd known they were dominant men, not that they were Doms. God help her, she wanted his touch on her puckered nipple so bad, she didn't care about their sexual preferences or who saw them. He inched lower, taking the stretchy material with him, and grazed the aching tip. Instant, searing pleasure forced her breath out in a *whoosh* and she couldn't help but push against his caressing finger as he stroked back and forth over the turgid tip.

"Master Damien isn't happy with you, and neither are we." Trevor tightened his hands on her hips before sliding them up her waist until he reached the hem of her banded top. With a sharp tug, her breasts popped free, the wraparound now bunched underneath them.

"*Son of a dipshitiot!*" Paige exclaimed in a shocked whisper of arousal.

Trevor's deep laugh vibrated against her spine, but she didn't have time to say anything else since Troy was dipping his head to her bare breasts. The strong suction on her left nipple robbed her of cognizant awareness and she didn't give a fig who might be looking, not when her fantasy of feeling one of the Carlson brother's hands and mouth on her had come to fruition. *Correction, both men*, she amended when Trevor cupped her fullness, lifted the small mounds and offered her nipples to his brother. The carnal scene the three of them made implanted itself in her roaring mind.

"I do enjoy hearing your colorful expletives," Trevor whispered in her ear as the two of them gyrated their hips faster against her.

"Keep it up and you'll hear a lot more." Sparks of fiery heat zinged from her nipples down to her sheath with each tug from Troy's mouth, every swipe of his tongue. He still kept his other hand pressed against her lower back and every time she automatically attempted to free herself, the inability to do so added to Paige's escalating arousal. The sensory overload was almost too much, making her forget her purpose for being here.

Their admission they were members of Sanctuary had caught her off guard. Paige hadn't considered the brothers were of the same mold as the men Penny enjoyed meeting here at the club. Yes, they were dominant, and she'd suspected they could be controlling when allowed, but they'd never hinted they were into this kinky lifestyle. It unnerved her how easily she could picture herself strapped to one of the apparatus along the back wall with one—or both—of them preparing to sexually torment her.

Troy reclaimed her attention when he sank his teeth into her already throbbing nipple, the quick, there and gone again pain wrenching a cry from Paige's throat and another gush of cream between her legs. Lifting his head, he stated above her mouth, "That's just a sample of what'll happen if you continue with this folly. The next time you try to interfere in my investigation, I'll paddle your ass, regardless of where we are or who's watching. Now," he nipped her lower lip again, sending another lightning bolt south, "be a good girl, allow us to walk you out and stay away from here."

His softened tone matched the concern reflected in his eyes when he gazed down at her. Cool air wafted over her damp, exposed breasts, tightening the throbbing buds even more. She didn't know whether to be relieved or irritated when Trevor pulled up the top and both men stepped back, leaving her shaking on the brink of unfulfilled lust.

～

"LET'S GO." Troy slid his hand from behind Paige's back to enfold her hand in the warm clasp of his while Trevor took hold of her other hand. Together, they steered her back into the foyer, helped her slip on her shoes and then led her out to her Jeep.

Struggling to keep himself in check, Troy replayed his terror when Damien had phoned, asking about the redhead he'd noticed leaving the hospital as he'd arrived. Being both observant and smart, the club owner had become suspicious when he spotted Paige in his club just days after he'd seen her at the hospital. The sisters weren't identical twins, but the familial resemblance was hard to miss. Troy promised Damien they'd take care of Paige, agreeing with the other man that she didn't portray a tendency toward submissiveness. Only Trevor believed the girl could be dominated by the right person.

Opening the Jeep's door, he glanced down into her flushed face and snapping gray eyes. Damned if that defiant look didn't get to him every time. The stretchy top molded to her pert breasts and clung to her turgid nipples, leaving every bump of her areola he'd felt under his tongue discernible against the cloth. Trevor wanted to tame her; he just wanted to ride her, over and over.

"Be a good girl, Paige, and go home." Admonishing her like a child raised her hackles, just as he'd known it would.

"You're not my boss." Whipping her head around to Trevor, she added, "You either." Pulling her hands free, she folded herself behind the wheel, grabbed the door handle and delivered one last parting shot. "And, you're certainly not my daddies."

Slamming the door, she left the parking lot amid a squeal of tires. A smirk lifted the corners of Trevor's mouth. "Huh. Think she's pissed at us?"

A rare grin split Troy's face. "Moron. Come on, I'm beat."

Trevor sighed and shook his head. "It's doubtful she'll back off. You know that."

Troy nodded as they reached his SUV. "Oh, yeah, I'm well aware of her stubborn streak, not to mention seeing how close the two girls are. But I'll be damned if this son-of-a-bitch gets another victim on my watch."

"Our watch," Trevor corrected, a hard glint replacing the light in his eyes.

CHAPTER 6

$\mathcal{R}$ ubbing her tired eyes, Paige reread the paragraph on the screen describing what she would have to agree to if she signed up for the auction at Sanctuary taking place the following afternoon. She reached up to rub one finger over a still-tingling nipple. After arriving home from the club with her body still humming from the thrill of being pressed between two tall, rock-hard male bodies, she'd known sleep was still hours off. Pouring herself a nightcap of Bourbon and water, heavy on the alcohol, she'd pulled up the information on the club's annual fundraiser. What she read both astounded her and added to the pulsing desire for two men she couldn't seem to shake. Last year's take from the auction set off alarm bells she was trying her best to ignore. If these men and women were willing to put out that much money to purchase a sub for a few hours, what on earth would they require their 'property' to do in return? And how would she be able to fake her way through their experience?

All buyers will be given a list of each participant's limits before bidding commences. Each submissive agrees to spend eight hours with their buyer, the time and place to be agreed upon by both parties.

Scrolling down to the form, she found a very thorough and

mind-boggling checklist. The options included the standard oral, anal and intercourse selections, but it was the 'not so standard' choices responsible for the flood of heat warming her face. *Good grief! Pony play? Fisting? Erotic asphyxiation?* She didn't want to come across as a prude, or worse, get escorted off stage due to a lack of bidders. God, wouldn't that be the height of humiliation? She'd never imagined pretending to be a sexual submissive could be so difficult.

You loved *Troy and Trevor's take-charge attitudes tonight.* "Yeah, yeah. Shut up already yet." Sometimes, her inner voice could be damned annoying when it lectured her on those two. Paige admitted she hadn't counted on the men she'd been fantasizing about for months showing up at the club tonight. And definitely hadn't expected her off the charts response to having their hands on her. Her first taste of public exposure had enhanced the experience instead of withdrawing from it, another startling revelation to deal with. The activity going on in the club before Troy and Trevor arrived had drawn her curiosity, and she'd found voyeurism titillating, but she'd garnered no real interest in trying out anything she witnessed. Not until those two arrived.

Doubts about her ability to fake her way through eight hours with a dominant stranger kept her from filling out the form for another ten minutes. By the time she'd finished her drink and then conjured up the image of Penny's bruised face and close call with severe brain trauma, she found herself checking boxes and signing her name. No sex, but she enjoyed both giving and receiving oral. Anal play only since she thought she could handle a little teasing back there. She'd never understood the draw of including that orifice for sexual fun, but most of what she'd learned about her sister's kinks baffled her as to the appeal for so many people. It wouldn't be the first time she faked an orgasm, so the only thing she'd have to overcome would be the urge to exert her natural independent nature if the 'bossiness' got to her before the time limit ended.

Best case scenario: the son-of-a-bitch who hurt Penny came after her next, following the auction, and she wouldn't have to go through with it. Tomorrow, before stopping in to visit Penny on her way to Sanctuary, she'd spend an hour at the gym, honing her kickboxing skills until her confidence in the skill returned.

Paige hit send before she could change her mind, vowing to ignore her inner voice telling her this was a stupid thing to try. Since doing nothing wasn't an option, setting herself up seemed to be the only way to draw this guy out without waiting for weeks for him to strike again. The cops had failed to find him in months, so she refused to rely on them. Remembering Troy's warning about not getting involved drew a shiver as she padded down the hall to her bedroom. "What he or Trevor don't know, won't hurt them—or me, for that matter," she muttered. The two men who'd dominated her midnight fantasies for months without exhibiting a shred of personal interest in her had no right to dictate to her now, or interfere if she wanted to explore their alternative lifestyle for herself. They didn't need to know her only interest lay with avenging her sister.

Paige plastered on a smile before entering Penny's hospital room the next day, the note she'd discovered on her windshield that morning hidden in her purse. *Back off, bitch.* That's all it said, but it was enough to let her know she'd caught someone's attention last night. It worried her whoever it was knew her address; she hadn't counted on that. But knowing what Penny had suffered, and how close her sister had come to serious brain injury, or worse, hardened her resolve. There was no need to trouble her twin with either the note or her plans for later that day, or to reveal the nerves crawling under her skin like a swarm of insects determined to annoy her. She knew her sibling like the back of her hand; they could practically read each other's thoughts. Penny would blow a gasket if she thought Paige had drawn her assailant's attention, even though she would understand Paige's need to get justice for her.

"Hey, sis. I heard from your nurse you might be released to go home in the next day or two." Breezing over to the bed, she bent and kissed Penny's forehead. "It'll be so good to have you home. No more headaches?" She sank onto the chair next to the bed, relieved when Penny shook her head.

"Not in the last twenty-four hours. I still hurt all over, and my left side is still weak, but I know how much worse it could have been." A delicate shudder shook her slender frame where she sat propped up in bed. "All in all, I'm pretty lucky. What have you been up to?"

Paige waved an airy hand. "Oh, this and that. The greyhounds went home yesterday after I left here, and I think I'll hold off on taking in any more pet sitting jobs until you've reached a full recovery."

Penny shook her head. "I know you need the extra money, so don't turn down work because of me. I'll be fine. The sooner I'm up and moving around, the sooner I can return to work. With tax season upon us, I'm needed ASAP. I've already agreed to do a few filings from home."

Unlike Paige, Penny had finished college, earning a degree in accounting and then landing a prestigious job at a large firm. The income from all three of Paige's jobs didn't equal what Penny brought in, another glaring difference between them. There were times she'd asked herself if she should return to school and get a better, more stable job, but nothing appealed to her. She liked being her own boss, answering to no one, even if the tedious, mundane work of cleaning houses was starting to chafe. Bar tending was fun, and she enjoyed conversing with the regulars, shooting a game of pool during her break and eyeballing the city's finest gathered together in one room.

"Only if the doctor okays it. And I'll be there to make sure you don't overdo," Paige warned. She hedged, then posed the question uppermost in her mind. "So, has Detective Carlson been in this weekend?"

Her sister sent her a shrewd glance, brushing her hair off her cheek with the back of her hand. "Is there something you're not telling me about him? Or his hunky brother?"

She averted her eyes from Penny's probing gaze. Her twin could read her like a book, as easy as Paige could her. She hated keeping secrets from her, but there was no way Penny would approve of what she planned to do, and if she mentioned coming across the Carlsons last night at Sanctuary, she wouldn't hear the end of it. There was no point in Penny reading more into that encounter than existed, or for her to encourage Paige to remain open-minded about a possible relationship with one of them. Troy and Trevor's sudden interest in her stemmed solely from their investigation and keeping her out of it. It would be best if she remembered that.

"No. I barely know either man. They've been in the bar a few times, but they're not regulars like some. When they have come in, they've been friendly, but kept their distance, no personal over-tures." Paige looked at Penny again and pulled up her cheeky grin. "But, I agree, they are hot, aren't they?" She fanned herself and blew out an exaggerated breath.

Penny giggled. "At least you have the good sense to notice."

"A girl would have to be blind not to notice those two. Here, I brought us a snack to share before I leave." Digging through her purse, she produced two large candy bars. The sugar high was more for Paige's benefit than Penny's since her sibling didn't have the sweet tooth and junk food habit Paige did, but that didn't mean Penny wouldn't appreciate the chocolate and nut bar after eating bland hospital food for the past week.

"Oh, God, how pathetic is it that I'm drooling? Thank you." She snatched the treat out of Paige's outstretched hand and wasted no time ripping off the wrapper and taking a bite.

"Any time." They gabbed while eating, but Paige's apprehension over the auction wouldn't allow her to relax. The desire to confide in Penny, get her advice on the subject her sister was so familiar with, almost convinced her to reveal her plans.

Desperate to get going before she blew this last chance to see her sister avenged, she stood and adjusted her purse on her shoulder. She needed to get to Sanctuary in time for the detailed instructions from the staff, and before she lost her nerve. The extra online research she'd taken time to do this morning revealed how mind boggling the scope of the BDSM world was, and a good deal of it panty-melting. She was neither blind nor deaf and maintained a healthy sexual appetite despite the long dry spell she'd been mired in. It would be impossible not to get turned on a little by some of those pictures and stories. That sure as hell didn't mean the lifestyle was for her, which was the one thing she'd have to hide best from a buyer.

"I'll let you rest and be back tomorrow in between my houses. I've picked up a third place on Mondays, so it may be late afternoon."

Penny licked chocolate off her fingers as she asked, "When are you going to turn your job into a business? I've told you I'll help."

Paige laughed. "You know that would mean I'd have to grow up. I'm not sure I'm ready, or want the responsibility." She couldn't deny Penny's offer to help expand her business by taking on more homes and offices and hiring crews to work for her was tempting, but she needed to be sure that's the next direction she wanted to veer toward.

Penny rolled her eyes. "Whatever, just think about it. Now, get out of here."

Twenty minutes later, Paige pulled into the parking lot at Sanctuary and cringed at the number of vehicles already there. With her heart pounding out a mad rhythm, she hightailed it inside before she could change her mind. The same receptionist greeted her before pointing to a different door to enter than she'd taken last night.

"Go through there and down the hall to the next door. That'll lead into the room behind the stage where you can prep and get the final instructions. Good luck and have fun!"

"I'll try," Paige quipped with no intention to do so. Fun was not high on the agenda for the next few hours.

A background of low music followed her down the hall and continued into a large room teeming with half-dressed women. The palpable vibe of anticipation rubbed off on her as she watched the unabashed way the girls paraded around the room in front of the two men giving instructions. The good-looking blond bouncer caught her attention and beckoned her over, sizing her up as she padded toward him.

Paige's hackles rose at his blatant inspection of her from head to toe, but she reined in her temper with a reminder of what was at stake. "Name?" he asked as soon as she reached him.

"Paige… Johannsen." *Damn.* She'd almost given him her real last name instead of her mother's maiden name. She needed to get on the ball, but that was proving more difficult than she'd imagined. The girls already in line to parade on stage waited with obvious excitement, appearing unashamed with their bared breasts, butts and mounds. Paige hadn't considered she would have to stand in front of the room full of strangers with all her privates put on display. She'd assumed there would be a choice of scanty attire to pick from.

"Okay, I've got your form. To be clear, you agree to bondage, light pain, oral, anal play only and toys. No intercourse. Correct?"

She was not a shy person, but listening to a man she'd never met before listing off the sexual things she'd agreed to allow another stranger to do to her sent a wave of heat over her face. "Yes, correct."

"Okay. Breasts, pussy and ass bare, otherwise you can don any of the garments over there." He nodded to an array of hanging outfits along the wall. "You'll be up in about fifteen minutes. Don't hold us up."

The man's indifferent, business-like attitude helped her stay committed to this endeavor as she padded over to the rack of skimpy outfits. "No, no, no," she chanted, discarding everything she came across. Conscious of the time, and the threat in the bouncer's voice when he'd ordered her to be ready, she hurried and selected a black, lace-up corset with cups to hold her breasts and sheer stockings to hook to garters. Since the room offered no privacy, she moved to a corner and dressed as fast as possible, refusing to think about the eyes already gazing upon her nudity. The deep baritone of the auctioneer filtered through the cracked door, as did the occasional laughter and the louder rounds of applause. Paige refrained from peeking out on the stage, afraid if she did she would run away from this opportunity. Given her anxiety level, if she didn't portray enough vulnerability to catch this bastard's attention tonight, then she never would.

"Johannsen! You're up next."

"*Oh, doodledrawers,*" she mumbled, padding across the room to the other bouncer manning the door. For the first time since she'd begun waxing, she regretted how the remaining strip of pubic hair emphasized the rest of her bare labia. He swept her body with an appreciative glance before winking and nodding his approval.

"You'll do well, relax. Remember, it's for a good cause."

His friendlier mien helped ease the tension in Paige's shoulders until he waved her through the door onto the stage and she saw the emcee was none other than the same man she'd caught entering her sister's room at the hospital the other day. Stopping halfway onto the stage, she wrestled with what to do as she realized the owner of the club was also Penny's new interest and now stood waiting for her with a tight, disapproving look. *Shit, now what?*

With a crook of his finger and a gleam in his vivid blue eyes, Master Damien beckoned her toward the spotlight, calling out, "Don't be shy, Paige. You're not new to the club scene or the lifestyle, are you?"

Paige squared her shoulders against the knowing taunt that revealed he was on to her and shored up her nerve. Two could play this game. Conscious of her propped-up breasts, pert nipples pointing straight ahead, and bare mons and buttocks as she crossed the stage, she didn't know how she managed to keep her head up and her eyes on his. Thank goodness the audience sat shrouded in darkness as she stepped onto the spotlighted stage.

"The lovely Paige." Damien introduced her by taking one clammy hand and lifting her arm to twirl her in a slow circle. "This sub is offering her delectable body for light pain and anal play, oral consumption and usage of toys." Yanking her against his side when Paige faced toward the audience she couldn't see again, he wrapped one steely arm around her waist and bent to her ear. "I'm not happy with you, even if you are doing this for your sister. I don't tolerate subterfuge in my club."

Paige shivered from the warning in his tone but couldn't resist snarling back, "Then let me go and I'll leave."

"No, that would be too easy." Reaching up with his free hand, he plucked at one distended nipple, drawing her shocked outrage and chuckles from the bidders shrouded in darkness. "It looks like whoever gets this tasty piece will have his hands full." He pinched her nipple and admonished, "Behave, girl."

Paige had never struggled so hard to keep her temper in check. Maybe she should've watched a few of the participants on stage before her and gotten a heads-up on what to expect from the emcee. At least his actions were helping to keep her mind off the room full of ogling eyes. High priced bids rang out, surprising her with the amounts. A different sense of awareness crept over her skin, one that worried her with the small thrill of satisfaction she hadn't expected. Then Master Damien turned her around again and doused the warm sensation generated by the interested bids by squeezing her right cheek.

"Come on, people. Look at this supple ass. What'll you give the Children's Miracle Network for hours of play with these round, malleable globes?" He slid his hand over to her other buttock and kneaded her flesh.

Drawing in a breath, she scowled at his smug face, her whispered, "Back off," met with a frown of his own. Without warning, he pulled back and delivered a sharp smack that sent pain ricocheting through her entire lower half, his deep voice drowning out her gasp of outrage.

"This one may take two Doms to handle, starting with a well-deserved spanking. Any takers?"

Before Paige could state her objection, two other voices called out a simultaneous bid that outdid all the others by over a thousand dollars. A shock wave of recognition almost sent her to her knees, but didn't keep her body from responding with its usual heated rush from knowing the Carlson brothers were near, and eyeing her naked butt.

Master Damien spun her back around in time to see a small spotlight illuminate Troy and Trevor seated in the front row. Troy's displeasure with her mimicked the club owner's while Trevor's sensuous lips turned up at the corners in his usual, amused expression. Her buttock burned and her nipple throbbed, but those uncomfortable sensations changed to a pleasurable warmth and pulse as she gazed upon the two men she couldn't seem to get out of her system. Paige noticed no one else now, heard nothing else as they finalized the transaction, and sure as hell possessed no clue what she'd just agreed to as the bouncer led her off the stage.

~

TREVOR LEANED against the wall outside the stage dressing room, crossed his arms and regarded his brother's agitated pacing with amusement. "Relax, would you? Damien caught her enrollment in time to call us."

Troy blazed him with a look of irritation. "I'm pissed she went against our orders, again, not worried about the interfering minx."

"Uh, huh. You keep telling yourself that, bro. In the meantime, I'll admit I'm itching to get my hands on Red, and have been for some time. It's nice she fell into my palms. Want me to handle her from here on out?"

"Fuck that, Trevor," he snapped so fast Trevor knew the moment Troy realized he'd just given himself away. "You're a sick bastard."

"Yeah, but you love me anyway. Now, what are we going to do with our acquisition for eight hours?"

"I know what we will not do, and that's let her off the hook this time. I plan to shave off thirty minutes by tossing her over my knees as soon as she gets her sweet ass out here. After that, I say if she's so interested in BDSM, we introduce her to the things she agreed to tonight. That might be enough to scare her off this vendetta and keep her out of our hair."

"Or," Trevor drawled, the image of Paige draped across his brother's lap searing his brain, "given her unpredictability, our efforts just might backfire and reveal she has a small thread of submission inside that lean body."

"If that happens, God help all three of us."

They both straightened when the side door opened and Paige stood there dressed in jeans and a bright yellow tee with black lettering reading: *People say you can't live without love... I think oxygen is more important.* Her face reflected a myriad of emotions, indecision being the most blatant. Straightening her shoulders, she stepped forward and that cocky grin Trevor enjoyed appeared.

"So, I'm guessing Damien ratted me out and assume he was the one who sent you after me last night. If you think I'm paying you back for what you bid, think again. I don't owe you anything."

"Wrong, sugar." Trevor snatched her hand and yanked her against him. "You owe us eight hours of your time. The contract you signed clearly stated if you renege on your end of the bargain, *then* you must repay us every dime. You did read the fine print, didn't you?" He could tell by her widening eyes and struggle to swallow that she hadn't. "Oops."

Paige averted her eyes and muttered under her breath, "*Addlepated dim doodle.*"

Trevor grinned at Troy. "Did she just call me an addlepated dim doodle?"

Troy nodded, a gleam replacing the irritation in his eyes. "I believe she did. I'll add that infraction to her punishment."

"This way, Paige." Tightening his hold on her hand, Trevor followed Troy back into the playroom where the auction was still underway.

"Where are we going?" Paige demanded with a tug of her hand.

He looked back to see her cast a frantic look around the room and felt her shudder when Troy halted at an armless chair situated on a small, raised dais. "Right here," he answered. "Your choice, sugar. Honor your signed agreement or agree to pay us back our donation." When she hesitated, the wary trepidation in her eyes at odds with the outline of her puckered nipples against her shirt, he said, "Come on, Paige. Be adventurous. You know us well enough to trust we won't do anything you'll regret. You say one word, red, at any time, and we halt whatever we're doing. That was also in the contract. What do you have to lose?"

She glanced from him to Troy, who remained silent, then back to Trevor again, her dove-gray eyes turning flinty with grim determination. "I'll honor the contract, as long as you promise to honor the safeword."

"Of course," Troy replied, stepping onto the dais. Sitting on the chair, he held out his hand. "For your punishment tonight, we'll keep it the simple stoplight colors in the contract. Red means stop, yellow, pause for a question or reassurance, green means you're good. If you want to change it later, we can. Ready?"

She eyed his lap with a cute dip of her brows. "No, but I'll do it anyway."

"That's our girl." She flipped Trevor a startled look at his words then stiffened when he reached around in front of her and unsnapped her jeans. As he lowered the zipper, he could tell from her audible indrawn breath, she hadn't expected them to mete out her punishment on her bare butt.

With a shove, he lowered the jeans and her panties to mid-thigh before handing her over to Troy. They intended to catch her off guard a lot during the time she would be under their control. He'd always suspected there was more to his favorite bartender than her flirty, independent nature. Neither he nor Troy had been blind to the interest she couldn't hide whenever they were in the bar. Since she wasn't a regular player, they'd both steered clear of any personal involvement, but that hadn't been easy for him. Trevor's attraction to the feisty redhead began upon first meeting her, and had increased each time he saw her. Troy, he suspected, also found himself drawn to Paige, but less inclined to either admit it or act upon it. Whatever they ended up planning to do with her during their allotted eight hours should prove interesting and enlightening for all three of them.

Right now, he enjoyed the hell out of watching his brother ease her down over his lap until her hands clutched his leg for balance. With a brush of his hand up her back, he left the t-shirt bunched around her shoulders and neck, her unfettered, pert breasts free to dangle and her surprisingly plump ass propped up. His own hands itched to be the one caressing those soft globes as Troy cupped one white buttock, but standing by as voyeur came with its own rewards. Like being able to read the expressions crossing her face in rapid succession. Surprise replaced irritation as soon as his brother touched her, followed by a glaze of arousal in her pewter eyes when Troy took his time exploring her malleable flesh with one palm while keeping his left hand pressed between her shoulder blades.

Yeah, they made an enticing scene to watch, and introduced a whole slew of future scenes to consider after tonight.

CHAPTER 7

*O*nly sheer stubbornness kept Paige from saying red when Trevor pulled her jeans down. Her natural inclination to protest this indignity with 'no way, no how', fell to the wayside the minute her mons pressed against Troy's muscled thigh and she looked up to see raw lust and rich approval etched on Trevor's face. Then Troy palmed her butt cheek, his calloused palm brushing against her bare skin, setting off sparks of pleasure that commanded her attention. She'd yearned for their attention for months, and now had it in spades.

Few of her lovers had ever bothered with ass play, so she'd never imagined that part of her anatomy could be so erogenous. But the more he explored her buttocks, squeezing then caressing, the hotter she became. A curl of arousal took up residence between her legs, softening her pussy, dampening her slit until embarrassment forced her to tighten her thighs.

Closing her eyes, Paige tuned out the voices from the ongoing auction and shoved aside fretting over whether anyone else's eyes were on her. The tantalizing caresses eased her into relaxing then prodded her to wiggle her butt and loosen her thighs in a teasing hint to do more, to touch her where she ached.

"I think she's ready."

The amused inflection in Trevor's voice snagged her attention one second before his words sank in. Before she could register the full meaning of that comment, Troy halted the soothing, arousing strokes of his hand and delivered a sharp swat to rival the one Damien issued on the stage.

Her head reared up in startled astonishment at the abrupt switch from coaxing pleasure to blistering pain. Before she could say anything, he swatted her again, adding an identical throbbing burn on her other cheek.

"Take a deep breath, Paige, and lie still. It'll be over before you know it."

Shaking her hair out of her eyes, she glared up at Trevor as Troy peppered her buttocks with an array of slaps that robbed her of breath. "Easy... *ow!...* for you to say," she gasped, her mind consumed with the fiery heat spreading across her entire backside and the deep throbbing encompassing her abused skin and spreading to her pussy.

"You should've heeded our warnings, and remembered I mentioned consequences if you continued with your harebrained scheme to interfere in my investigation," Troy admonished without slowing the rapid volley of spanks.

It was hard to think straight, to pay attention to what either man said, but she managed to stick up for herself with a quick rebuttal. "I don't take orders from anyone... *holy shit!*" Crap but those last two hurt! "Damn it, I'm not one of your little groupies, willing to let you walk all over me." Desperate to deny her body's heated response and the pleasure inching its way past her resistance to this degradation, she tried to wriggle away from his descending hand, but Trevor reached out and clamped his hands over the tops of her thighs. Between Troy's imprisoning hand braced between her shoulders and Trevor's tight told, they left her no choice but to endure and accept her surprising reaction or say red and pay the hefty price tag of ending this now.

Then Trevor's face swam into view in front of her as he squatted down and winked. "Be a good girl and we'll reward you."

"Says who?" Troy asked, pausing to trail his fingernails over her buttocks.

Paige's response to the prickling scrape across her sore skin turned out to be another eye-opening revelation. Tingles of pleasure erupted along her abused flesh, overriding the pulsating waves of discomfort. "*Oh,*" she breathed in astonishment.

This time it was Troy who chuckled, but before she could enjoy the sound, he whacked her sore butt three more times and her penchant for uttering nonsensical words slipped out. "*Asshattery douchnozzle!*"

Trevor's smile split his craggy face. "God, you're a delight." He glanced up and nodded. She braced herself for another painful smack, but instead, two pairs of hands roamed freely over her aching flesh, igniting a firestorm of sensation throughout her entire body she couldn't control.

Her breath whooshed out of her lungs as the pain entwined with unbelievable pleasure to the point she couldn't differentiate between the two sensibilities. An embarrassing whimper spilled from her mouth, the heat covering her butt spreading to fill her pussy with damp warmth.

Fingers teased the inside of her thighs, enticing her to open them wider. Other fingers glided down her crack in a stupefying exploration of receptive nerve endings she'd never imagined could be so titillating. Paige's gasp lodged in her throat when the hand on her inner thighs inched up and fingers stroked up the seam of her vagina. "More," she demanded, her tone laced with need as she lifted her hips.

Troy, she assumed, pinched her right cheek, the sharp sting earning him a glare as she flipped her head around and up. "What was that for?"

"For daring to give orders. Subs don't call the shots." He rubbed the offending spot then ruined the soothing caress with another swat.

"I'm not a sub," she grumbled in instant denial.

"Your sign-up sheet says you are, at least for a full eight hours spent with us," Trevor interjected.

He followed that reminder of her subterfuge with the insertion of two fingers into her pussy, derailing her objection. How the heck was she supposed to think straight with their hands all over her? Shaking her head in bemused stupor and escalating lust, she slammed her eyes shut and bit her lip to remain as docile as possible. Even if it killed her. At this moment, she wanted a climax more than she needed to exert her independence.

"I thought you might see it our way," Trevor purred.

"Oh, bite me." So much for remaining docile. There were times Trevor's humor at her expense grated on her, with Troy's silence doing the same.

"Well, if you insist." Troy raised the knee under her hips, lifting her buttocks before their mouths descended on the quivering globes.

Dual nips on her already pulsating flesh drew a resonating cry from Paige's throat and a wave of intense pleasure to add to the arousal stirred up by the continued movement of their fingers drifting over her anus and deeper inside her pussy. The bastards didn't stop with one bite, but traveled across her buttocks delivering several sharp teeth pricks on top of her well-spanked skin. Wiggling against their tormenting mouths did no good as they never let up on tormenting her in a way she'd never believed she'd allow, proving what a sexually manipulative force the two of them could be.

Finally, desperate need overrode all other emotions and insecurities, and left her no choice but to plead with them. "Please, enough already." She shifted and whispered with a cringe, "*Please.*"

"Damn, a heartfelt, breathless plea does it for me every time." Troy pushed his thumb against her anus, just enough to prod the opening and send another crashing deluge of sensation throughout her entire pelvis.

"Go ahead, Paige. Come for us." Trevor pulled back from the grasping clutches of her pussy only to fill her with three fingers and an irresistible glide over her aching clit.

Paige trembled under the onslaught, splintering apart as the pressure against her clit mirrored that against her puckered hole and set off a skyrocket of explosive pleasure. Ecstasy racked her body, her sheath spasming against his pummeling finger strokes while their mouths continued to roam over her clenching buttocks. She didn't know how they managed, and didn't care, instead choosing to enjoy the sweep of sensations giving her the best orgasm she'd ever experienced.

She kept trembling as Troy sat her up and wrapped his arm around her waist. Looking up, she blinked at the shadowed concern in his eyes as he held her close. It wasn't the humiliation and pain they'd just subjected her to that kept her sitting docile and vibrating on his lap, but her astonishing response to both men. Until Jim had shown his true colors with his fist, Penny had been the most content person—with both her personal and professional choices in life—Paige had ever known. Yet, for years, Paige had lamented over her sister's sexual preferences, not understanding the draw. Now, she possessed an inkling of what she'd been missing all this time, which required some serious thinking.

WITH A RELUCTANCE he couldn't recall feeling before, Troy allowed Paige to slip off his lap when she shrugged his arm off. Standing her between his knees, he kept his hands on her hips to steady her when she wobbled, ensuring she could handle the aftereffects of her first taste of kink. Despite the protests and back talk, she'd come apart under the painful stimulation they'd both wrought. Unlike Trevor, he'd held on to his misgivings about her, and never believed she would submit to any man, under any circumstances. She challenged him, and normally he didn't care for that when it came to sex. His job often left him drained, and more times than not, frustrated with a legal system that treated criminals better than victims. When he needed to unwind and set it all aside, he wanted a biddable woman who enjoyed what he liked to dish out.

Paige's slender frame vibrated under his hands, her silver eyes unwavering as she gazed down at him with a perplexed frown tightening her brow. She appeared as confused by her responses as he'd been surprised by them. Maybe they both had some rethinking to do before this went any further. His face was eye level with her heaving chest and turgid nipples. The rigid projection of the pretty pink buds proved how affected she'd been by her first spanking and taste of their domination, and were an irresistible temptation for his mouth.

Leaning forward, he drew on one nipple and then pulled back with a strong suction and tongue rasp over the tip before taking his time to nibble on the tender bud. Troy noticed Trevor standing behind her, his hands doing something to her ass he envied. The girl had a nice, soft but firm backside. It had been his pleasure to punish and turn it a beautiful shade of crimson.

Her eyes glazed and she tried to shift her pelvis, but he tightened his grip, keeping her still. Her enticing, bare labia shone with her still oozing cream, another sign they could get her off again with little effort. Too bad for her he was more in the mood to get her dander up once more. "You know," he stated around her nipple when she pushed her breast closer to his mouth, "you should be on your knees, thanking us."

"What?" Just as he'd thought, her face flushed and her eyes snapped with annoyance. "Why should I do that? Do you have any idea how much my butt hurts?"

Troy caught Trevor's attention, waited for him to slide his hands up to her shoulders then, in sync, they urged her down. "Unless you're ready for round two, kneel."

"Oh, for..." With a disgruntled huff, Paige went to her knees, and Troy damn near came in his pants like an adolescent teen. The t-shirt had fallen back down, outlining every nub of her areolae against the soft fabric that skimmed right above the enticing swath of pubic hair arrowed above her bare pussy lips. With her jeans still bunched around her thighs, her fiery hair in disarray around her face, and her eyes showing her displeasure clear as a bell, she presented a hell of a picture.

"As I was saying, you should be grateful because normally we don't follow a punishment with pleasure. We were nice because you're new to this. Next time, I wouldn't count on us being so accommodating if I were you. I don't always side with my brother in these matters."

She looked from him up to Trevor, her frown turning perplexed. "You... do you two do this often?"

Cocking his head, Trevor asked, "What, share a woman? Yes."

"Huh."

Troy could tell she hadn't considered that answer before, but her expression didn't reveal how she felt about their penchant for sharing.

"Well, if you think I'll thank you for whipping my butt, think again, doodle heads." She crossed her arms in a belligerent gesture of defiance.

Troy grasped both nipples between his thumbs and forefingers and then slowly squeezed, watching her eyes widen in alarm before she ceded the battle to him.

"Okay, okay, *Sheesh*. Thank you. Satisfied?"

Trevor reached down to help her stand. With a hand on her red ass, he held her next to him as he replied, "Not even close, sugar, but good enough for tonight."

Troy thought his brother's statement summed it up for both of them quite well. Stepping behind her, he pulled up her pants and reached around to zip and snap them closed before latching on to one hand while Troy picked up the other. "We'll walk you out and be in touch about when we can all get together for the seven and a half hours left of your agreement."

～

PAIGE WINCED as she stepped onto the stool to reach the high shelf along the fireplace wall. Every move she made this morning emphasized the lingering soreness encompassing her lower body. She'd spent most of last night tossing and turning, groaning when even the cool sheets brushing across her buttocks revealed the tenderness her first spanking left behind. If that hadn't been bad enough, each spark of warmth and discomfort zeroed straight down to fill her core with pulsing lust. Her response to Troy and Trevor's manhandling still boggled her mind as much as when she'd realized they were the ones who'd called out the winning bid for her.

She hopped down from the stool, clenching her buttocks on the landing. A twinge of tenderness made itself known and drew her groused muttering. *"Addlepated titweenies."* She almost smiled when she pictured their faces whenever she let loose with one of her inane lines. The nonsensical words had started popping out of her mouth at a young age, and the habit had grown and extended into her adulthood.

Stretching her tired, achy body, she scanned the great room of the two-story home she'd finished cleaning, ensuring she left nothing unfinished. The Morgans were among her first clients, and owned one of the most profitable, and tiring, homes on her list to clean. Thank goodness she could call it a day now.

As Paige gathered her supplies, she tried not to wonder what else Troy and Trevor had in store for her, or when they would demand she pay her debt. It may have taken a year, and risking their wrath by trying to interfere in their investigation, but she'd finally gained the hot brothers' attention. Sometime between the humiliation of bending over Troy's lap bare-assed and exploding in a body-encompassing orgasm, she'd thought about milking this turn of events for every drop she could get. Since they'd shown little personal interest in her before, their demand she abide by the auction rules or pay up had taken her by surprise, but she wasn't one to question the giving of an unexpected gift too long or too hard.

They thought they were teaching her a lesson and ensuring she pulled no more stunts like last night by enforcing the terms of that contract. She knew their sudden interest in her was to ensure she kept out of the investigation, reinforced by showing her what she'd been setting herself up for by coming to the club under false pretenses. But after experiencing what those two could do to a woman's body, she decided to jump on board with whatever reason would allot her more time with them, and with any games they wanted to play. Maybe after eight hours of indulging in decadent sexual practices with the two, she could rid herself of this unreciprocated infatuation.

Now, if she could just handle the whole 'submit to me' thing, she'd be able to relax and get more out of the short time she would have them to herself. Kneeling between them had gone against her nature, and she'd found that part of the scene last night unacceptable. Then she recalled Troy's tight pinch of her nipples, and his intent, probing gaze. A shiver rippled down her spine and her pussy clutched remembering that sharp pain, and the quick uptick of arousal it had generated.

She needed to talk to Penny, but she couldn't say she was looking forward to seeing her smirk at Paige's dilemma. Paige locked the Morgans' door behind her then opened her purse to drop the key in. The folded paper she'd found on her windshield yesterday morning reminded her of the threat she likely didn't have to worry about now. It still troubled her he knew their address, but since Damien was sure to ban her from Sanctuary, it looked like the bastard would win this round. She would continue to be diligent about watching out for herself, but wait until Penny came home and recovered more before revealing how close she'd come to her assailant. No sense in upsetting Penny, or ruining the few hours she would have with Troy and Trevor by showing it to anyone now.

After returning home to shower and change, Paige drove to the hospital and found her sister in physical therapy. Dressed in loose gym shorts and a plain t-shirt, Penny ambled up and down a set of parallel bars, her gait slow and uneven, but much improved from the last time Paige had seen her up.

"Looking good, sis." She smiled as the therapist pulled a wheel-chair up to the end and Penny eased down with a sigh. "No pain, no gain, isn't that how the saying goes?"

Penny gave her a scathing look. "Just wait until I've recovered my full strength."

"I live for the day, and the challenge." Paige looked at the thera-pist. "I'll take her back upstairs, if that's all right?"

"Sure. Good workout, Penny. We'll get in one more tomorrow morning before you're discharged and then we can set up an outpa-tient schedule."

"Tomorrow?" Paige asked as she wheeled her sister toward the elevator. "For sure?"

"That's what Dr. Matthews told me this morning after another scan. I swear, I could line a room with the number of scans this place has of my head." Penny reach up and grazed the bandage still covering half her forehead. "It's a miracle I have any brain cells left functioning."

"Yes, it is, so let's not push it. Are you sure you're ready to come home?" Backing her into the elevator, Paige reached around and pressed the button for Penny's floor then stood at her side, watching her closely.

"If I don't get out of here, I'll go bonkers, Paige. I'm mobile now, enough I can take care of myself. I'll have meds for the lingering headaches and you to make sure I do my exercises but don't overdo it."

"Damn right." The door pinged open and Penny wheeled herself across the hall into her room with an airy wave toward the nurse's desk, Paige following behind. When she went to assist Penny into the bed, her twin shook her off. "I'm not an invalid. I've got this." She sat on the side, appearing content to sit up for a while longer. "Tell me what you did on your day off, besides come up here to see me."

Leave it to Penny to hand her a tidy opening for what she wanted to discuss but didn't want to. Settling into the chair facing her, Paige stated, "You likely won't believe me."

"But, you'll tell her anyway, won't you?"

Both women whipped their heads toward the door and that intruding, steel-edged voice. Damien leaned against the wall in a negligent, deceiving pose, his face taut, his eyes sharp and assessing when they scanned Penny from head to toe.

Paige found her voice first and scowled. "You keep turning up like a bad penny."

"You keep insinuating yourself in my club under false pretenses," he shot back.

Penny gasped, her eyes wide with shock and anger when she swiveled her gaze back to Paige. "You, what? Paige, tell me you didn't."

"She can't, not without lying." Damien sauntered in and stood at the foot of the bed, crossing his thick arms. "You don't plan on lying to your sister, do you, Paige?"

Irritation slithered under her skin as guilt pricked Paige's conscience. She never kept secrets from her sister, but given Penny's condition, she'd refused to burden her with her plans. That, and she hadn't wanted Penny to talk her out of them. "My conversation with my sister is none of your business, or your concern." Paige ignored Penny's gasp and refused to look away from Damien's icy glare.

"Penny, sweetheart, tell Paige what happens when she exhibits such disrespect to a Dom. Oh, wait." He snapped his fingers and a wicked grin ticked up one side of his mouth. "That's right. Last night, you learned firsthand the consequences of going against me, and other Doms, didn't you?"

"What's he talking about, Paige?"

Paige disliked the flush that spread over Penny's cheeks and the way her eyes rounded when the jerk called her sweetheart. How could her sister fall for a man so similar to the one who had turned abusive all those months ago? Seeing no way around it, she came clean with her.

"I was trying to help. I thought if I could get your assailant to focus on me, I could draw him out into the open again."

Penny's eyes snapped with anger. "At a huge risk to yourself? What were you thinking?"

Paige pushed to her feet and fisted her hands on her hips. "I was thinking I'd do anything, risk anything to nail the bastard who hurt you. Are you telling me you wouldn't move heaven and earth to avenge me if the situation were reversed?"

Penny hesitated, and Paige could easily read her answer on her face. Seeing the way Damien frowned, she assumed he also caught the guilt now reflected in her eyes.

"You know I would, but Paige, you... you're not submissive!" Penny's exclamation revealed her astonishment at the lengths Paige had gone through to avenge her.

Damien snorted. "You wouldn't say that if you'd seen her response to her punishment last night. Your sister went off like a firecracker, draped over one of her buyers' lap while they both played with her."

With a giggle, Penny quipped, "Oh, to be a fly on the wall. I can't picture you in such a scene, and with two men no less!"

Another voice intruded with, "It was a hell of a scene."

With a low, muttered curse, Paige looked toward the door and Trevor's slow drawl to see both Carlsons striding in. The small room shrank even more with their overpowering presence. Her heart, that traitorous organ, went pitter patter, and her vagina, the faithless bitch, went all damp and happy at seeing them. It seemed she couldn't win. Somehow, that didn't faze her with annoyance as it should have.

"Oh, my God—them?"

Paige grinned at Penny's astonishment. It was only fair her sister get blindsided as well. "Yes, them."

"Make your questions quick," Damien told Troy and Trevor before dropping another bombshell on Paige. "I need to talk with Penny about coming home with me tomorrow when she's discharged."

"What?" Penny gasped at the same time Paige cried, "No way!"

Damien met their objections with a determined glint in his eyes. "Penny, we'll discuss this in private. Paige, you don't get a say so, this is between me and your sister. If you argue," he added, playing a trump card, "you'll upset your sister."

Glancing from Penny's tense face to Damien's smug look then over to the Carlsons' knowing gazes, Paige knew when she was beat and did the only thing she could.

Muttering, *"Bunch of dimwitted doodledrawers,"* she stomped out with a backward toss, "I'll call you later, Penny."

TREVOR NODDED to Troy and Damien before joining Paige at the door. He enjoyed the way she frowned at him when he clasped her hand and said, "Come on, potty mouth. I'll walk you out."

She followed him with a huff that widened his grin. "I don't know why you and your brother think I can't walk to my car by myself. Believe it or not, I've been managing that feat for a long time."

"If I didn't know better, sugar, I'd think you had something against us. You don't, do you?" His smile turned sardonic as the elevator doors whooshed closed.

"Only that you're overbearing pains in my ass all of a sudden.

What happened to you barely knowing I exist?" The taunting look she tossed him mimicked his and drew a chuckle.

Bending down, he whispered in her ear so the other two people in the lift didn't hear. "Speaking of your lovely ass, how is it today? Any problems?" She stiffened against him, but not until after she leaned into his side with a soft sigh.

"None of your business," she hissed, but he caught the glimmer of amusement in her eyes.

Trevor tugged her out of the elevator when it opened on the ground floor and kept quiet until they exited the hospital. "I'm making everything about you my business for now, so get used to it. Are you free next Sunday?" he asked when they reached her Jeep.

"Yes. That's my only day off." Paige tried, but couldn't suppress the leap of excitement pumping her pulse up.

"Good, we'll let you shave off the remaining seven and a half hours of your contract then." Just to see those gray eyes glaze with passion again, he pinned her against the vehicle with his lower body pressed against hers and drew her hand behind her back. Her eyes widened and her body softened as he bent his head and took her mouth in a tongue exploring kiss meant to arouse and leave her with something to think about.

Those soft lips clung to his, her small tongue giving back stroke for stroke as she arched against him. He noticed she didn't shy away from the public place, but he doubted if she caught the significance of that. His body went hard from the feel of her soft curves against him, her low moan of surrender and the way she nipped at his jaw when he released her.

"Until Sunday, Paige." He flicked her nose and walked back inside.

Bemused, Paige stared after Trevor, wondering how she'd make it until Saturday since her vibrator no longer held any appeal for her.

CHAPTER 8

$\mathcal{P}$enny tensed when Paige left her alone with the
detective and Master Damien. She still couldn't wrap
her mind around her sister's ploy to draw out her attacker, or
Paige's involvement with the Carlson brothers. Not that the two
men weren't eye-catching, but she could have warned her about
their BDSM involvement had she come to her first. She'd known
the second she saw Paige in physical therapy something was on her
mind, but she never would've guessed she'd spent time last evening
receiving her first spanking, at Sanctuary, no less.

Then Master Damien had to go and derail her a second time by
tossing out that tidbit about going home with him tomorrow. What
was he thinking? With every visit, he'd left her increasingly flustered. She didn't understand his sudden interest in her. Since
someone had assaulted her leaving his club, she understood his
sense of responsibility and even his overprotectiveness, a trait most
Doms shared. But to push her into spending time recuperating in
his private home went above and beyond the scope of their limited
relationship and sent jitters jumping around in her abdomen.

With a wary eye, Penny watched Detective Carlson move
toward her, his face calm and understanding where a few minutes

ago, when he'd looked at her sister, he'd shown the countenance of a hard-edged Dom. "Any news?" she asked him when he stopped in front of her. She could see why Paige's face had reflected such interest, even though she tried to hide it. Tall and imposing, Troy's soft tone always belied the stern set to his rugged features.

"I got hold of your ex, Jim Bates. He claims he was home, alone, the night of your attack, and he displayed genuine concern for you. He'll remain on my suspect list because he doesn't have an alibi, but I'm not looking at him for these assaults, not unless something turns up that points toward him. He's a member of a club in Savannah and never causes problems there."

"He never did in my club either," Damien bit out before switching his cobalt blue gaze to Penny. "That turned out not to mean much." She wanted to shrink under his scrutiny but held her head up. She knew she wasn't at fault for Jim's temper, and subsequent abuse, any more than she had been her assailant's.

"True," Troy sighed with a shake of his head. "But like I said, he's in Savannah, and the new branch he opened for the investigative firm he works for appears successful, and to keep him busy."

"He was always superb at his job, especially with cyber investigations like scams and computer fraud." Penny had always been in awe of Jim's computer skills.

"Yes, he mentioned that's his main expertise. I want you to know I've got volunteers in every club in Florida lined up for the upcoming weeks, good, trained people who will be diligent about watching for this guy. Let's hope he resurfaces soon and someone can nab him."

"I'd welcome him to try again at my place."

Penny shivered from the impact of the ice-cold rage swirling in Damien's eyes. She really needed to get herself under control when he came around. Blowing hot from sexual awareness and need one minute and then turning frigid when he revealed his ruthless side the next was getting tiresome.

"Be careful what you wish for, Damien." Troy noticed Trevor's return. Squeezing her shoulder, he said, "If I get anything concrete, I'll be in touch. In the meantime, take care of yourself."

"She will."

Penny did a mental head shake at Damien's arrogant insertion, waiting until the Carlsons left before turning to him and saying, "Aren't you carrying your sense of responsibility too far? I understand you feel guilty since my assault happened at your club, but no one's to blame except the perpetrator."

He cocked his head and eyed her with a brooding look that made her itch to run her fingers through his long black hair and over his furrowed brow. She squirmed under that intense, silent gaze, but refused to back down. They weren't at the club, nor was she his submissive.

"Your sister works a lot. It would be an imposition on her time, and finances, to take off for you. Spring break starts tomorrow, and I've instructed my assistant manager to take over at the club for the next two weekends," he stated with blunt reasoning.

She knew only too well the state of Paige's finances, and that her sister would neglect her jobs to cater to Penny's needs. "You act like I'm a complete invalid," she returned, frustrated because she wanted him, and couldn't figure out why his sudden interest in her after all but ignoring her for the past few years. "I'm getting around much better, I don't need a caretaker."

"You may not need one twenty-four/seven, but you're getting my help anyway, either at my place or yours, you decide."

Penny pushed to her feet in agitation, unable to get a read on him, her mind replaying the scene on the Sybian and the way she'd responded to his dominant takeover of her senses. Her weak leg gave out on her, forcing her to grab his arm as he rushed forward. She shuddered from the sudden impact of falling against his large body then feeling his arm wrap around her waist. His low chuckle, the first time she'd heard one from him, vibrated down her spine and echoed in her ear as he bent his head.

"See, you do need me. Quit fighting it, little one."

"I don't understand you," she whispered, her voice tremulous.
He sighed. "I know."

～

AN AFTERNOON CRUISE. *On a private yacht. With not one, but both men
I've been lusting after.* Paige scanned the busy Friday night crowd
with a mental head shake. As if she didn't have enough to fret over
with Penny ensconced at Damien's house, her sister's decision to
take up with a man she met under the same circumstances as her
abusive ex weighed heavily on Paige's mind. Now, Penny's misfor-
tune in getting assaulted may have inadvertently gifted Paige with a
fantasy come true opportunity, but that didn't negate the fact she
might have gotten herself in over her head with the Carlson brothers. Every time the memory of having their hands and mouths all
over her butt and inside her popped up, she craved a repeat of
being the sole focus of their attention. Then reality would stick its
rude nose in her business and remind her nothing could ever come
of messing around with the pair, except maybe one more erotic,
off-the-charts sexual encounter to remember when they returned
to being polite customers.

A female cop sitting at the end of the bar lifted her glass for a
refill, reminding Paige she had a job to do. Drawing another
brew, she tried not to think about Trevor's call yesterday, and the
plans for Sunday he and Troy had come up with. March wasn't a
bad time to spend an afternoon on the ocean, and who wouldn't
enjoy sailing on a fancy mega yacht with two hot guys? Oh, and
another couple, friends of theirs. It was the fun accoutrements
Trevor mentioned that turned her palms damp, and hearing about
the other couple that sent a wave of heat through her. Always
before, she'd known what she was getting into when she
succumbed to the urge to have sex with someone, but not
this time.

Best-case scenario: She got both Troy and Trevor out of her

system on Sunday. Worst case: She walked away yearning for more, maybe nursing a tender heart.

"Hey, quit daydreaming and get me another." Detective Evans snapped his glass down on the counter.

Paige sent the refill down the bar top with a slight push before acknowledging her nemesis' belligerent demand. She returned Evans' glower, surprised at his red-rimmed eyes considering the watered-down drinks she'd been serving him the past two hours.

"One more, Detective." Picking up his empty, she turned away to get a clean glass, but he stopped her by latching on to her wrist with a bruising grip.

Leaning forward, Evans snarled so no one else could hear, "You're not my keeper, bitch. Quit cutting back on the booze."

"It doesn't seem to have mattered since you're still a drunken ass. Let. Go. Of. Me," she enunciated slowly.

He tightened his grip until she winced then released her and sat back with a taunting sneer. Resisting the urge to rub her throbbing wrist, she turned her back on the jerk and mixed the weakest drink yet. *Take this, you mother fucking titworm.*

"Is there a problem, Paige?" Mel asked, sidling up to the bar and flicking the surly cop a warning look.

"Not at all," she replied in her sweetest voice that earned her another glower from Evans. "I was just telling our good detective he's met his limit with this refill."

Mel said something to Evans, but Trevor snagged Paige's attention when he entered The Precinct and maneuvered his way through the crowd toward the bar. It was the first time she'd seen him without his brother, but the lustful impact of his potent gaze struck her the same. The detective stalked off with a disgruntled huff, Mel winked and gave her a smile before turning to make the rounds again, and Trevor slid onto the bar stool in front of her.

"Hey, sugar. Can I get a beer?"

"Of course." Damn it, Paige didn't get flustered around men, but from the way Trevor's eyes skimmed down to her chest then back up to her face, she knew he was picturing her shirt rucked up to her shoulders and thinking about the way he'd enjoyed her bare breasts last weekend. She remembered too, every, single, vivid detail.

"Where's your sidekick? I've never seen you in here without Troy." Sticking a frosted glass under the spigot, she pulled the lever, willing her body to calm down with a warning they weren't getting together again for another day and a half.

"We do manage to have our own separate interests and down time." His slow drawl curled her toes, and made her wonder if she was a separate interest, or just a thorn in both their sides because of her determination to avenge Penny.

"Here you go, then. Enjoy your evening."

Paige swiveled but Trevor halted her with one, low-voiced word. "Stop." She wasn't sure if the goosebumps racing over her skin were due to irritation from her immediate compliance or the warmth his tone always produced. Sucking in a deep breath, she pasted on her friendly bartender face and swung back around to face him. "Did you need something else?"

He cocked his head with an amused grin. "Really? So formal after I had my mouth all over your ass and your cream gushing over my fingers?"

Frantic, she leaned forward and hissed, "*Shh!* What if someone hears you?"

"Please," he whispered back. "Give me a little credit. No one is near enough to hear what we're saying over the noise in here. I stopped by to see for myself if you were being honest and you're on board with Sunday's plans."

She hadn't expected such solicitous concern as she heard in his voice and noted on his face when he kept those probing eyes leveled on hers. If she hadn't already figured it out, that look would have confirmed she lacked the ability to pull much over on him, or his brother.

"I still don't get what's in it for you," she returned, hoping he would answer the one question plaguing her most.

Trevor sipped his beer before answering, his gaze remaining focused on her over the glass. "Troy and I will have an attractive redhead all to ourselves, miles from shore, on a yacht filled with endless possibilities to torment you with. What's not to look forward to?"

"Neither of you showed an interest in me before Penny's assault," she reminded him, attempting to ignore her tight nipples and the sudden way her bra felt too confining under his piercing gaze.

He hesitated before replying, "Lucky for all of us you decided to tread where we warned you not to then, isn't it?"

She couldn't win with verbal sparring, so her only hope would be to shock the heck out of both men by submitting to their every demand on Sunday. With any luck, she would leave them aching for more, as they'd done to her last weekend. She should've come up with that plan days ago; it would've saved her a lot of grief.

"Yes, it just might be." Paige grinned at the way he startled before masking his reaction to her quick agreement. "Two, or in this case, three can play your game, Trevor. I'll see you and Troy Sunday." This time he didn't stop her when she moved away from him, but she felt his eyes on her until he left fifteen minutes later.

The following afternoon, Paige slowed her steps to the Jeep when she noticed another note fluttering on the windshield. With a hand that shook, she jerked it off and opened it. *Last warning, back off before you end up worse than your sister.* A slither of unease rippled down her spine and she cast a quick look up and down the street before hopping behind the wheel. She'd be a fool not to heed the warning, but since she couldn't return to the club now they'd found her out, she labored to swallow down the lump lodged in her throat and calm her racing heart as she pulled out of the drive. What was done was done, and even though she regretted not being able to lure this son-of-a-bitch out of hiding and take part in taking him down, she'd be only too happy to drop off his radar with her absence from Sanctuary.

She pulled up to Damien's house to find Penny waiting for her on the front porch swing. As she started to get out to help her sister, Penny surprised her by walking over to the Jeep with a much stronger, surer gait than the last time she'd seen her only a few days ago. After waiting until she shut the passenger side door, Paige got right to the main reason for their lunch appointment.

"Okay, give. What's going on between you two?" Backing out of Damien's drive, she didn't miss the discomposure crossing her sister's face before Penny smoothed out her features. "Don't you even think of lying to me, sis."

"I'm not, Paige, but there's nothing to tell. Damien feels responsible for what happened, is all."

"Then why do you look so despondent? Are you feeling bad? You seem much stronger." The two had made plans to go out for lunch before Paige reported for her shift at the bar. The timing worked well since Damien had been called into the club because of a problem and wasn't around when Paige picked Penny up. She held nothing against the man except his high-handedness in dictating to her sister.

"I'm feeling good, and yes, I'm doing much better. You noticed how much easier I'm walking? Damien has me working out on his weight machine, and it's been helping."

"I did and am so proud of you. I know these last two weeks couldn't have been easy. Any nightmares?" The bistro they'd selected wasn't far, and Paige pulled over to park in front of the popular cafe. A short, wrought-iron fence surrounded the front outdoor patio with its round, checker-clothed tables under colorful umbrellas. Sitting outside in the pleasant, mid-seventies temperature and mild breeze would be enjoyable after being cooped up all week.

Penny hedged before admitting, "Just one, but... I was fine."

Paige put the Jeep in park with a sigh. "Come on Penny," she said, swiveling in the seat to face her. "Talk to me. I can tell when something's bothering you. Are you ready to come home?" She hoped so, but wouldn't push.

"No, yes... damn it, that man has me twisted into so many knots, I'll never get them untied," Penny burst out in a rare show of frustration. Of the two of them, she was usually the most easygoing.

"I thought you liked being tied up," Paige teased before turning serious again. "What's he doing?"

"I do like being bound, and that's the problem. He's not doing *anything*! I'm sleeping in the guest room and he waits on me hand and foot in between turning all Dom when it's time to exercise, eat, or rest, which means he's in Dom mode most of the time." Penny rolled her eyes. "When he's not dictating to me, he's being too... nice."

Shaking her head, Paige opened her door and slid out, saying, "Men. If we could figure them out, we might not want them. Ever think of that?"

"No, but now I will." Penny followed her to a table before confessing, "He's everything Jim wasn't, which I figure is why I'm attracted to him. But it's one-sided so, yes, I'm planning on returning home soon. All I need to do is get up the nerve to go against a Dom's wishes for the first time. And get that smirk off your face. It's not as easy as you think. If you haven't found that out yet with the Carlsons, you will if you're around them much longer. Your turn to give. I want to hear details about your punishment, and what it's like to have two men fawning over you."

"They're hardly fawning," Paige returned with a wry twist to her lips. "The only reason they pulled that stunt the other night was to keep me from going back to Sanctuary. Now that Damien, and Troy and Trevor, know what I was up to, they'll bar me from the club. Which is why I can't figure out why they're insisting I meet the obligations in the auction contract." She shook her head, as confused over their motives as Penny appeared over Damien's. "But I'm going through with it. I've spent the last year trying to figure out which man I fantasize most about, without an ounce of encouragement from either. If nothing else, I'll use those hours with them to get a little recompense for the sleepless nights they've given me."

Penny giggled, a sound Paige relished after all her sister's suffering. "I don't blame you, but I still can't picture you letting them tie you up, or you taking orders from them, even if it's limited to sexual submission."

With a rueful exhale, Paige admitted, "Me either, which is why I plan to distract them with flirtatious teasing, to keep them as on their toes as they put me. I wonder who will end up enjoying the upper hand."

They took a seat at an empty table and Penny hid her face behind the menu, but Paige still caught the humor lacing her voice with her reply. "My money is on them."

Paige tried not to put much stock into Penny's words as she worked her way through another shift at The Precinct that night, but her sister's remark did nothing to boost Paige's confidence for tomorrow. It helped that the bar boasted a larger than usual Saturday night crowd, keeping her so busy she didn't have time to stress over what the guys might have planned or what her response might be to their dominance. That was, not until Troy walked in, zeroed in on her from across the room and then nodded before joining a group in the back corner.

Over the next hour, Paige's job ran her ragged filling orders while conversing with the clientele, all the while leaving her conscious of the thrill of one man's constant scrutiny. Where was that focused interest all these months when she'd been pining over him and his brother? Yeah, she was looking forward to tomorrow, and pulling out all the wiles she could muster to keep them off guard as they'd been doing to her.

$\sim$

TROY SIPPED HIS DRINK, listening with half an ear to the conversations and joking from his cronies. He'd worked late last night, but Trevor had phoned when he got home from checking in with Paige and said she appeared calm about going out with them tomorrow. But he didn't trust her, not when it came to this abrupt about-face over submitting to them. He didn't deny he'd been as drawn to the spunky redhead as his brother, but it had never entered his mind to act on it. He enjoyed limited down time, and when given the chance to meet up with the gang of seven for an innocent game of poker or an evening of BDSM play, he didn't want to waste time catering to a newbie or arguing with a defiant sub.

Paige fell into neither category—at least that was what he believed after having the pleasure of her draped over his lap and the feel of her ass reddening and heating under his hand. Her cries of surprise and pleasure were genuine, her responses enough to leave him hard and hurting. She intrigued him and was turning out to be a puzzle with missing pieces he'd enjoy filling in.

They had asked Zach and Sandie to join them tomorrow, limiting the extras to one couple in deference to Paige's inexperience and the way they'd coerced her into complying. Neither he nor Trevor felt guilty over enforcing the terms of the contract; she had a way out by paying them back. She didn't need to know they wouldn't have pushed repayment had she balked. But they'd both noticed the gleam of interest in her eyes and the obvious signs of arousal when they'd discussed fulfilling the remaining seven plus hours.

Bringing his glass to his mouth, he hid his grin when Paige said something to the people lined up at the bar that made them laugh. Following with a silly grin and pirouette, she entertained her customers with flirtatious glances no one found fault with. When the crowd thinned, he downed the last swallow of his drink and rose, making his excuses to his friends.

"Excuse me. I believe I'll get a refill then head out. Catch you guys later."

Troy wound through the tables, passed the pool sharks off to the side and slid onto a stool at the bar, his cock twitching when Paige stepped over to him with a wary frown and that cute dip of her brows. She tossed her head, swaying her chin-length hair around her jaw, her gray eyes snapping with awareness and determination.

"What can I get you, Detective?"

She didn't know Trevor had relayed every word of their encounter last night. Amused, Troy leaned forward and cupped his hand on her nape, drawing her torso across the bar to meet him halfway. Against her mouth, he whispered, "So formal after giving me the pleasure of smacking your delectable ass then feeling your pussy grip my finger with your orgasm." She stiffened and tried to pull away, but he held her still long enough to press his lips hard against hers. Sitting back, he held up his glass. "A small refill, please."

"You..." Flustered, she cast a quick look around and he could see the relief replacing her annoyance when she noticed no one stood close enough to hear, or even pay them any mind. "Sure." He made sure their fingers brushed when she took the glass and enjoyed the flare of heat spreading over her pale cheeks.

"When do you get off?" Troy asked when she set his refill in front of him.

"Mel's nephew is picking up extra cash by taking over for me at ten. Why?"

"I'll wait and walk you out."

"Here we go again with your fetish for walking me to my car. I'm a big girl, Troy, and know how to take care of myself."

He grinned and leaned forward again, this time letting her meet him halfway on her own, which she did without hesitation. Damn, maybe big brother was right, and the girl possessed more than an inkling of submission under that layer of feisty independence. "I thought to tell you in private about another fetish. It includes fitting you with a pair of nipple huggers and small butt plug before we drive down to Miami tomorrow. Have you ever used either?"

Her breath hitched and her eyes widened, but a teasing smile ghosted across her lips followed by her tongue darting out to lick it off. "No, Detective, I haven't." She stood back, adding, "But I'll discuss the possibility with you in," she checked the time then raised a brow, "ten minutes, when you walk me out."

Troy shifted on the stool, his jeans growing tight around his semi-erection as he watched her work cleaning up her station. Snug denim hugged her ass, and he itched to get his hands on her again. Her quick turnabout after he'd shocked her with their plans caught him off guard, a rare thing for anyone to accomplish. As soon as her replacement arrived, she reached under the counter, waved to Mel and strolled around the bar to meet him.

"I'm ready."

He grasped her elbow and they walked in silence out the side door, down the short, narrow hall to the back exit and into the rear parking lot. "I need to talk to Mel about getting better lighting back here," he stated, leading her over to her vehicle and taking the keys from her to open the door.

"About tomorrow, do I have a say in anything?"

"You have the safewords, or you can pick your own, either of which will stop anything we're doing. And you can still change your mind about participating at all any time between now and when we reach the marina in Miami. Believe it or not, you hold the power to make all the decisions. I told you about the toys to prepare you, and give you time to think about this overnight, before we arrive at 1:00."

He caught the gleam in her eyes even in the meager light. Paige leaned into him and brushed her lips over his, the 'barely there' kiss enough to send a frisson of lust straight to his groin. "I won't change my mind. In fact, I'm looking forward to it, Detective. Goodnight."

"Paige." She halted before sliding behind the wheel but didn't look around at him. Pressing against her back, he instructed, "Wear a skirt, and leave off your bra and panties." He felt her stiffen, but she nodded without a word before settling in the Jeep.

She had guts, he'd give her that, Troy thought, watching her drive off. He hoped that bravado lasted through the afternoon. For the first time in years, he was looking forward to introducing a newbie to the lifestyle.

CHAPTER 9

"*Y*ou'll enjoy them, I promise."

Penny's words echoed in Paige's head as she padded to the front door, her buttocks clenching at the thought of invasion. The first thing she'd done upon waking this morning was call her sister and ask about what to expect from the two toys Troy mentioned. Her nipples were virgins to anything other than human fingers and mouths, and no one had dared touch her between her cheeks until last week. The brush and press of Troy's thumb against that taboo orifice had delivered an eye-opening array of new sensations, which left her open to exploring other possible pleasures that untried body part offered. Penny's assertions about the nipple huggers and plug helped ease Paige's mind over trying them, but she still balked at parading around naked under her skirt.

It had taken a supreme effort on her part to bite back a negative retort to Troy's clothing dictate last night. Reining in the urge to exert her independence this afternoon may prove to be the biggest challenge. Her libido, the traitorous bitch, wasn't helping matters by being unable to decide which brother she craved more, regardless of their dominant high-handedness.

She ran clammy hands down the white denim skirt she'd purchased that morning along with the blue and white striped knit top and then reached for the door handle. Straight up 1:00 she opened the door to the mouthwatering sight of Troy and Trevor on her doorstep.

"Ready and dressed for an ocean cruise," Trevor stated before tipping up her chin with two fingers and brushing her mouth with his. Sauntering inside, he used those same fingers to graze over her nipples without pausing a step, the light touch enough to leave the nubs puckered and cause her breath to stutter.

Troy stepped forward, and before she could wrap her mind around his intent, he gripped her hair and tugged her head back for his hard lip lock. The sharp yank on her scalp tightened the coil in her abdomen and drew a small drip of cream from her pussy lips. Together, they presented a potent concoction Paige wanted more than anything to stir up before tasting.

Turning from his perusal around the small living area, Trevor cocked his head and regarded her for a solemn moment before asking, "Do you still want to come with us today?"

The hint of mirth dancing around his mouth drew her attention to the double entendre she knew he intended with the word 'come'. The fact Paige grew as warm under Trevor's amused regard as she did with Troy's sterner approach still baffled her. "Yes, of course." She waved a hand down her skirt. "As you can see, I wore what Troy instructed, and," tossing both men a teasing, impish grin, she flipped up the front of the skirt, "I left off my underthings." Dropping her skirt, her look turned smug until Troy wiped it from her face with a few, succinct words.

"Excellent. That means you're ready to bend over the sofa."

Taking her hand, Trevor led her to the small couch. "Come on, sugar. Let's get you decked out and on the road. We have a thirty-minute drive ahead of us."

Paige could tell by their watchful gazes they expected her to argue, so she did the opposite and bent over, bracing her hands on the sofa without a word. A pregnant moment of silence followed and then Troy's angry voice whipped out, startling her with his low growl.

"Who did this?" Lifting her right hand, he held out her wrist with the small purple bruises surrounding it.

Paige had completely forgotten about the marks Evans' grip had left behind, but she wasn't about to turn over his name to the two men regarding her with affronted scowls. The cop with an attitude toward her was her problem, one she could handle just fine without the brothers' interference.

"A customer got grabby last night. I took care of it, so let it go. Please," she tacked on when they stood there in ticked off silence while preparing to debate the issue. Pulling her hand from Troy's light grip, she bent back over the sofa and flipped them another taunting grin. "You were saying?" She didn't have long to wait until fingers skimmed up the backs of her thighs, hiking up the skirt as they traveled over her exposed buttocks.

"We'll discuss that later. Now, relax. Exhale, and it'll be easier." Troy dug his thumbs into her cheeks and spread them to expose her puckered, private back entrance.

Paige wiggled her hips in embarrassment, attempting to dislodge his grip while saying nothing, but all that earned her was a sharp slap on her thigh. "Ow!" It wasn't pain that drew her startled cry, but the shock of burning pleasure traveling up her core. Mortified by that quick response, she tossed a glare toward Trevor's smug face, and forgot about her plans to turn the tables on them as she snapped, "That was uncalled for."

"I disagree. Now be still. We're using the smallest plug, so there should be very little pain." He reached into his jeans pocket and extracted a short chain with two rubber loops attached at each end. "I'm looking forward to seeing what your nipples look like dressed up in these huggers."

Since the burn on her thigh had the audacity to travel into her sheath and distract her, Paige ignored him and faced the seat again.

She didn't try to figure out whose fingers now held her cheeks apart and who was prodding her anus with a slick, round bulb until Troy uttered another command.

"Deep breath, Paige."

She inhaled, and the object entered her untried orifice with a plop and a pinch of discomfort that gave way to a slow, burning stretch as he pushed forward. Her chest grew tight with her held breath. Tingles raced up and down the walls of her rectum while goosebumps popped up on her skin. Another plop and she could feel the round flat rubber base resting against her opening. Paige released her pent-up breath on a *whoosh* as they helped her stand, and then sucked it in again when the plug rolled inside her, setting off sparks she was ill-prepared for.

"*Oh,*" she breathed in surprise at the myriad of sensations spreading throughout her lower body.

"I think she likes it, bro. Let's see if you enjoy the nipple clamps as much, sugar." Trevor pulled the short top up, exposing her unfettered breasts. The sudden brush of cool air puckered her nipples into even tighter nubs, but it was their hot gazes responsible for the slow rise of arousal swirling through her body.

They dipped their heads, their breaths fanning over her nipples before their mouths latched on to the aching buds. "*Holy shitnoodles!*" She felt the tugs on her distended tips all the way to her curled toes, and she gripped a wad of their thick hair in each hand, desperate to anchor herself against the light starbursts of pleasure. Teeth nibbles followed, the stinging nips soothed by dual tongue strokes that robbed her of much needed air. Trevor's whiskered scruff scratched her tender skin, the little prickles both ticklish and arousing. She wasn't ready for them to cease their erotic torture, but that didn't stop them from pulling back and looping the rubber clamps around her now damp, swollen nipples. A quick tug, and the loops tightened enough to keep them in position, leaving her tips to throb with a dull ache. Troy yanked her top back down, stopping her from reaching up to rub over the dull throbbing.

Trevor didn't give Paige time to object or complain before leading her out the door. "You'll be fine, now let's go."

Nestled between the brothers on the front seat of a four-door, dark blue SUV, the press of their hard thighs and arms against her, the constant, dull throb of her nipples and the unaccustomed full sensation of her rectum kept her too distracted to enjoy the scenic drive down the coastal highway. A slow hum of pleasure seeped into her veins, the warm sluggish flow robbing her of conversation until Troy broke the silence upon leaving the city.

"I like your house, Paige. Have you and Penny lived there long?"

"Ever since we moved in with our grandmother when we were toddlers. It was just us, Mom and Nana when we were growing up."

"Where are they now?" Trevor asked, turning toward her, his fingers toying with the ends of her hair.

Paige tried to shrug off the pang of loss, but from the close way these two watched for her reactions to both their touch and their probing questions, she doubted she could hide anything from them. "Dead. What about you? Do you have family nearby?"

"There's just Ray."

Troy's short, blunt answer didn't invite prying, but that was too bad. If they could, she could. "And who's Ray?"

She couldn't miss the way Troy glared at Trevor over her head before he stated, "You started this."

"Troy doesn't like to talk about our parents' death in a car accident when we were fourteen. Zachary Allen-Vancuren, whom you'll be meeting soon, is one of five guys we met the summer we turned fifteen." He paused a moment, shifted his gaze to Troy, who frowned but said nothing, and then added, "At a camp for juvenile delinquents."

That tidbit was enough to snatch her attention off her tormented body long enough to notice neither man appeared comfortable discussing that time in their lives. Their willingness to share such a personal part of themselves affected Paige with an expanding melting sensation covering her chest. To lighten the sudden tense silence, she teased with a grin, "Are you telling me the big bad cop and the 'by the rules' DA were once wild, rebellious teens?"

"Losing everything in the blink of an eye can turn even good kids bad," Troy returned, his cool, reserved tone revealing he didn't joke about that stressful time in his life.

Feeling for them, Paige murmured, "I can sympathize with the loss of family, but you have each other, and whoever this Ray is. We were twelve when we lost Mom, but Nana was with us until five years ago. I like to think that put more check marks in the lucky column for Penny and me compared to the unlucky."

"I like the way you look at things, sugar. Maybe you and I can work on Troy," Trevor said before reaching up and tweaking her right nipple. "But today is just for fun. We're here."

With the change of subject, her attention switched back to the unaccustomed pulsations the toys delivered to her nipples and rectum. With Troy's help, she slid out of the SUV on the driver's side after he parked in the Gold Star Marina lot, her balance teetering against a jolt of arousing awareness, forcing her to lean against him. She was used to hearing Trevor's deep chuckle, but not his brother's. She shivered in response to Troy's quiet laugh vibrating against her chest.

"The toys might be too much for her," Troy stated above her head before he slid a hand down her arm and grasped hers.

These two might be too much for me. Paige would never admit that out loud, so she tossed her head back, reached for Trevor's hand and swung both arms as they strolled up the pier. "It'll take more than a few toys to get the better of me, boys. *Oh. My. God.*"

Stopping with an abruptness that drew a questioning glance from both men, she stood with mouth agape at the largest, most luxurious yacht she'd ever set eyes on. As a lifelong resident of Florida, she knew her way around piers and boats, but she'd never been out on anything close to the three-tiered cruiser sporting shiny teak decking and sleek lines.

"Wait until you see all the big toys to play on," Trevor whispered in her ear before leaping aboard and hauling her up after him.

Paige braced her feet and swayed with the slow, barely discernible rocking, her gaze going to the helm where a tall, sandy-haired man waved them over. Leaving the seat next to him, a young woman approached her with a beaming smile of welcome that lit her green eyes.

"You must be Paige. Welcome aboard. Shoo, you two." Snatching Paige's arm, she waved the brothers away. "Go help Zachary get us going. I'll show her around."

"When did you get so bossy?" Troy reached out and yanked on her short brown hair that showed hints of blonde and red in the sunlight before calling over to Zach, "Get your girl under control."

Zach snorted. "I've been having fun trying for months. Maybe I should turn her over to you two for a lesson."

"Shit." The young woman blanched. "Let's go, Paige. Oh, I'm Sandie."

Bemused, Paige followed Sandie up a spiral staircase as the purr of the motor stirred to life under them, praying the three men couldn't see her bare butt. "Whoa," she exclaimed as they reached the top level and the sudden shift of the vessel leaving the slot sent her stumbling against the rail. Her breasts swayed, and the plug rolled inside her with the sudden, jerky movement. She turned her head as a flush stole over her face with her damp response.

Sandie giggled with a knowing smirk. "What are you sporting under that top and skirt?" Without embarrassment, she flipped up her camisole top to reveal clamped nipples in similar loops as Paige's. "Zachary's also tormenting me with a butterfly which I have a love/hate relationship with, depending on how long he makes me wait for an orgasm." She pushed her top back down. "How long have you been seeing Troy and Trevor?" she asked with a casualness that helped Paige relax.

Taking a cue from her relaxed, open dialog, Paige cocked her head with a small grin. "You don't seem surprised at my accompanying both men to join you today." The idea would shock Paige herself if she hadn't known they were just going through this today to show her how wrong she'd been to go against their dictate to stay out of the investigation.

Sandie shook her head. "After witnessing my stepfather ordering a man's murder and fleeing my home in fear of him catching me, it takes a lot to shock me."

"Oh, tell me more," Paige insisted, intrigued by Sandie's admission.

"Come on. I'll give you a tour while I tell you how I snuck aboard this decadent boat and ended up spending four days with Zachary, all alone." Striding to the rear, Sandie waved her hand toward the lounges. "I didn't have a guide when I first saw the restraints on the chaises." She pointed to a bar folded back against the side of the covered outdoor kitchen. "That pulls out and a chain will dangle from it. I had to tease Zach into restraining me there."

Paige remembered only too well the hard press of Troy's hand between her shoulders, holding her over his lap while Trevor clamped his hands on her thighs. At the time, she'd refused to give much credence to the undeniable thrill she experienced from their hold, but picturing herself cuffed on a lounge with their hands and mouths on her again delivered that same charge. She may soon have to admit Penny's sexual preferences just might hold merit.

"Ooh, your turn to give. I can tell by the look on your face you were remembering something those two did."

Paige liked Sandie. Laughing, she relayed her first spanking and Sandie, in turn, told her about the first time Zach, now her husband, had bent her over, all the while walking around and pointing out the games of skeet shooting and shuffleboard. Paige had been so engrossed in hearing about Sandie's antics to entice Zach to fuck her after he'd discovered her in his bed, miles away from port, she didn't hear the guys come up.

"Did you leave anything for us to show her, Sandie?" Trevor slid his arms around Paige's waist and pulled her back against his rock-solid chest.

Her breath caught before she remembered her plan and pulled away from him with a flirtatious smile. "We've been comparing our first spanking scenes. I think you two came out on the short end." It took every ounce of willpower she possessed not to burst into hysterics at their startled faces. She could tell they hadn't expected her to be so open today. In all likelihood, they probably thought they'd have to coax her into cooperating this afternoon, another reminder they'd been blind and deaf to her growing interest in them this past year.

Trevor smirked and Troy frowned, their usual expressions when they regarded her with those identical probing looks. "We can always remedy that." Troy reached for her but she sidestepped him with a quick skip.

"I want to see the rest of the boat," she quipped.

Zach's low growl followed by Sandie's delighted, "Uh, oh," drew Paige's attention.

"What?" she asked, perplexed.

"Zachary has this thing about calling his toy a boat." She turned a beaming smile on her husband. "Maybe you and I should go..." she paused for dramatic flair before finishing with, "up front and leave them alone."

Paige admired the way Sandie didn't flinch from her husband's thundercloud expression. "Starting a little early, aren't you, baby?" he drawled in a silken, menacing whisper.

Sandie backed away with her hand held out as if to ward him off. On an unperturbed laugh, she admonished, "We have a guest. You have to be nice."

"Like hell. She's their guest, not mine."

Sandie sent Paige a droll look. "Did I mention my husband can be an ass?"

Paige's lips quirked in amusement. "No, but I'm getting the picture."

With a pointed finger at Zach, Sandie backed away from him as he stalked her with a dark look that belied the light of mirth in his cobalt eyes. "See, you're giving Paige a bad impression. Come on let's go downstairs and we can watch for dolphins from the... front rail."

Paige shook her head as Sandie took off with a squeal, Zach hot on her heels. Looking toward the brothers, she encountered the same feigned, thundercloud expressions on their faces as they approached her with slow, measured steps. With a hasty step back, she asked, "What? I don't get what they were going on about."

"Sandie likes to mislabel parts of the yacht on purpose to get Zach's attention," Trevor explained. A loud, flesh smacking sound reverberated from below, followed by Sandie's high-pitched cry. "It looks like she received her punishment before you," he taunted with a smirk.

"Me? What'd I do?" Unable to resist, she turned and wiggled her hips before skipping behind the front end of a lounge, putting the chaise between herself and them. She didn't see the wide expanse of wavy blue ocean spread out around her; only the dark intent etched on their faces and the identical gleam of anticipation in their eyes. Her heartbeat kicked up a notch as they approached her from both sides. She'd intended to have a bit of fun at their expense, but she hadn't counted on how fast they could turn the tables on her.

"You disparaged our efforts concerning your spanking last week," Troy said. "And that's after we were so nice to you and let you climax. You know what that means? We have to do better today. Starting now."

Okay, so deep down, she'd known this was where her teasing would lead. In her mind, she'd rather break the ice early and get down to whatever they had planned so she could set aside her doubts and insecurities and go about enjoying this brief time with them. Sandie had played right along with her, and Paige wished the two of them could remain friends after today.

Trevor caught her as she tried to bolt over the lounge, but instead of sitting down on it, he bent her over one arm and flipped up her skirt with his other hand. The ocean's balmy breeze wafted over her exposed flesh, stirring up a sexually charged shiver of awareness. The unexpected titillation forced the air from her lungs on a long groan. Her buttocks tightened around the plug, the pulsing of her nipples increasing when Troy rucked up her top and pulled it over her head.

"Hey! I didn't mean anything by it!" she exclaimed, bracing for the first painful swat, praying for a less demoralizing response than the heated rush she'd experienced last week.

"Tsk, tsk, now you're lying," Trevor admonished before delivering a resounding slap on her right cheek. "You redden as nicely as I remember."

Paige lost her breath from the sting of that sharp smack the moment his hand connected with her flesh; her heart skipped a beat with the next swat and sent a wave of heat over her face; her pussy fluttered and her mind turned to mush with the third, blistering spank. At this point, she didn't know whether to beg for more or demand for him to stop. Then he soothed a hand over the flesh he had struck, the soft caress easing the ache and calming her rioting senses until Troy stirred them up again.

Reaching under her, he plucked at Paige's distended nipples, the constant tightening and loosening of the huggers with her every movement driving her insane. "What's nice about these clamps is that you can leave them on for long periods, but now it's time for something a little more confining. Deep breath."

Before she could comply, Troy tugged the loops off and blood rushed back into her engorged nipples. Another swat accompanied the tiny needle pricks of pain stabbing at the tender nubs. "*Asshattery numbnuts!*" It wasn't the pain that drew her startled cry, but the shock of burning pleasure spreading up her core.

"Such a potty mouth. What are we going to do with you?" Trevor chided while delivering a smack right in the middle of her buttocks that pushed the plug deeper and added to the fiery streak of pleasure darting from her quivering anus into her sheath.

"I can think of several things." Troy replaced the huggers with metal clamps that reignited the pain Paige refused to give in to. When he reached into his pocket to withdraw long, colorful metal feather weights to clip on to the loops, she slammed her eyes shut with a shudder.

"Are you still with us, Paige?" Trevor asked with another calming caress over her burning backside followed by a teasing glide up her damp seam.

Dawning a cloak of confidence she was far from feeling, Paige flipped her head around and pulled up a taunting smile to go along with a butt wiggle and her reply. "I can handle whatever you dish out, Trevor."

One of those conspiratorial looks they were so good at passed between the brothers before Trevor returned her smile. "Then start by addressing us properly." Out of the corner of her eye, she saw him reach down and bring up a leather paddle just as a tug on her right nipple pulled her breast down with a heavy object. She didn't have time to question how she'd missed seeing the implement stashed under the lounge before he instructed, "It's Sir, or Master from now on."

Oh, I don't think so. "Shit!" Paige screeched when he brought the paddle down with a resounding *whack* that jarred her entire body. Troy attached the other feather weight, and now her breasts swayed with the laden jewelry that elongated her nipples and increased the throbbing intensity in the tender buds.

"There goes that mouth again. Trevor, let's move to the lounge," Troy suggested as Paige watched him loosen his pants.

Without warning, her discomfort took a new, exciting turn as Trevor guided her onto hands and knees on the padded chaise before settling behind her again. Her mouth watered when Troy knelt in front of her, cock in hand, an enticing pearl drop beading on the smooth crown. Another swat from the paddle covered her butt as Troy gripped her hair and lifted her face until she gazed into his lust-filled eyes. Power surged through Paige from the need he'd done nothing to hide, a need she'd stirred to life inside him.

"Yes or no?" he demanded, nudging her lips, rubbing the pre-cum droplet over them.

"I signed on for oral, didn't I?" she returned before darting her tongue out and swiping over the smooth mushroom cap. "So, yes."

"Yes, Sir," he insisted in a hard tone.

Since attaining orgasm was now a priority, Paige complied without argument. "Yes, Sir." Uttering those words triggered a small thrill that caught her unaware, but with his cock tempting her mouth, she saved delving into the why of her response until later. Opening her mouth, she wrapped her lips around his cockhead, wondering when the ache encompassing her buttocks and pulsing around her nipples had morphed into such sweet arousal. And then she ceased to think at all.

Troy kept her head immobile with his grip as he dipped further into her mouth. Trevor lightened up on the paddle, spanking her with just enough force to rock her already heightened senses while maintaining the tingling burn covering her cheeks. In an effort to regain control, she licked under the rim of Troy's cap and laved the sensitive spot most men enjoyed until his hand in her hair loosened.

Hiding her triumph, she sucked him in deeper and traced over the throbbing veins along his shaft, feeling the pump of his blood against her tongue. The spanking stopped, followed by Trevor's hands roaming over her throbbing buttocks, alternating between kneading and caressing until she couldn't differentiate between the soreness and the pleasure encompassing her entire lower body.

"Son of a bitch," Troy growled when she moaned around his flesh and then released him to suckle his balls.

"If she's tormenting you that much, I'll distract her."

Paige was too busy working Troy's cock again to heed what Trevor meant until she felt his wide shoulders pushing her knees further apart, his hands gripping her hips and lowering her to his mouth to nuzzle her pussy. His whiskers scratched the delicate skin of her inner thighs and sent a distracting rush of heat up her core. She faltered and held her breath when his thumbs slid up between her legs and spread her labia. Warm breath blew over her tender folds before he stabbed his tongue into her quivering sheath. Sparks of pleasure ricocheted up her core, making it difficult to concentrate on pleasuring Troy. She fought back the arousal, determined to prove they couldn't get the better of her, and focused on driving Troy crazy. Closing her eyes, Paige broke from his light grip of her hair and sucked hard and deep, never letting up on laving up and down and around and around his thick shaft. Drawing up with a strong suction, she clamped her lips around his crown and glided her tongue over the smooth surface. Releasing a moan of savoring pleasure, she lapped up his seepage then dipped down again with an even tighter clasp of her mouth.

Paige's concentration scattered as her body heated from the inside out and her pussy swelled from Trevor's constant licking, the deep probe of the finger he added into the mix and the brush strokes over her clit. Awash in lustful sensations and manipulation, she came close to whimpering for the first time in her life when Troy took charge again by clamping her jaw and holding her still as he pulled from her grasping mouth. She shivered from his withdrawal and Trevor's continued assault on her sheath, her body and mind threatening to combust from the myriad of sensations.

"Now, bro," Troy ordered, his guttural tone zeroing straight down between her legs where her pussy rested against his brother's mouth.

In sync, and without warning, they removed the clamps and butt plug, sending Paige off like a firecracker. Rocking her pelvis against Trevor's marauding mouth, she rode the undulating waves of pleasure until every ripple ceased, every muscle clamp around his tongue and finger eased. Before she could return to her senses, Trevor shifted out from under her, pulled her back to sit on his kneeling, denim-covered thighs and brought his arms around her waist. Blinking her eyes open, the first thing she saw was Troy's fisted cock aimed at her heaving breasts, his grip moving up and down the hard flesh that had just filled and stretched her mouth. She grasped Trevor's thick forearms, but that didn't stop him from sinking two, then three, and then, God help her, four fingers into her pussy and setting up a pounding rhythm while Troy spewed his semen onto her reddened nipples with an echoing shout.

Ceding to their dominant wills, she broke apart in another climax as soon as Trevor whispered in her ear, "Come for us, sugar," and pummeled her sheath with clit abrading thrusts.

CHAPTER 10

*P*aige fought off returning to earth as long as possible, instead choosing to relish the aftershocks of pleasure still coursing through her before facing the two men who had once again knocked her back on her heels with their sexual control. Her plan to string them along this afternoon with her own brand of sensual teasing had backfired when nerves kicked in after viewing the boat's accoutrements and wondering what those two had in store for her. With a sigh, she returned to her senses and surroundings, slowly tuning in to the rough abrasion of Trevor's jeans against her sore buttocks and the tingles from the scratchiness against her sensitive skin.

"This is in my way." Trevor unzipped her skirt and pushed it down before helping her to stand and step out of it.

The afternoon sun warmed skin never kissed by its rays before; the outdoor exposure coupled with the brothers' ever-watchful gazes evoked a gush of cream along with new tingles inside her still quivering pussy. Trevor picked her up, sending the vast panoramic view spinning in a dizzying circle around her as he strode toward the bow. "Where are you taking me?" she questioned, a touch of worry taking up residence in her abdomen over how nice his arms felt holding her and with Troy keeping step beside them. Being the object of two men's focused attention would be a heady experience if she thought she meant more to them than a thorn in their sides during an investigation.

"Right here." With a wicked grin, Trevor dropped her with a loud splash into the largest, deepest hot tub she'd ever seen.

Sputtering, Paige scrambled to right herself on the bench, conscious of the way the hot swirling water over her abused buttocks and nipples brought back to life the discomfort they'd heaped upon her. "*Crap on a schnoodle!*" she mumbled under her breath while squirming in the bubbling water to get comfortable.

"Lay your head back and be still," Troy ordered from behind her as his hands landed on her shoulders and pressed her back.

She had no choice but to obey, but couldn't fault him for his high-handedness when he sent her into euphoric bliss by kneading her shoulders and using his thumbs to rub up and down her neck. "*Oh*, oh God, that feels good." Trevor, standing in front of her, reached in to treat her thighs to the same wonderful manipulations. Mimicking his brother, he dug his long fingers into her tense muscles and worked out the tightness with a mixture of deep presses and lighter rubs. "I'll give you all day to stop," she sighed.

Troy slid his hands down her chest to cover her breasts, scissoring his fingers over her nipples then closing and twisting. "You have ten minutes, and then we'll get something to eat."

Paige's stomach took that moment to rumble, drawing Trevor's chuckle and his hands up to the crease where thighs met hips. With his eyes leveled on hers, he executed a slow glide of his thumbs toward her parted labia and dipped inside her sheath with both thick digits. One brush over her clit, along with the small tugs on her nipples, had her primed and ready for more, and growing increasingly worried about their rising sexual hold on her.

"Not yet, sugar," Trevor chided with a knowing grin when her hips jutted toward his hands without her permission. Damn feckless, unfaithful body.

"And here I always thought you were the nice one," she said, pouting.

"I am. I'll show you how nice after we eat."

She let need override caution and pulled out all her wiles to entice them into giving her what she wanted: another climax. Reaching up, she trailed her fingers up and down Troy's arms, and when he released her breasts to move back up to her shoulders, she followed. Arching her chest forward brought her breasts out of the water to bob in an enticing display of soft, wet creamy mounds topped with rigid, protruding nipples. Widening her legs, she thrust her hips up again, this time giving her body permission to taunt and beg.

"C'mon, boys, play nice," she purred. A giggle threatened to escape when Troy cursed behind her.

"You've just earned a lesson in consequences. Come on, out you go now. There's Zach with lunch."

They hauled her out of the decadent tub and then each man snatched a towel hanging on the side before driving her crazy with brisk rubbing, taking their time over her breasts, butt and between her legs. She swayed into their hands as her body warmed and her blood heated. By the time they draped the towels back over the rack, her breasts ached, her buttocks were clenched and her pussy dripped, leaving Paige to question how simple lust could have combusted into a never-ending, aching need in such a short time.

Taking her hands, they headed toward the dining area in the center of the deck where Zach stood unloading hoagie sand-wiches onto a table and Sandie sat, naked, pouring lemonade. Paige balked before they reached the other couple, sudden awkwardness over her nudity holding her back. At the club, the room had been shrouded in darkness and she couldn't make out individual faces in the crowd gathered for the auction until the spotlight landed on Troy and Trevor in the front row, and then they had commanded her complete attention. Here, being exposed in the bright light of day in front of one other couple seemed to put more emphasis on both her and Sandie's nakedness.

"Where are my clothes?" she asked, looking toward the lounge they had used earlier.

"Sandie probably has them folded somewhere. You can get them before we return to port, not before." Troy's tone brooked no argument as he and Trevor picked up the pace again.

Shoring up her resolve and nerve, she tossed her head, the damp ends of her short hair tickling her neck. "Well, I wouldn't want Sandie to be the only one drawing attention since you three are still dressed."

"Because we're the boss," Trevor quipped before pointing to the bench opposite Sandie's seat. "Slide in there."

"I saw you in the hot tub," Sandie remarked with a lustful sigh. "That massage looked wonderful."

"It was." To Paige's wonder, after Troy placed a sandwich in front of her and Trevor slid a glass of lemonade over, the men conversed between themselves, touching upon topics such as sports and recent events. She didn't know whether to be glad they weren't ogling either of the women, or miffed about it until Sandie winked with a quirk to her mouth.

"Go figure," her new friend said, drawing Paige's sheepish grin for being so transparent.

"Are you talking about Miles and Hope?" Zach asked his wife before he looked back at Troy and Trevor. "Did you hear those two eloped yesterday?"

Neither could hide their surprise before Troy returned on a dry note, "Leave it to Miles to find a woman willing to avoid a big gathering to celebrate their wedding. Jackson's going to be pissed."

"He'll get over it," Trevor stated with confidence. "That doesn't mean we can't celebrate. I say we plan something, maybe a surprise party. That'll irk Miles and appease Jackson." Trevor's glee at the prospect was written all over his face.

Curiosity overrode unease at calling attention to herself as Paige asked, "Who are Miles and Hope? And Jackson?"

Troy looked down at her and ran a finger over one nipple, a casual caress that ignited a firestorm inside Paige. "Friends of ours. Miles is a former Martial Arts champion and owns a gym downtown, and Hope manages a homeless shelter a few blocks from it. Jackson runs an animal shelter and veterinary clinic outside of Miami."

"If you can make another trip down Tuesday evening, Paige, you're welcome to come to our girls' night out. This week, we're meeting at our place, and Hope will be there," Sandie invited.

The unexpected invitation warmed Paige as much as Troy's light touch and Zach's blue gaze, but there was no sense in getting involved deeper with the brothers' friends after today since this was a onetime get-together. Something their omission of an invitation to the planned surprise party reminded her of. Ignoring the pang clutching her chest, she pasted on a regretful look and opted for an evasive reply.

"Thank you. I can try, but make no promises. My sister's been laid up and should move back home this week. I need to be there for her." That last remark was wishful thinking on her part, but worked well for an excuse.

With an abruptness that caught Paige off-guard, Troy clasped her right hand, avoiding the bruises, and hauled her up. "Since it looks like everyone's done eating, it's time for the consequences of teasing us in the hot tub and not addressing us as instructed." His stern gaze switched to Zach. "Would you mind meting out ten swats?"

"What?" Paige's eyes flew to Sandie's husband as Zach rose from the table with a glint of mischief in his gaze and one raised brow. It had been one thing to flutter over his eyes on her. Bending over for a punishing reprimand by a stranger was another.

"Not as long as you and Trevor don't mind taking Sandie to task for me," Zach agreed.

"What did I do?" Sandie's incredulous look toward Zach mirrored what Paige felt.

Zach shrugged. "Nothing. I simply enjoy seeing you bent over and your ass turning a lovely shade of crimson. Be careful, baby," he warned in a silky tone Sandie heeded by clamping her mouth shut and averting her eyes.

Much to Paige's astonishment, the moment Troy pushed her torso down on the table, leaving her hips pressed against the side, the edgy arousal that had been simmering since the hot tub bubbled into a full boil. When Sandie landed a few feet away from her, they traded rueful grins the guys wiped off their faces when they reached over them to take hold of their wrists. Troy and Trevor flanked Sandie, each shackling one arm and pinning it to the table while Zach stood to Paige's right and went for her wrists before stopping short with an angry curse.

"What the fuck?"

Apparently, Zach could tell a tight grip had caused the bruises circling her wrist as easily as the brothers could. "Hey, don't look at us. She's the one not talking," Trevor returned.

"You can tell me later why you're allowing that." With a firm grip below the bruises, Zach pinned her arms to the table and held nothing back from his first swat. Paige sucked in a breath at the painful burn, refusing to cry out or complain. Turning her over to another man for her 'punishment' negated the warm fuzzy Troy and Trevor's overprotective concern had drummed up, but determination to ride it out without a word settled inside her, over-riding embarrassment and unease. *I'll show them*, she chanted over and over.

The rapid-fire, flesh-slapping resonated around them, punctuated by Paige and Sandie's harsh breathing and low groans. Fire blazed across Paige's buttocks and not once did Zach pause to rub the painful burn like she'd grown used to after just two spankings. She bit her lip, hating each smack even if her traitorous libido jumped on board with the pain induced pleasure winding its way through her body by the time he delivered the tenth stroke on the tender skin of one sit-spot.

"I think you were mistaken," Zach told Troy and Trevor as they helped Paige and Sandie up. "Paige here is very well-behaved."

The taunt hit its mark and Paige whirled on him, her body vibrating with annoyance. Before she could let loose with the irritation slithering like a snake under her skin, Trevor clamped a hand over her mouth.

His voice laced with humor, he told his friend, "She can be." Reaching down with his free hand, he caressed her throbbing cheeks and Paige couldn't keep from pressing against his soothing hand, a shudder quaking her body from the arousing rub. "Come along, sugar."

TREVOR USHERED Paige down the spiral stairs, Troy right behind them. He couldn't wait to bind her and torment that lean, supple body some more. He'd known right away, as had Troy, she was trying to throw them for a loop by suppressing her feisty nature and pulling out all her wiles. They'd nipped those efforts as soon as they'd left the marina and could strip her of her defenses. The way she had bounced back after regaining a clear head from her climax had drawn his admiration, and prompted the urge to act again. She appealed to him on so many levels, he didn't know where to begin. After today, he suspected Troy wouldn't be able to walk away from her either.

They both knew those bruises circling her wrist had resulted from a tight grip, and every time he saw them, his rare temper rushed to the surface, begging to be unleashed on the fucker who had dared to put them there. He knew what it had cost Troy to hold back when they were at her house, and he was glad his brother refrained from marring the day by pushing Paige for answers. She wouldn't have backed down like the subs they were used to playing with.

Holding open the door to the playroom, Trevor paused a moment to enjoy a slow sweep of Paige's naked body; the breasts that were a perfect soft handful, nipples red and puckered; a slim waist that flared to hips wide enough to cradle his body; the eye-catching thin line of hair arrowing to plump, glistening folds that tempted his mouth again.

"You going to stand there all day, or move?" Troy grumbled.

Trevor flashed him a grin and waved Paige inside. "Come on, sugar. Little brother is impatient."

Troy snorted. "And you're not?"

"Oh, I am."

Trevor wondered if Paige knew her every thought showed on her expressive face. Those striking gray eyes darted around the playroom, skimming over equipment she'd likely seen at Sanctuary, such as the spanking benches and newly added St. Andrew Cross, and then widened with shock when she spotted the medieval fucking chair and hanging fucking swing. In a flash, interest and a sly cunning replaced the surprised jolt, and she tugged on his hand as she moved toward the chair.

"Tell me about this," she insisted without an ounce of embarrassment when the three of them stood before the wood and leather high-backed chair. The cutout in the seat would leave a sub's pussy and ass open and easily available for use, but she didn't flinch from that embarrassment; instead running her hand over the arm as if testing the sturdy oak before flicking the leather restraints that would ensure the occupant couldn't move until the Dom allowed.

Testing her bravado, Trevor grasped her hips and pressed her onto the seat and spread her legs with his. Grabbing her hands, he placed them on the arms, saying, "Once you're bound, a Dom has effortless access to both your pussy and ass. Want to try it out?"

When he removed his hands and stepped back, she popped up as fast as a jack-in-the-box and sidled away from them.

"I don't think so." Paige looked away from his knowing smirk and watched Zach steer Sandie over to the spanking bench, then looked away when he bent his wife over, keeping her in place with a leather strap over her hips. Her gaze scanned the room again, touching upon the plush, curved sofa along the back wall and the arched porthole windows letting in a stream of late afternoon sunlight before stopping on the center, floor to ceiling poles. Pointing, she asked, "Those. What do you do there?"

"I like showing instead of telling." Troy led her over to the poles and Trevor followed with anticipation drumming a steady beat in his pulse. Years of indulging in the same kinks together left them both able to set up a scene with little verbal communication.

Paige remained silent until they positioned her between the poles, raised her arms above her head and tethered her wrists. "I'm not sure about this," she admitted with a deep indrawn breath and reflexive jerk on the cuffs. Uncertainty crossed her face for the first time since entering the room.

She hid her initial panic well and then covered it with a bravado Trevor couldn't help but admire. Cupping her face, he replied, "We are," before brushing his lips over her mouth. With a yank on her hair, he squatted down next to Troy to secure her ankles, their faces level with the proof of her arousal glistening on her damp folds.

"My turn," Troy murmured. Leaning in, he swiped his tongue up her seam with a hum of appreciation. Paige's hips jerked, both men chuckling at the quick change to eager acceptance before Troy rose, pulling a blindfold from his back pocket. "Some things are better experienced without looking."

She shook her head in automatic denial. "I don't—"

Trevor stopped her with a finger pressed over her mouth. "If you're too afraid, or can't handle it, say red. Otherwise, keep quiet." The instant squaring of her shoulders and tight set to her lips proved the goading remark worked as he'd planned.

While Troy wrapped the black silk around Paige's eyes, Trevor reached into the small bag he doubted she had noticed and pulled out two gloves. "Good guy or bad guy?" he asked Troy, holding up a supple leather glove with short, sharp spikes lining the palm and fingers and another mitt covered with soft bunny fur.

"Need you ask? I'll take the vampire glove."

Paige whipped her face toward their voices, a small tremor shaking her bound body. "*Vampire* glove? What... *ow!*"

"I told you to keep quiet." Trevor ran a finger over the red slash his swat on her thigh left behind.

"And you failed to address us by our proper titles again." Troy followed the reprimand with a matching smack on her opposite leg.

"How am I supposed to remember things like that when... *holy addlepated titweenie!*" Paige ended on a gasp when Troy scraped his gloved hand over her reddened skin.

Trevor brushed the area with his fur-covered hand, soothing the pinpricks even though he knew his brother had put no pressure behind the stroke. Ignoring her outburst, he followed Troy's lead up to her arched neck and trailed his palm down, skimming her shoulders before inching toward the fleshy undersides of her breasts.

"WHAT *IS* THAT THING?" Paige quaked in the bonds, tuned out Sandie's cry that followed a smack on bare skin, and concentrated on the myriad of sensations the two opposing objects drummed up. The light scraping pinpricks over her skin were more startling than uncomfortable, the soft brush of fur following in their wake drawing tiny, pleasurable pulses.

"Sir." Troy punctuated his stern rebuke with the increased pressure of one gloved finger over her nipples.

Paige groaned, the pain just sharp enough to crumble the edges of her resistance. "Sir."

"That wasn't so hard, was it?" Trevor whispered in her ear, soothing the sting with a soft brush of fur over her nipple. "Your nipples say you like the dual sensations between the vampire glove and my rabbit furred one." Another finger-glide over each nipple sent a zing of pleasure between her spread legs. His amused voice echoed in her ear, adding a shiver of pleasure she was beginning to crave more than her next breath. "Now, be quiet and let us play."

She hated it when they dictated to her like that, but loved it when they touched her where she ached for them the most. The darkness enhanced the sensations running amok as they pinpricked and soothed their way over her nipples, down her quivering abdomen and around to her buttocks. A harder press scraped over the fleshy mounds of her butt, leaving behind a tingling pain that ignited a firestorm of heat deep inside her quivering pussy. Her pulse spiked at the delay of a softer caress, the pause giving the discomfort just enough time to seep into her muscles. Paige bit her lip, refusing to voice a complaint or plea, wanting to prove she could handle whatever they did. She hadn't counted on the swift rise of arousal clouding her senses even more than Trevor's belated caress over her warm, throbbing buttocks now tingling from an amassing of minor stings.

"*Shit on a cracker,*" she muttered as they ventured a diabolical journey down the back of one leg and up the front of the other, leaving behind a warm, prickly trail covering her skin. Perspiration broke out in the wake of blossoming pleasure-pain exploding over her skin. Troy rested his spiked-gloved hand on her upper right thigh while Trevor paused on her left, and then they pressed their lips to her ears, tugging on her earlobes with sharp teeth before drawing goosebumps by tonguing the sensitive whorls inside the shells. Their dual torment left her vibrating in the restraints, aching for more... more, more.

She arched her head back, the teasing stroke of ungloved fingers playing a soft tune over her labia shattering the last of her resistance. Thrusting her hips forward, she whispered a tormented plea. *"Please... please touch me."*

"We are." Troy's calm, smug voice came from behind her and she ground her teeth together to keep from snarling at him. "But if you want more, then by all means..."

Paige screamed with the burst of tempered, needle-sharp pricks blazing over the tender flesh of her folds. Instead of the calming stroke of fur soothing the torment, fingers spread her labia and delved deep enough to tease her sweet spot. She cursed long and low as they withdrew and then almost choked on a startled gasp when one spiked finger brushed very lightly against her sensitive clit. As welcome as the sun after the rain, several orgasms rolled through her, unraveling so fast, one after another, they robbed her of breath and left her body steeped in pleasure, her mind numb with it. The greediness of her need shocked her. Then two mouths latched onto her nipples and bare fingers slid through her slick folds to pummel her depths with body-jarring plunges aimed at keeping the onslaught of climaxes going, and all she could do was hang on and ride out the consuming pleasure.

TREVOR KNEW the moment the fog of ecstasy lifted and the need to wrestle back control took over. As soon as they released her hands and ankles, Paige flung off the blindfold and, with a calculating, determined gleam in her eyes, dropped to her knees in front him.

Looking up, she smiled despite the way her hands shook when she moved to free his cock. "Your turn," she said before taunting him by running her tongue over her upper lip.

"Hey, what about me?" Troy asked with feigned insult.

Trevor bit back a laugh when she flipped her head around and quipped, "You already had your turn." The slow swipe of her tongue over his cockhead erased his amusement, the instant lick of pleasure from her touch forcing a deep, indrawn breath.

Troy reached down and tugged on a nipple, a rare, indulgent look on his face as he said, "Haven't you learned you're not the boss yet?"

God, it pleased him to see his brother lighten up for a change, Trevor thought as he clasped Paige's bright red head. "I'd say for about the next ten minutes she is."

Paige's hot mouth engulfed his aching flesh, forcing him to tighten his jaw and hands on her head as she threatened his composure. Kneeling before him, naked, her skin dotted with the pink marks they'd left behind, she posed an erotic picture as stimulating as watching her earlier when she had sucked off his brother. Hot combusted into scorching heat with the scrape of her nails down his shaft, his long, low moan resonating around them. He didn't know if it was her suckling lips and stroking tongue or the woman herself that could claim responsibility for his quick response, but he saved his analysis for later. Right now, the moist recess of her mouth threatened to hijack his brain cells as heat engulfed his cockhead and traveled a searing path down his shaft to pool in his groin.

Trevor switched his gaze from Paige's bright, bobbing head to his brother, who was packing up their toy bag. "Christ, you could've warned me," he ground out.

"It's more fun to watch you struggle," Troy returned with a smirk.

"And you didn't?" he shot back. Troy grunted without answering and then one soft hand cupped Trevor's sac, forcing another deep, indrawn breath. She flicked him a sultry, dove-gray glance before closing her eyes and rolling his balls in her palm, shredding his control with the switch from soft tongue strokes lapping around his dick to tiny nibbles over the blood-pumping veins. *"Fuck!"*

Troy raised a sarcastic brow and reached down to swat Paige's ass. "Hurry up, girl. Zach just returned to the helm to take us in."

Trevor would take him to task for rushing her, but the strong suctions around his cockhead worked too well at pulling his climax from his balls. He swayed with the sudden glide of the yacht, his body jerking as he spewed into her greedy, never ending mouth. Mind-blowing ecstasy consumed him for endless seconds, and it was only when Paige released him and cool air wafted over his damp cock that he could pull his head out of the clouds of euphoria.

CHAPTER 11

"We need to talk." Troy glanced from Paige's slumped head resting on Trevor's shoulder to his brother's face.

The sun had set by the time they'd sailed into the marina and hit the road back home. He'd waited for Paige's obvious exhaustion to take over before talking with Trevor. To say the girl had thrown him for a loop today would be the understatement of the year. He hadn't believed Trevor whenever his sibling would hint their favorite bartender held more submissive promise than what showed on the surface. Troy had always enjoyed her friendly flirting, her silly phrases and, yes, even those sparks of temper every redhead seemed to possess. And after seeing the lengths she'd been willing to subject herself to to avenge her sister, his admiration of her rose several notches despite his irritation over her meddling and fear for her safety. But not once in all the months she'd been working at The Precinct, had he believed she possessed a submissive streak.

Sometimes, it really irked him when Trevor was right.

"You don't think she'll quit setting herself up?" Trevor whispered over Paige's head.

"She'll have to now that Damien knows about her subterfuge. He won't let her into Sanctuary. I'm not as concerned about that as I am about where we go from here. You and I, with her," he clarified when Trevor's brows dipped in confusion.

A slow grin creased Trevor's cheeks, revealing straight, white teeth their parents had sunk a small fortune into. Lucky for Troy he'd been spared braces, something he used to enjoy tossing in his older brother's face.

"It took a little longer than with me, but she got to you too, didn't she?"

Troy shook his head. "Let's just say now I'm willing to explore how far we can take her." He wouldn't admit to anything else until he knew for certain this was more than a desire for a different flavor of ice cream after choosing the same tastes for so long.

"That's good enough for me. For now. Ray will like her."

Troy slammed the brakes on going down that road. "Sex, bro, that's all I'll agree to. No reason to introduce her to family."

"Have it your way, for now."

It had taken Troy years to call Ray family. The beat cop had picked up their rebellious asses off the streets, sent them to that summer camp for juvenile delinquents and then petitioned the courts for legal guardianship, catching them unawares with his determination to set them back on the straight and narrow. He and Trevor were the luckiest of all the boys they'd bonded with the summer they were fifteen. Their home lives had been picture-perfect, growing up with both loving parents in a nice, upper middle-class neighborhood. The two of them attended a small private high school where they'd excelled in grades and sports, Troy landing on the varsity soccer team while Trevor shot hoops with the senior basketball players.

After their parents' sudden deaths in a car accident, they'd landed in foster care and a different school. Consumed with grief and anger, they had lashed out at anybody who tried to help, run away numerous times, and ended up getting caught when buying drugs for the first time. Alcohol hadn't worked to ease the pain of their loss and they'd never gotten the chance to sample the drugs. It wasn't until they'd met five other boys whose tragic home lives were worse than what Troy and Trevor had lost, followed by Ray picking them up at the bus depot and announcing they'd be coming home with him that their hard shells cracked for the first time.

Pulling into Paige's drive, he cut the engine and looked over at his brother again. The look on Trevor's face as he gazed down upon Paige portrayed more than caring concern for a sub they'd put through the paces. A touch of longing softened his brother's craggy features, and Troy found himself hard pressed not to feel the same yearning when he looked at the sleeping redhead now. What had happened, or changed, to make him feel for her something he'd never experienced with another woman? *Sex, bro, that's all I'll agree to.* He hated to admit it, but that statement came across as an obvious protest against someone who just may have snuck under his skin a while back without him knowing it.

"C'mon, sleepyhead. You're home." Troy shook her shoulder and enjoyed watching the grogginess clouding her eyes change to slow awareness when the overhead light flicked on as he opened the door.

"Already?" Paige blinked in confusion before her mind cleared and she sat upright with a rueful smile. "Wow. That's never happened before. I'm used to staying up late, not conking out before nine."

"Multiple orgasms will do that to you," Trevor teased, taking her hand and helping her out.

They walked her up to the door, Troy insisting on unlocking it and taking a visual sweep of the interior before asking, "Are you okay, or do you want us to stick around?" She'd slept through the residual aftershocks of their intense scene, but he wanted to be sure none lingered to upset her after they left.

Paige rolled her eyes and held out her hand for the key. "I'm fine. It'll take more than several orgasms to rattle me. As I said, I can handle whatever you toss at me."

She averted her face with that last remark, a small furrow appearing between her slim brows. Troy glanced at Trevor and he shrugged. Odds were she was tired and out of sorts from all the sensation play. For a newbie, Troy had to admit her responses had surprised him. In that regard, Trevor had been right, the girl possessed hidden depths he now wouldn't mind diving into. Of course, he'd never admit that to his brother.

"Then we'll say goodnight." Trevor cupped her face and kissed her long and hard before Troy did the same. They left her with swollen lips, a bemused expression and a look of regret in her eyes neither understood.

PAIGE LOCKED the door behind Troy and Trevor and leaned against it with a tired sigh. The afternoon had gone better, and worse, than she'd expected, and she didn't know how to deal with it. Never in her wildest fantasies had she imagined herself submitting to two men the way she'd caved on that decadent, floating vessel. It had helped instead of hindered her to have Sandie and her husband on board also, with Sandie enduring similar torment to what the brothers had heaped upon Paige. Misery loved company and all that. Only, it hadn't turned out to be miserable, just the opposite, as her still swollen, pulsing vagina, tingling nipples and sore rectum attested to.

By applying their skills together, they'd revealed a part of her she'd never known existed. She didn't know whether to hope the remnants of debauchery lasted a while for her to savor or disappeared fast so she could put the day behind her and move past the regrets.

Pushing away from the door, she padded into the kitchen to raid her stash of chocolate as she tried to ignore the too quiet house and the pang Penny's absence wrought. She could use a heart-to-heart with her sister about now, but didn't want to disturb her if she was resting. Dipping her hand into the jar on the counter, she pulled out two mini nougat bars, unwrapped one and bit into it with relish. The flavor burst over her tongue much the same as Trevor's cum, and she recalled her groan of appreciation at the taste of him. She'd relished every drop almost as much as she savored getting in the last word when they'd released her from the cuffs.

But somehow, now that the glow was wearing off, that small victory was no longer enough. Between Trevor's light-hearted cajoling and Troy's hard-edged demands, she'd been lost the second they had touched her, and that was a first for her. By the time she finished the candy, tiredness pulled at her and she decided to wait until morning to deal with that.

Paige's entire body continued to twitch with sensitive awareness as she walked down the hall to the bathroom, still feeling the remnants of itchy pinpricks from that wicked glove. Troy had been careful not to press too hard, just enough to scrape her skin with small pricks that were only uncomfortable until Trevor soothed them into pulsating throbs with his softer glove. Her arousal from the contradictory sensations had gone ballistic in a way she'd never dreamed could happen.

After filling the tub, she stripped and stepped in with a tired sigh. She winced as the hot water lapped over her bare labia, reminding her of the pinpricks on that tender skin. She glanced down, surprised to see no marks marring her flesh, only lingering pinkness around the protrusion of her still puffy clit. "Oh, no, no more tonight, you betraying little slut," she groaned aloud. Paige remembered how the two of them had reduced her to this pathetic state without even fucking her, and a wave of despondency washed over her. She regretted that the most. Since she'd fulfilled the terms of the auction contract, and the chances of her returning to Sanctuary before anyone caught Penny's attacker were nil, odds went against getting the chance to fulfill that fantasy with either brother.

In fact, Paige doubted she would see or hear much from either Carlson now. God, she wished her sister was home. She could use a sympathetic shoulder to cry on right about now.

~

"WHERE DO you think you're going?"

Penny's heart skittered to an abrupt stop at hearing Master Damien's deep, commanding voice before resuming with a rapid, panicky beat. Shoulders slumped, she turned to face him standing in the doorway. She'd been so close. A warmth had filled her chest when he'd announced earlier he would be gone for a few hours visiting his mother who resided in a retirement home. Who wouldn't grow enamored of a man who took such good care of his elderly parent?

"I've taken enough of your time," she choked out around the lump caught in her throat. His thundercloud expression didn't bode well for that excuse. Her plan to have her things packed and be out of his house by the time he returned wasn't going too well. When he slowly crossed his arms over his wide chest and continued to stare her down with his icy blue gaze, she fidgeted from foot to foot and cast her eyes down before adding, "You have to admit, I'm much better. I don't need looking after." Damn it, why was he the only man her backbone turned to water over?

He kept silent for another thirty seconds before knocking the breath out of her with his next words. "As your Master, it's up to me to decide what you need. Or, has it been so long since you've lived with a Dom, you've forgotten that?"

Penny's gaze flew up, and she stared at him aghast before a kernel of anger tightened her stomach. The infuriating man had featured in her nighttime fantasies for years, yet had never once showed the slightest personal interest in her until the attack. She didn't need a pity Master, or a guilt-ridden one.

"My Master? Isn't that carrying your guilty conscience a bit far? As I've told you several times, I don't blame you or anyone else for the assault on me." *Uh, oh.* She took a hasty step back when he narrowed his eyes and his large hands slid to his waist, his long fingers caressing the black, braided leather of his belt. How many times had she eyed that accessory with a longing to feel the lash of a painful spanking searing her skin again?

Master Damien wasn't a Dom many dared to cross, not even away from the club. Every sub he welcomed into Sanctuary learned quickly not to sass him or disobey a rule, not unless she wanted to end up over his lap or strapped down on a spanking bench. He'd sent countless women running from the room in tears, but Penny had craved that strict dominance for as long as she could remember. She had to remember his actions hadn't given credence to his claim of being her Master.

He cocked his head with his direct stare. "Is that what you think? That I brought you here because I feel guilty?"

That silken tone sent shivers up and down her body, but Penny refused to look away from him. "I... you put me in your guest room!" she blurted, her face heating from what that confused, tortured announcement revealed. Every night she'd lain awake aching for his rough possession, for something other than demands to eat or rest, for him to show he wanted her, even if just for a short time, like all his other subs. Every solicitous touch this past week had delivered a jolt of hot sexual need down to her empty, aching pussy, a need he'd appeared oblivious to. She was so desperate for the man, she found herself willing to take crumbs to satisfy the hunger she'd carried for him for years.

"Tell me something, Penny," Master Damien continued in that same, soft voice while he continued to stroke his belt. "What else did Jim do to you, besides give you a black eye?"

Penny stumbled back in sudden agitation, frantically searching her mind for something she'd said or done that might have given away the depth of Jim's self-centered fixation on her. Clenching her hands into fists, she ignored Master Damien's sardonic lift of one brow when he noticed her unease. "I-I'm not sure what you mean. He… it was just that one time he hit me, and then I left him."

"That's not the whole truth, sweetheart. I can see the fear in your pretty eyes, in the way you're trembling." Keeping his gaze level on hers, he unbuckled his belt with slow intent. Penny's mouth went dry, her buttocks clenched and her sheath swelled with damp need. She yearned to feel the painful proof he cared more than she needed her next breath.

That relentless, laser-sharp gaze left her no choice but to tell him what she hadn't even told Paige. "He was angry because I was sick, nauseous, and couldn't…" Penny waved a hand toward his crotch, too mired in humiliation to say the words.

Damien reached out and pinched her chin, lifting her face up, refusing to let her look away. "Couldn't what? Fuck?"

She tried shaking her head, but his restraint prevented even that slight movement. The urge to lean into his large frame threatened what little composure she was still holding on to.

"He wanted oral, but, since I was too sick…" The memory of Jim flipping her over and pressing her down into the mattress with his bulky weight on her back as he took her from behind rose to the surface after she'd been so successful at keeping it buried and forgotten for so long. Her ex hadn't cared about her comfort, or the fact she'd been sick. Like always, his own gratification had taken precedence. That, and he'd never let an opportunity to exert his control over her pass. As soon as he'd rolled off her, she'd packed her bags, his parting gift a black eye. "And, before you say anything, I didn't fight him, or even say no, or my safeword." Penny had allowed her submission to overrule common sense and accepted part of the blame for that night because of that mistake.

"That's because he made sure you knew it would do no good," Master Damien replied with an undertone of steel. "And that's why

I put you in the guest room. You weren't ready for anything more intimate."

"I rode the Sybian," Penny returned in her defense. Master Damien was one of the most astute Doms she'd ever met, so the fact he'd suspected something of that nature had occurred didn't surprise her. Neither did his insight into her psyche.

Releasing her chin, he stepped back and pulled his belt from the loops, refusing to release her from his gaze. "That was before the assault. You left the playroom when I was called away. That was your first infraction. Pull down your pants."

A wave of heated longing swept aside a tremor of unease as Penny loosened her slacks and pushed them down. It never occurred to her to say no or walk away from him. Her eyes went to the belt, now folded over and gripped in one strong hand, and her nipples peaked from the remembered pleasure-pain of leather snapping against her tender skin. Why deny what she knew she wanted, what she needed?

"You let your past influence the trust I asked for when I brought you here. That was your second infraction. Turn around and brace your palms flat against the wall and present your ass for your punishment. If you're good, I'll reward you. If not, you won't sit for a week," he threatened.

The mention of a reward made it much easier to comply, her pulse spiking with the hope he meant to fuck her. Nothing short of feeling his pummeling cock invading her pussy would assuage the ache she'd lived with for so long. As soon as she placed her hands against the wall, she pushed her hips out, spreading her legs as far as her pants would allow. He didn't make her wait; the first lash came fast and hard, blistering a line across her buttocks with fiery heat and pain.

Penny bit her lip to keep from crying out as she responded to the building pain with a gush of cream. The next stroke landed below the first, then another covered her sit-spots. Within seconds, her buttocks throbbed, her skin burned and tingled, and yet she craved more of the blazing lashes while through it all, her pussy remained empty, untouched... needy.

"*Please,*" she pled on an aching whisper, unable to hold back any longer.

Master Damien wielded a strike across her upper thigh in response, throwing her mind into a tailspin of disbelief when he growled, "You've led me a merry chase since the moment I approved your membership, sweetheart. Why should I let you off easy now?"

Easy? He calls this easy? Merry chase? "What are you talking about?" she gasped after the next swat threatened her position. "You barely noticed me until I returned a few weeks ago."

"I've never *not* noticed you." Dropping the belt, he pressed his jean clad crotch against her sore butt, gripped her hair and turned her face toward his until he could breathe against her mouth, "It's been you for so fucking long, I can't remember when I didn't ache for you. Do you know how fucking hard it was to sit back and watch you with that prick?"

Surprised wonder replaced shock. "Why didn't you say something before?" Tears burned her eyes, arousal pulsed through her entire body and her butt *hurt*. She couldn't recall the last time she'd felt so good.

Master Damien reached between them and she heard him lower his zipper before feeling his hot, hard cock pressing between her buttocks. "You were a newbie. I had to give you time to find your bearings and discover what you wanted. Then you took up with the asshole." Disgust laced his voice.

"I never knew. I... *oh!*" Penny sucked in a deep breath as he filled her with one deep plunge, driving her up on her toes with the womb-nudging thrust. Master Damien's stunning revelation was nothing compared to the mind-numbing pleasure of his possession. He wrapped one hand around her wrists, holding them above her head as he bulldozed her pussy and her senses over and over, the jackhammer thrusts abrading her clit and drawing more copious juices to aid his possession.

"Now you do. Come for me, baby. Squeeze my cock with your sweet pussy, show me how much you want me, and this." He reared back and slammed home again with a low grunt.

Unable to hold back, Penny screamed, responding to his guttural command with a burst of pleasure so intense, her head swam and her body went numb. By the time she came down from the euphoric high, he was pulling slowly out of her still quivering sheath, his breathing as heavy as hers, the press of his body against her back a welcoming comfort she hadn't known she needed to erase the remnants of her last time with Jim.

"Thank you, Master Damien," she whispered on a shudder as he turned her to face him.

Dropping a kiss on her trembling lips, he stated, "Don't thank me yet. I'm not done with you. And from now on, just Master will suffice."

A thrill added to the lingering pulses of pleasure tickling her insides. With a dip of his torso, he flipped her over his shoulder and brushed a hand over her tender buttocks before pushing one long finger deep inside her core and carrying her to his bedroom.

"I'LL BE STAYING with Damien a while longer."

Paige plopped down on the front porch swing with a glare toward Penny leaning against the rail. Lifting her beer bottle, she took a long swig of her one after work indulgence before asking, "For how long?" She tried to squelch the envy her sister's announcement stirred up, but all she could think about was how quiet and lonely the house had been the last few weeks. "You told me Saturday you were ready to come home." She winced at the accusation in her tone, but couldn't help feeling betrayed over

Penny's decision to stay with Damien for an indefinite period of time.

"On Saturday, I was. Yesterday, he changed my mind." Penny fidgeted with the hem of her summer tank but didn't look away from Paige's disgruntled stare. "He said he's wanted me for years."

Paige snorted. "Before or after he fucked you?"

"During, if you want to know," she snapped back before her despondent sigh broke through Paige's selfish attitude. "Look, I know you don't understand the dynamics of my sexual lifestyle, but—"

Paige's laugh cut Penny off before she sobered with her own sigh of regret. "That's where you're wrong, sis. It seems yesterday was an eye-opener for both of us, only your day ended on a higher note than mine. I'm sorry, I shouldn't have taken my pissy mood out on you." With a push of her bare foot, she set the swing swaying, the hint of spring in the air wafting over her bare legs. She was tired after scouring two large houses and in honor of the warmer late-March temperature, had traded her work clothes for a sundress as soon as she'd gotten home.

Penny straightened, the angry glint entering her eyes warming Paige where she'd been so cold all day. "What did they do?"

A humorless laugh burst past her lips. "Everything, and not enough."

"They knew you weren't submissive. Were they disappointed, mad?" Penny shook her head as if she couldn't believe either Troy or Trevor would have portrayed either emotion after a scene.

Paige sucked in a breath and prepared to shock her twin as much as she'd been stunned yesterday by her responses to what the brothers had put her through. "That's just it, Penny. You'll love this confession. Much to my displeasure, I've been harboring an unknown streak of submissiveness." She tried picturing herself with another man, allowing him to spank her, tie her up, boss her around, and the image wouldn't pop up. Neither would the same thrill she could still get today whenever she thought about Troy and Trevor.

Her beloved, double-crossing sister threw her head back and burst into hysterical laughter that proved contagious. Paige's lips quirked before she giggled like a teenager. "Okay, I admit it is damn funny when you consider all the lectures and eye rolls I've tossed your way over the years." A mock frown replaced her humor. "You could have warned me."

"It wouldn't have done any good," Penny replied before bursting into laughter again.

"I don't need to put up with this." Paige stood, feeling better just from being with her twin again. "Go back to your new boyfriend. See if I care."

She turned to go into the house, Penny hot on her heels saying, "I'll stop. Promise. Tell me why you're so grumpy if you had fun yesterday."

Paige waved an airy hand as she padded into the kitchen and tossed the empty bottle into the recycle trash and then reached for the cookie jar. "I orgasmed several times. Just because it was under their hands and mouths doesn't mean anything, right?" She bit into a chocolate chip cookie without looking at Penny.

"They didn't fuck you? That's what's bothering you? I've told you plenty of times BDSM is not about fucking. If you have a good Dom, he'll concentrate on seeing to your needs, not his." Penny's look turned sly. "Unless there's more to the relationship than sharing a scene or two."

Paige didn't like the tidy corner Penny had backed her into so she answered with a flippant reply. "Then I guess I'm lucky, because they sure as hell met all of my needs, and then some." Like those she never imagined she'd been harboring.

"C'mon, Paige, give," Penny cajoled. "Which one do you have your sights set on? Maybe I can help."

Since Paige herself couldn't figure out which brother got her motor running the hottest and fastest, Penny's offer would do her no good. "You can't, so let's leave it, okay?" She swallowed the last bite of cookie before hugging her caring sister. "For the record, if you're happy with Damien, and you trust him, then I'll work at being happy for you. Just be careful. I couldn't bear to see you get hurt again."

"Thanks, sis." Penny returned her embrace. "I already know Master Damien is nothing like Jim, which is why I'm open to exploring what he's offered. Now, I need to get back."

Paige followed her back onto the front porch then almost bumped into her back when she came to an abrupt stop. "Are you sure there's nothing else going on with you and either of the Carlsons?" Penny tossed over her shoulder with a wicked grin as she trotted down the steps toward her car.

Paige ignored Penny's parting remark, her attention riveted on watching Trevor exit a sporty Mazda he'd parked at the curb, wondering what had prompted this unexpected visit.

CHAPTER 12

With an absent-minded wave to her sister as Penny backed out of the drive, Paige waited for Trevor on the porch, her heartbeat picking up speed with every step that brought him closer to her. Damn the man for showing up out of the blue and turning her insides out with one sweep of those soul-searching, dark brown eyes. The closer he got, the faster her blood pumped through her veins until it pooled between her legs in a hot, molten puddle by the time he stood before her.

Leaning against the post, she crossed her ankles hoping to keep her slutty vagina under control and pasted a neutral look on her face. "Trevor. What brings you here?" Her blunt greeting drew a slight frown, but the tilt of his mouth remained in place.

"I'm checking up on you. Troy would have come also, but he caught a case." He moved up the steps and stood before her, his height dwarfing her five feet seven inches. She'd always liked that about both him and Troy. Not anymore.

"As you can see, I'm fine." Paige waved a hand down her body. "You can run along now and report back to your brother you've done your duty. Thanks for stopping by." She pivoted, needing to get away from him before she did something foolish, like ask him inside, but he caught the door before it shut behind her.

"I see you have your temper up. Do you want to discuss why out here or inside?"

His calm tone and implacable gaze added to her irritation, and she held her breath for the count of ten before exhaling with a huff. "Look, I appreciate the thought, but I'm a big girl. I did everything you and Troy demanded, meeting the terms of the contract I signed to take part in the auction." Wanting a little payback, she tilted her head and kept her eyes pinned on his as she ran her tongue in a slow, provocative sweep over her lips. Placing one hand on his chest, she murmured, "All of them, including... oral." She could tell from the way his eyes darkened he remembered her mouth wrapped around his cock as well as she did.

Appearing unfazed, he returned, "We can discuss that at dinner. Where do you want to go?"

Flustered again, she stepped back enough for him to push past her into the house. Rounding on him, she fisted her hands on her hips, set aside pride and revealed the reason for her pent-up discouragement. "What the hell is with you? Neither you nor your brother showed a lick of interest in me this past year and now I can't keep you out of my house!" She threw up her arms in disbelief.

"You could if you wanted to, which you don't. I'm starving. I can go grab something if you don't want to go out." With a casualness that grated on Paige's nerves, he leaned against the wall and folded his arms across his chest. "What'll it be, sugar?"

"Don't call me that," she snapped, her temper nearing boiling point. When her stomach growled loud enough for him to hear, she came close to stomping her foot.

Trevor straightened, walked toward her with a predatory gleam in his eyes she couldn't turn away from, and reached out to draw her against him with his hand on the back of her neck. "Hamburgers it is. Fries with it?" he asked before kissing her with a tongue-probing thoroughness that left her weak in the knees.

"*I'm a freaking addlepated twatwaffle,*" she mumbled when he released her. "Fries and a large shake, chocolate."

His pleased grin lightened his eyes. "Of course. I'll be right back." He chucked her under the chin and left her standing there a muddled mess. Dressed in tan slacks and a dark brown silk dress shirt sporting two open buttons at the neck, he looked the part of a successful lawyer, making her glad she'd changed into the bright yellow, thigh skimming sheath. *Thank goodness he didn't catch me in my grubby work jeans and tee*—she cut that thought off with a low curse. "What the hell? If he wants to feed me, fine, but he can damn well take me as I am, even if I was still a mess." She had never been ashamed of any job she worked and wasn't about to start now. No matter what it took, she wouldn't allow Trevor or his brother to get to her that way, regardless of what her betraying libido wanted.

"Tell me what you did today," Trevor insisted fifteen minutes later while pulling a burger and fries from a bag and setting them before her. Sliding over a large shake, he took a seat across from her at the corner kitchen table.

"I cleaned two houses." He raised one brow at the defensive note in her tone, which prompted her to grumble, "What did you think I did? You already know what my day job is."

"I thought you might elaborate a little. Penny looked good. Did you two have a nice visit?"

Paige bit into the burger and savored the juicy grilled taste while mumbling, "No."

"Why?" Trevor nibbled on a fry and she squirmed, wishing he would nibble on her instead. Damn the man.

"Because she's staying with Damien instead of returning home where she belongs."

She watched his Adam's apple bob as he swallowed before answering and her pulse went haywire. *Shit.* "You don't like Damien?"

"I don't know him, and neither does she." Paige picked up the shake and slurped through the straw, the creamy coldness sliding down her throat helping to throttle back her rising temperature over imagining Trevor naked and on top of her. *Double damn the man and the horny bitch living between my legs.* She had to remember he didn't want her that way.

"I do, and I can vouch for him, if you're worried he'll hurt your sister." He bit into his hamburger, eying her as he chewed.

"He's coming on as strong as Jim, her ex, did. I don't like it. She's vulnerable from Jim's abuse and now the assault, and he's taking advantage of that."

Trevor picked up his own shake and regarded her with a solemn gaze over the cup as he drank. "Want to know what I think?" he asked before returning to his burger.

"No."

He swallowed and ignored her succinct answer. "Okay, I'll tell you. I think you don't like Damien because he's dominant, just like her ex, and in your mind that means controlling. If you want your sister unhappy, keep pushing her away from a man who can give her what she needs."

Ouch. "You're controlling, and I like you," she defended then blanched when she realized what that statement revealed.

Trevor stood, leaned across the small table and cupped the back of her head. "I like you too." He whispered the satisfied purr in her ear and followed with a sharp nip on her lobe. The small sting zeroed straight down between her legs, forcing her to tighten her thighs to contain the surge of damp pleasure. Sitting back down, he popped a fry into his mouth and said while chewing, "There are different relationships within the BDSM lifestyle just as there are between vanilla couples. I have a good friend who enjoys a twenty-four/seven Dom/sub role with his wife. They are very happy and devoted to each other. Sandie, whom you met, only lets Zach get away with controlling their sex lives, and he's more than happy to indulge her. I don't know about your sister, but if I were to guess, I'd say she falls somewhere in between."

Paige hadn't considered that, and thinking back on the short cruise with the other couple, had to admit they'd both appeared happy, just as Penny had. Love for her sister prompted her to profess, "I don't want her hurt."

Trevor nodded, his shaggy hair brushing his neck. "Noted. But, like I said, I can vouch for Damien, and so will Troy. Are you finished?"

She leaned back in the kitchen chair with a contented sigh. "Yes. That hit the spot, several in fact. Thanks."

"You're welcome." He pushed his chair back from the table and his voice took on a commanding edge. "Come here, Paige."

Her heart jumped into her throat and her nipples beaded just from his tone alone. Resisting the urge to run to him, she tried to portray a calmness she didn't feel. "Why?"

"Because talk time is over and I said to. Please don't make me repeat myself."

The polite phrasing didn't fool Paige. Irritated he would think he could come into her home uninvited and pick up ordering her around, she shoved back and jumped to her feet. Hands on hips, she struggled to ignore the inferno raging inside her. "I fulfilled my obligation to you and Troy."

"No, you didn't." The calm denial shocked her speechless long enough for him to explain. "The contract was for eight hours. Including the hour driving time down to Miami and back, you only completed five of those hours. Last chance. Come here."

Her bare feet moved of their own accord, taking her to stand between Trevor's spread legs and leaving her struggling resolve to get over both him and Troy in ashes. He nailed her in place with his piercing gaze and skimmed his palms up the backs of her thighs, lifting the sundress while caressing his way to her silk-clad buttocks. With a tug, the panties fell to her feet and Paige kicked them aside, her pussy swelling, aching for his touch. Later, she would question how he'd turned the tables on her so fast. Now, the craving to give in to her body's demands surpassed even her desire to have her sister back home, and that was a hell of a lot.

Trevor palmed her buttocks, his touch igniting every nerve ending in her lower body as he tightened his hold, stood and lifted her onto the table. "Lean back for a minute," he instructed before resuming his seat and scooting the chair closer.

Falling back on her hands, Paige looked down at him situated between her spread legs, gasping in mortified excitement when he lifted both feet and placed them flat on the edge of the table. "What are you doing?" She trembled under his penetrating gaze and hard hands as he spread her bent knees further apart. With the sundress rucked up to her waist, her entire crotch was exposed, along with the blatant, damp proof of her arousal glistening at the seam of her vagina. By leaving them both clothed except for her panties and shifting his focused gaze to her gaping pussy, he'd reduced her to one body part. How could she not be ready to combust?

His lips quirked with amusement. "Looking at you." Trevor glanced up at her then back down between her legs again. Using just one finger, he traced over her pussy lips. "Touching you."

His face was close enough Paige could feel Trevor's warm breath feather over her labia. Leaning her head back, she closed her eyes and concentrated on the sweeping pleasure of his touch. Much to her frustration, he seemed content to toy with her, caressing her folds, dipping in between just far enough to tease her clit before retreating to spread her copious juices over her bare mound. Since discovering the myriad of nerve endings on her outer flesh, she'd never regretted keeping her pubic hair waxed. His touch on the puffy folds sent sparks shooting straight up her core, her slick vaginal muscles tightening around his finger when he returned with another slow press inside her. He proved stronger than her when he pushed in deeper, found her g-spot and caressed those sensitive tissues before pulling out and leaving her empty and on edge again. She blew out a frustrated breath after the third in and out foray, lifting her hips in a silent plea she knew her eyes reflected.

"Damn it, Trevor... *ahhh!*" The hard pinch to one tender fold halted her complaint, leaving her to shudder from the bite of pain that escalated her aroused state.

"Do you masturbate?" he inquired, lifting his gaze to hers.

Caught off guard by the abrupt question, she stuttered, "That... that's personal."

"So is what I'm doing. Answer me," he ordered with another teasing dip of his finger.

"Yes, doesn't everybody?" she snapped in frustration, wishing she could close her legs and rub the ache of unfulfilled lust pulsating between them.

"I don't know, I'm only interested in learning about you." He removed his hand and trailed damp fingers up and down the inside of her thigh, the light touch setting off tingles all over her body. "Show me."

She stiffened in shock and a surprising flare of additional heated lust. "What? No way..." Paige started to scoot away from him, fearing her response more than his demand, but he stood and clamped his hands on her hips, holding her in place with his tight grip and penetrating stare.

"You know, sugar, I'm fairly easygoing most of the time, but I do have my limits. Keep it up, and you'll get spanked again." His mouth tightened with the threat.

To prove he didn't scare her, Paige smirked and taunted, "You'd have to allow me off the table first."

She blinked twice at the rapid transformation of his taut-jawed look to one of pleased amusement. With a shake of his head and small smile, he warned, "Oh, sugar, you have so much to learn," right before searing the delicate flesh between her legs with a blistering slap.

"*Mothering...*" The blaze of red-hot pain startled her so much she couldn't even come up with one of her stupid phrases to cover her astonished reaction. The instant throbbing of her labia wasted no time seeping deep inside her quivering sheath. A lighter swat landed on top of the first, just hard enough to reignite the sting and entwine pain with pleasure until she couldn't differentiate between the two.

"Now," Trevor said, picking up her right hand and placing it over her burning folds before resuming his seat, "show me how you masturbate." He offered her a boon by explaining, "I want to see what works for you, where you like to be touched the most, where you don't."

"Crap, Trevor," she moaned with a dip of her middle finger between her still tingling, warm labia. "Anywhere is fine."

"Good to know, but I also like watching." To prove it, he gripped her knees and pressed them apart again, spreading her so wide she could feel the stretch of muscles.

The last of her resistance fell away under his penetrating gaze before he shifted his eyes from her face to between her legs. Leaning her head back again, she closed her eyes and concentrated on gaining relief by zeroing in on her clit, stroking over and over. The small bud hardened and swelled under her finger, her breathing increasing as small tremors racked her body and a light sheen of perspiration coated her skin. A deeper push put her in contact with the ultra-sensitive spot Trevor had located without difficulty. Playing around, she coaxed the tender nerve endings lining her sheath alive with pulsating, cream-gushing pleasure.

Lost in the throes of an impending climax, she jerked and her eyes flew open when Trevor joined in, using his thumbs to spread her labia and then rubbing the rough pads over the exposed flesh. With a grin she'd learned not to trust, he dipped his two middle fingers into his remaining shake and then tumbled her headlong toward climax by pushing the two cold digits past the tight resistance of her anus.

"*Trevor*," Paige wailed on a long groan that changed to a high-pitched screech from another stinging pinch on one delicate fold.

"You... what..." She stuttered to a stop, unable to come up with anything suitable as he spread the two fingers reaming her ass, the discomfort minor compared to the sparking heat of that forbidden touch.

"When we're playing, it's Sir, or Master Trevor," he admonished with a taunting grin that proved he enjoyed her struggles.

The word 'playing' reminded Paige he was just toying with her, finishing the time allotted him in that damned contract. With her body's demands now overruling all hesitation, and the chance he'd end this by fucking her, she couldn't stop from going along.

"Sorry, Sir," she returned, her voice dripping with sweet sarcasm. Her vagina clamped around her finger when she started to withdraw and the tiny tremors heralding an orgasm resumed. Eager for his cock, she latched onto her clit and milked the small bundle of nerves until her hips bucked against her hand and fiery pleasure erupted in a consuming wave that obliterated everything else.

Trevor couldn't remember when he'd enjoyed playing with a sub more. Watching Paige climax on her tabletop, her legs spread and affording him a close-up view of her pretty contracting pussy was worth the discomfort of holding back his own raging lust for a little longer. When she calmed and slowly removed her finger, he let go with his thumbs and pulled out of her ass. He soothed her with slow caresses up and down her thighs, feeling her muscles quiver under his palms.

"You are a delight, sugar." Pushing to his feet, he lowered her legs and helped her stand, catching her with a chuckle when she fell against him and clung for a moment. He longed for the time when she would cling to him for other reasons besides support while coming down from a euphoric high. Her hand snuck between them and wandered down, but before she could reach her goal and test his control, he grasped her wrist and held it between their chests. One touch on his cock, even over clothes, and he'd be unable to hold off until he and Troy completed their plans. It took no effort to inject sincere regret into his voice when he told her, "I have to go. Next time."

Paige stiffened and pulled away from him, keeping her face averted until he reached the door. "You just proved my earlier point. You don't want me, just temporary control over me."

Trevor spun about and strode back to where she stood with a stoic expression, her pink panties lying next to her bare feet. "You couldn't be more wrong." Snatching her hand, he gritted his teeth and placed it over his erection. "I want you," he rasped.

Perplexed, her brows dipped down as she gazed up at him. "Then why?"

"Because my brother wants you too, and we come as a package deal." He waited a moment and saw the dawning of understanding on her face when she paled and then reddened. "Exactly. That is not something we jump into with a newbie. You have to know and want what you're getting into before we move forward." He kissed her, a quick, soft brush before striding back toward the door and tossing over his shoulder, "Troy will be in touch about finishing the last ninety minutes of your contract."

Trevor drove away from Paige's house more optimistic about their future and the odds whatever was between them would grow into something worth keeping. He and Troy had talked a long time about how to proceed with her now that she'd shown significant enthusiasm for submission. They'd agreed to push her individually by dividing the remaining time left on the contract, check the waters of compatibility as a couple before introducing her to the possibility of a three-way relationship. The last-minute case Troy picked up had worked in their favor, giving Trevor a good excuse for showing up alone to see how she'd fared after they'd pushed her so hard yesterday. Their initial intent with her first spanking had been to drive home how foolish she'd been to try to pass herself off as submissive at Sanctuary, and to set herself up as bait behind their backs. Her response that night had encouraged Trevor to pursue the matter of how far he could take her, and Troy's unhesitating agreement had signaled he was more open about the feisty redhead's possibilities of being a good match for them. They'd both suspected she'd agreed to honor the contract thinking to use those hours to get them out of her system, never imagining they would end up desiring more from her.

He loved the thrill of catching a new sub off guard and unaware of her submissive streak. Jackson and Julie's wedding was this coming weekend, and if all went well, and Trevor had his way, Paige would accompany him and Troy. Meeting the rest of the gang of seven and their significant others at the marriage of one of their own would be akin to being introduced to family in the Carlsons' book. He could take the good-natured ribbing sure to come their way from the guys—in fact, he was looking forward to it. Troy, on the other hand, might not. Little brother had never taken being wrong well.

STILL SHAKING from her powerful climax and Trevor's revelation, Paige leaned against the door, wondering if she'd ever be able to eat at her kitchen table again without remembering what she'd done on it. *They both want me?* She shook her head in bemusement. That was a first for her, a mind boggling, panty-dampening first she didn't know how to react to. Finding two men attractive was normal; she wouldn't even label lusting after two men at the same time odd for a thirty-one-year-old, sexually active woman. But she couldn't recall a time when two men had reciprocated those fantasies. Given the way Trevor and Troy had kept their distance the past year, she still couldn't wrap her mind around Trevor's departing words.

She needed to be careful not to read too much into those words though. He'd only mentioned her finishing the hours owed them from their auction bid, nothing more. On one hand, she couldn't help but admire their noble restraint from fucking her until she accepted they both wanted her; but on the other, the wait was frustrating the hell out of her. There was no commitment between them, so why would they care if she had fucked Trevor today and Troy whenever he showed up to finish the terms of the contract? It sure as heck wouldn't have bothered her.

More confused and horny than ever, Paige padded into the bathroom and flipped on the shower, vowing to put the shield back up around her heart that had protected her thus far. She needed to neutralize the pang she'd experienced when Trevor turned to leave without fucking her, and fast. After losing her father before she'd ever known him and then her mother before she'd hit her teens, she'd learned not to risk further heartbreak or loss by allowing herself to get close to anyone except her twin. There was no use second-guessing what those two might do next, or fretting over where she'd be when they finished with her. Like she'd always done, she would keep her feelings close and find a way to move on after Troy finished with her.

CHAPTER 13

"*W*hat the fuck are you doing here on a Thursday night?" Detective Evans snarled under his whiskey-laden breath so no one else could hear.

She didn't need this, Paige thought in disgust as she backed away from the irritable cop. After being up all night with the pitiful whining lab she'd agreed to dog sit for two days followed by rising at 5:30 this morning to squeeze an extra house into her cleaning schedule, she had been in no mood to fill in for Mel's nephew tonight. And she certainly didn't intend to sit back and allow a patron with a stick up his ass to browbeat her.

Crossing her arms, she returned Evans' glare without flinching under the cold malice reflected in his red-rimmed eyes. "Tell me something. Do you resent me because I'm the only one besides Mel who refuses to mollycoddle you and your addiction, or because your wife left you and she and I are the same species?"

His jaw tightened as he clenched his hands into fists. "You and that bitch could've been taken from the same mold. She did nothing but nag me about drinking too until I got tired of hearing it."

"Well, feel free to walk away from me anytime you want." She set a coke in front of him. "You've already imbibed your limit. Take it or leave it." Turning her back on him, she strode down the bar to wait on the couple seated at the other end. She could feel the hate emanating off Evans when he returned to his table empty handed.

For a Thursday night, the bar brought in a decent crowd which helped Paige keep her mind off the real reason for her irritable mood. When she didn't hear from Troy on Tuesday, she figured he and Trevor had plotted to give her breathing space before launching the next assault on her senses. She spent the day Wednesday enjoying the anticipation humming through her veins until night had fallen with no word from Troy. The disappointment she'd gone to bed with reminded her what always happened when she let her guard down.

As if her thoughts held the power to conjure him up, Paige sent a beer sliding down the bar just as Troy sauntered inside. Awareness flooded her system, sending her pulse into overdrive as she watched him head straight toward her while combing his fingers through his hair in an absent-minded gesture. Her vision narrowed to his loose-limbed walk, and conversations and music dimmed until the only thing she heard as he slid onto a stool was his voice.

"It's a good thing Penny knew where you were," he stated by way of a greeting. "I'll take a whiskey on the rocks."

Gritting her teeth to fight back her instant response at seeing him again, Paige pasted on her bartender's smile, the one that said be nice to the customers. "Sure thing, Detective." She heard him greet people while she dropped a few ice cubes in a glass and poured the amber liquid over them. He was alone when she returned to set his drink before him, his dark eyes scrutinizing her features with one of those intent gazes that drew tingles down her spine.

"Thank you." He frowned. "You look tired. Everything okay?"

"Yes, and thanks for pointing that out. Anything else I can get you?" Since he'd looked her up at work, she could only assume he wasn't here to see her home to fulfill the time she owed him. Why that bothered her so much, she refused to question or delve into.

"No, thanks. Tell me how you liked the vampire glove. You fell asleep so fast on the way home, I didn't get a chance to ask."

Paige's face heated, and that disconcerted her as much as Troy asking that question here and now. Casting a cautionary look around, she breathed a sigh of relief when she verified no one stood within hearing range. Leaning over the bar toward his smug face, she hissed, "Don't ask me about such things in here," before straightening back up.

His piercing gaze remained steadfast. "You answered Trevor's questions, and no one can hear us, so give. Any lasting effects, scrapes I need to know about?"

"He didn't pester me in public, and you know there aren't, so change the subject. Or better yet, go away." She didn't really want him to leave, but she also didn't care to air what had occurred on that decadent yacht at her work place.

"No, and he will if you stick with us long enough."

What that cryptic comment and the rapid increase of her pulse meant, she didn't dare speculate. Thank goodness he changed the subject without batting an eye.

"How's Penny? I haven't had time to follow up with her this week."

Since he seemed sincere, Paige didn't mind that question. "She's good. Damien treats her well, or so she says."

He sipped his drink before asking, "You don't believe her?"

"I do, but I still don't like how fast he's moved with her." *Crap.* Paige fidgeted when Troy gave her another long, probing stare, this one putting her on edge while curling her toes.

He nodded, stating with confidence, "You envy her ability to move on."

"What? That's absurd," she scoffed, averting her eyes from his. She missed her twin, that's all there was to her unhappiness with her sister's decision to remain with Damien for longer.

"Is it? Be honest, with yourself, if not with me," he insisted.

Paige didn't know what it was about his quiet demands that

compelled her to comply without hesitation, but she found herself doing just that when she admitted she had missed Penny when she'd lived with Jim, but had never resented their separate living spaces or felt put out over the relationship. After Jim had shown his true colors and Penny didn't hesitate to leave him, Paige only recalled being grateful her sister hadn't suffered worse and that she'd washed her hands of the bastard. She didn't want to believe she envied Penny's new relationship, or the contentment her sibling couldn't hide, but knew it was something she needed to consider. Later. When one of the men who had figured prominently in her nighttime fantasies for so long was sitting in front of her, her body insisted she think of other things.

Two customers strolled up to the bar and Paige turned to Troy with relief. "I have customers. Like I said, I'm fine, no lasting effects from your debauchery last Sunday," she drawled, a teasing hint of appreciation for those hours they'd tormented her seeping into her tone.

She turned away, intent on leaving with the last word, but his sharp command halted her without conscious thought. "Stop."

A shudder accompanied her quick compliance, unsettling Paige as much as his presence and leaving her to wonder how she'd ever get over either Troy or his brother. "What now?"

Troy ignored the irritation lacing her voice as he answered in a calm, unperturbed tone. "You're off in less than an hour. I'll walk you out."

"That's not necessary," she insisted.

"Yes, it is. There's still time on your obligation to fulfill."

Reaching into the M&M bag stashed under the counter, Paige tossed a handful of chocolate morsels into her mouth, hoping the sugar burst would distract her from the ripple of pussy-dampening longing rushing through her body. The banked heat in his eyes and underlying suggestion he meant to use up that time when she got off work added heat to the mix, reaffirming she needed to finish with that contract—and the Carlsons—as soon as possible. Her ability to move on, to get over them, not to mention her sanity, depended on it. Without replying to his comment, she strode over to her customers, praying the next thirty minutes flew by fast.

IT WASN'T like Troy to enjoy spending his free time bantering with a woman, trying his best to get under her skin, rile her just to see the sparks in her gray eyes light up or relish the uncertainty crossing her face from her reaction to him. He couldn't say he liked that big brother had been right about their fiery bartender, but wouldn't fight the inevitable any longer. His insistence that whatever this was between the three of them was just sex had lost momentum with each passing day this week and every time he caught himself thinking about Paige non-stop. Her obvious love for her sister, along with her over-protectiveness, reminded him of his close bond with not only his brother, but with each of his friends. There wasn't anything he wouldn't do for any of them, just as Paige had proven she would set aside her own convictions to get justice for Penny.

But he hadn't been doomed until he'd witnessed the signs of submission she possessed without even knowing it. He hadn't been ready to admit that a few days ago, but in this case, the short absence between then and now had worked to open his heart to other possibilities besides sex. Since he intended to fluster her more when he escorted her out, Troy let her finish her shift in peace, and slid off the stool to join a detective he knew well at his table.

By the time he saw her retrieve her purse from under the counter after Mel dimmed the bar lights, shutting down service, Troy debated whether he could go through with his plans he'd run by Trevor without caving and fucking her. Only Mel and his employees parked in the back alley, and tonight it was just the owner and Paige working. Once Mel took off, they should be ensured privacy for a short time. Should being the operative word, he thought with glee. Pushing her boundaries was proving to be his favorite pastime.

~

"GOODNIGHT, MEL." Paige lifted a hand to her boss as he got into his car, Troy's warm tight grip of her other hand keeping her close to his side as he opened the door to her Jeep. She noticed his SUV squeezed into a space in the small back lot also and surmised he'd planned ahead to walk her out.

"See you tomorrow, Paige. I've got you covered for Saturday," Mel called out, shutting his door before she could ask him what he meant. As far as she knew, she wasn't scheduled off this weekend.

"I mentioned I'd like to take you out," Troy said as he pressed up against her.

Only one small light above the back door illuminated the few parking spaces behind The Precinct. The dull orange glow left the two of them shrouded in shadows and the sudden silence following Mel's departure revealed her rapid breathing, proof of her uneasiness over accepting Troy's invitation. Since she couldn't choose which brother she wanted the most, any relationship beyond these few hours would lead to heartbreak. But *holy douchnozzle*, she'd never been so tempted to shuck consequences and risks and go with her libido.

Her temper flared from the position he'd cornered her into. "You could've checked with me first," she bit out. "I don't appreciate you going to my boss before talking to me."

"You will. We'd like you to attend our friend's wedding in Miami and then join us for a short cruise after the reception. You'll like everyone," he assured her.

She lifted one brow in inquiry, goosebumps racing over her skin at the mention of another cruise. "We?" she asked, needing clarification.

Troy's lips curved in one of his rare smiles that warmed her enough to melt in a puddle at his feet. Good thing she could control herself.

"Trevor and I, of course. He told you we both want you, and we don't have a problem with that."

"Do you two tell each other *everything?*" She wondered how many women they had double-teamed and then shoved that thought aside as a road best not traveled.

"Yes." Sliding his hands under her short hair, he cupped her skull and brought her mouth up to his.

Paige cursed her weak resistance then gave in to it. For whatever reason, both Troy and Trevor claimed to want her now. The time she'd spent with them thus far had only whetted her appetite for more and barely dented the lust she'd been harboring for the brothers for close to a year. As long as she remembered this was just a fling, a temporary walk on the wild side of coveted but forbidden fantasies, she could reap the pleasures they offered and move on when it ended, as she'd always been able to do before.

Sinking into the kiss, and against his muscled frame, she savored the taste of him on her tongue, the forceful possession of his mouth, and couldn't help but compare the difference to Trevor's kiss. His brother used a softer, coaxing manner backed by an underlying thread of dominant insistence that got to her every time. Troy didn't mess around, just turned hard and demanding when he was ready to reel her in. Two opposite approaches, yet she responded with equal fervor to both. *I'm doomed, fucking doomed,* was the only coherent thought she could conjure up.

Proving her point, Troy released her and spun her around so fast, her head swam. Then he whispered in her ear, shocking her with his order. "Bend over and brace your hands on the seat, Paige."

The dark seduction wrapped around the command in his voice stripped away all hesitation, making room for an illicit thrill that shook her.

"We're out in the open," she whispered back, scanning the alley even though she already knew they were alone back here. There were lit up windows high in the building opposite the bar, but even if someone peeked out, the car would block their view. But the risk of getting caught, being seen by strangers, remained. Putting need before caution, desire before prudence, she placed her hands palm down on the seat and held her breath in expectation.

"I love your ass." Troy ran his hands under her calf-length skirt, drawing the garment up as he traveled up the backs of her thighs until he reached her panties. He draped the skirt over her back and lowered her panties to mid-thigh, the bare exposure to the sultry night air producing a flutter of awareness in her abdomen. "And I love playing with your ass." He filled his hands with her malleable flesh, kneading the soft muscles until Paige squirmed with the need for more.

"I kind of figured that out already." She gasped when he spread her cheeks and prodded her back orifice with a slick, rubbery bulb. "Here?" she exclaimed in disbelief as he pushed past the tight resistance of her anus. Hundreds of sensations shook her body, shock at her behavior and response the least among them. God help her, she didn't care where they were, or if anyone was watching. He'd already set up a pulsing ache in her sheath that demanded assuaging.

"You're a bright girl. Deep breath..." he pushed until he'd embedded the rounded object, "and release."

The plug didn't feel as big as the one they'd used before, at least not until she heard what sounded like pumping air and the thing inside her expanded. Her breath caught as she stuttered, "You... you could have warned me!" She trembled from the sudden fullness, those new nerve endings they'd introduced her to turning ultrasensitive. "What is that?"

"I like surprising you better. It's an ass pump. You can remove it when you get home. Here, let me take your mind off it."

A resounding smack that threatened her position and composure followed, the burn having its usual effect. Lowering her head,

Paige quit trying to make sense of her responses, and her feelings, and gave herself over to the pleasure. Several more rapid slaps covered her buttocks before he invaded her pussy with a deep, three-fingered thrust that brought her up on her toes. She pushed back against his marauding hand, mewling with frustration when he explored her entire sheath yet avoided putting pressure against her clit, right where she needed it most.

"The plug makes your pussy even tighter, and from how wet you are, I'd say you like it." Troy tugged on her clit, one quick squeeze before pushing deep again. But it was enough to leave her shaking with palpable need, aching for him to fill her as deep and stretch her as wide as the plug in her ass.

Paige wiggled her hips, bore down on his ramming fingers, accepting each jackhammer plunge with a groan of pleasure. She forgot their surroundings, forgot she wasn't submissive, forgot she was a temporary diversion for both him and his brother. Falling to her elbows from the forceful finger-fucking, she pleaded in a breathless voice, "Please, Troy… Sir, I need…"

"That's all I wanted, baby," Troy crooned.

He pulled out of her and then latched onto her clit with two fingers, milking the tender piece of engorged flesh until her climax exploded without the usual slow build-up. She muffled her scream, but feared it still echoed down the alley. Paige wobbled when he helped her rise, her labored breathing sounding harsh in the otherwise quiet, dark night. The slight breeze cooled her perspiration damp skin and caused a delicate shiver to ripple over her exposed flesh.

Not knowing what to say, she turned from his focused gaze and slid behind the wheel. "I have to go." She reached for the door handle, but he placed his hand over hers to stop her.

"Not yet. Wait here a minute." Troy strode to his vehicle, reached inside and withdrew a small pink gift bag. Handing it to her, he said, "A gift from Trevor and me. We'd like you to wear them under your dress Saturday."

"And if I don't?" she couldn't help asking since he hadn't insisted.

"Then you'll have trouble sitting during the ceremony and reception. Drive carefully. Goodnight, Paige."

She didn't open the bag until she got home. Sinking down onto the sofa, she held up the black vibrating panties with a sense of fatalism. *Do they mean to arouse me in public? And why does that idea sound appealing?* No matter what they threw at her, it seemed her body was on board. Just imagining what these would feel like turned her on; picturing herself at a wedding, surrounded by people she didn't know and trying not to react to the soft pulses from the garment terrified her. Surely those two would wait until after the ceremony and reception to torment her, wouldn't they? With them, she never knew, and that meant she'd spend two nights of restless sleep over what they had in store for her before Saturday.

~

"You look amazing," Penny announced when she breezed into Paige's bedroom on Saturday, ten minutes before Troy and Trevor were due to arrive.

"Thanks, sis." Paige eyed her twin in the mirror, her abdomen tightening when she noted Penny's flushed face and sparkling eyes. *Oh, God, could Trevor be right? Am I envious of Penny's ability to move on with her life following not one, but two traumatizing experiences?* "You look good, too, happier than I've seen you in a long time." She turned from eyeing herself in the gray silk sheath she'd chosen to wear to the wedding today to face Penny. "Living with a dominant man really does agree with you, doesn't it?"

"It's more than that, Paige." Penny sat on her bed and leaned back on her hands with a contented sigh. "I like a strict Dom, but also a caring one, and that's where I went wrong with Jim. He didn't care about me as much as he did about controlling me.

Master Damien's been all about learning what I need and giving it to me while pampering me at the same time. God, I love that!"

"I get it. He's a prince among Doms," she returned on a wry note.

Penny regarded her in silence until Paige turned away. She needed to get over her reluctance to accept their relationship if she didn't want to jeopardize the special bond she and Penny shared.

"I wouldn't go that far, but he isn't Jim. If I can remember that, why can't you?"

"You're right, Penny." Paige sank down next to her. "Would you believe I'm jealous?" Admitting that wasn't pleasant, but it helped loosen the tight knot in her stomach.

Bolting upright, Penny stared at her in disbelief. "Jealous? You have *two* of the hottest Doms in the city chasing after you. How can you be jealous of me?"

"Because I'm just a thorn in their side they're trying to pluck out. I saw the way Damien looked at you in the hospital. You're right, he's nothing like that asshat, Jim. He was into you before you went home with him, before he touched you. That says a lot."

"I think you're doing what you always do when someone gets close. You're shutting yourself off, too afraid of what *might* happen down the road to take a chance on letting someone into your life." Penny stood and padded over to Paige's closet to retrieve her black heels and bring them to her. Dropping them at her feet, she pointed to them, sounding a lot like Troy and Trevor when she instructed, "Put those on, they'll showcase your long legs and you'll go from stunning to knockout. Have fun today, and don't think about tomorrow, or the next day, or next week or next month. Just today. Tomorrow, start over and just think about what you want that day." Spinning on her heel, she got to the door before turning back with a cheeky smile. "I saw the package to the vibrating panties. Now I'm the one who's envious. You'll freaking *love* them."

Shaking her head in bemusement, Paige slipped on the fuck-me shoes and stood, the inflatable butt plug shifting inside her a reminder of what might happen after the reception today. She'd only inflated the toy enough for a snug fit. The drive to the church in Miami would take almost forty minutes, and sitting on the plug that long would be enough of a distraction without having it stretching her to the point of discomfort, and arousal. The panties were a perfect fit, which somehow didn't surprise her. Determined to take Penny's advice, she vowed not to fret about where she'd be with the brothers come tomorrow, and go with the flow today.

Who didn't like weddings? she thought as the doorbell pealed and set her heart to racing with expectation.

CHAPTER 14

At least they let me sit in peace during the ceremony. Paige squirmed in her seat at the reception table, her face flushing from the panty vibrations Trevor had just flicked on. As if being seated between both him and Troy during their friends' Jackson and Julie's wedding and now at the reception wasn't distracting enough. At least their group of close friends didn't act surprised to see the brothers sharing a date. Sandie and her husband, Zach, were the only other people she knew at the large table, but the best man's wife, Hope, had greeted her with genuine pleasure. After pointing out her husband seated with the bridal party, Paige wondered how the soft-spoken woman handled the scarred, tough-looking martial arts instructor.

Seeing the dressy choker adorning the doctor's wife, Krista's neck had thrown Paige for a loop for a few seconds, since she knew the jewelry signified a stricter Dom/sub relationship than the brothers had introduced her to, but it hadn't taken long for the couple's friendly mien to set her back at ease. She knew there was a significant amount of her sister's lifestyle Paige remained clueless about, but didn't mind admitting she was now more open to exploring the possibilities than she'd been before Penny's attack. All because of Troy and Trevor.

Paige shifted on the padded seat again and slid Trevor a side-long glare, knowing it would do no good. "Can't this wait?" she whispered, praying the others didn't notice her sudden agitation.

"Nope," he whispered back without an ounce of pity.

Determined to ignore him and Troy, who smirked without looking her way, she leaned over to speak to Hope. "I hear congratulations are in order for you as well. Where did you elope to?"

Hope's blue eyes shone with happiness. "Where else? Vegas. But Miles chose a nice chapel and went out of his way to fill it with flowers. It was a lot of fun."

"We wouldn't know since you neglected to invite us," Sandie groused, sending her friend a disgruntled look. "That wasn't very nice."

"And here we all thought Jackson would be the one to opt for a quiet ceremony away from everyone." Sean, a black-haired psychologist and the last of the Carlsons' friends they'd introduced Paige to, shifted his silver gaze to Paige before explaining, "He much prefers his animals and Julie to people. We consider ourselves lucky Jackson is agreeable to hanging around us."

"I pet-sit in my home, and agree there are times I prefer my four-legged friends to anyone else," Paige returned with a smile. The tall veterinarian looked enamored of his gorgeous wife, and she thought it said something he'd been willing to put on this big splash for their wedding to appease her parents whom, from what Paige had learned, he wasn't fond of.

"Sean just gave me a cuddly Maltese mix from Jackson's rescue, and she's a big comfort when Sean's being a bully."

Alessa and Sean's relationship may be new, but from the look the two shared, the couple might be the next to announce plans to join their friends in wedded bliss. That would leave Troy and Trevor the last among the gang of seven uncommitted. Paige shoved aside the stab of pain at the thought of them moving on without her.

"I'm surrounded by strangers every day and love it," Hope said. "If I'd been isolated on the yacht for four days with just Zach for company, I would've gone bonkers. I still don't know how you stood it, Sandie."

Zach scowled at Hope. "Hey, I resent that."

Sandie just laughed and shook her head. "No, you don't."

The mischievous smile Hope gave her best friend hinted at something Paige didn't know about and a curl of envy over this group's close ties settled in her abdomen. Penny was the only person Paige shared such a bond with, and now she wondered what that said about her. Had her sister been right? Were the shields she'd erected after losing their mother and then Nana keeping her from getting close to anyone besides her twin?

The DJ announced the buffet, veering the conversation toward food. Late afternoon sunlight streamed into the hotel's banquet room through an array of French doors lining the outside wall. Paige's heels clicked on the marble floor as Troy and Trevor escorted her to the food line, the low hum of the panties keeping her on edge, waiting, wondering how far they'd take this in public. So far, the sensations remained a pleasant but distracting hum against her labia. Add in the shifting of the plug against those hypersensitive tissues and there was just enough titillation to keep her in a state of hyperawareness. Much more and she would refuse to allow anyone to hold her accountable for her actions.

"I like your friends," she commented as Troy stabbed a tender piece of rib roast and placed it on the plate she held out.

"So do we. Everyone will head to the yacht in a little while. Except Jackson and Julie, who will take off for their undisclosed honeymoon destination."

"What?" she returned in mock surprise. "We're not all joining in on the honeymoon?"

"She's caught on quick." Dr. Dax Hayes' amused voice came from behind Trevor.

Paige didn't realize she'd spoken aloud and her face warmed, but she didn't let that stop her from turning and smiling at the physician, intending to prove she could hold her own with these people. "It's been sink or swim since these two bought me at an auction. Swimming is much more fun than sinking."

"I'll bet," Dax drawled, his green eyes alight with approval that Paige basked in.

"Don't encourage her, Dax." Trevor yanked on her hair, drawing her scowl. "We have our hands full as it is."

With her plate filled with mouth-watering entrees, Paige opted to ignore them to appease the swift rise of the one hunger she still had control over. The other was a lost cause.

~

"Don't fret, Paige," Sandie said, laughing. "You'll get used to it, and us."

I'm not so sure about that. Paige looked down at her bare breasts and away from the other four women relaxing on lounges alongside hers who appeared unconcerned with their topless state. The day had warmed up enough to change into shorts after the wedding, but as soon as Zach had sailed them out of port, the men wasted no time divesting the women of their shirts before sauntering off the top deck to play a round of poker in the gathering room below. The light, tangy ocean breeze brushed across her skin in a tantalizing caress, her nipples reacting from the exposure without her consent. Even though Troy had turned off the vibrating panties an hour ago, her tender labia still throbbed from the soft pulsations and her pussy remained damp with swollen need.

She struggled to remain focused on the view, but caved and

glanced their way again when curiosity got the better of her. "Do you guys do this often?"

"What? Get naked in front of each other?" Krista's smile reached her light blue eyes. "Not a lot, maybe once a month the guys try to get everyone together. In case you haven't noticed yet, they're a tight-knit group. For them, our gatherings are as much about spending time with their friends as they are to indulge in their kinks."

Hope, who lay next to Paige, reached over and poked her on the shoulder. "Admit it. There's nothing like getting naked outdoors, especially when you have that and our guys as a view." She waved her hand toward the glistening sheen of blue water lapping in a steady rhythm against the hull of the rocking boat.

Alessa sat up and pushed back her long, strawberry-blonde hair. "The ocean's always nice, but I'll take looking at any of those guys without their shirts over it anytime."

Except for Paige, they answered Alessa's lustful sigh with nods and smiles of agreement. Since she'd never been given that privilege, she couldn't concur. Hell, she hadn't even viewed her own guys' chests yet. *Whoa! Back track that.* It wouldn't do to think of them as *her* guys, not even for a day.

"No fair discussing chests I haven't seen," she protested with a light laugh.

"Agreed," Sandie called down from her chaise at the end. "Instead, why don't you tell us what it's like being sandwiched between Troy and Trevor."

Paige wasn't about to admit she didn't know. Everyone had been open and nice, engaging with her as if she were a member of their select group. But she still felt like an outsider. Maybe that sense of not belonging stemmed from the past gatherings they'd reminisced about, or the way the men had looked at their significant others, as if they couldn't pull eyes conveying possessiveness, warmth and lust off them.

"Sorry, girls, I don't kiss and tell," Paige returned, hoping the teasing smile she tossed their way worked.

"It looks like we'll have to talk her into joining us for girls' night," Krista said. "Wine always works to loosen the tongue."

Paige didn't burst their bubble by admitting to her high tolerance for alcohol. It took a lot more than a few glasses of *vino* to get her talking. Deep male voices echoed up the stairwell right before Miles' coal black head emerged topside. With his midnight eyes pinned on Hope, he strode toward her while pulling off his tight tee, the intent etched on his face drawing a shiver down Paige's spine. She could only imagine what that look did to Hope. With barely a ripple of his impressive biceps, he lifted Hope off the lounge and tossed her over his shoulder before smacking her bikini covered bottom.

"Excuse us, ladies." Spinning on his heels, he headed toward the bow and the hot tub and fountain just as Sean stepped onto the deck.

Hope lifted her blonde head, giving them a cheeky wave that matched her smile, and the psych doc didn't hesitate to tug on her long hair. Paige didn't look away from Miles' broad back and Hope's excited face until the sudden return of panty vibrations heralded Troy and Trevor's reappearance topside. Not even Hope's squeal, "It's cold!" and Miles' deep chuckle could distract her enough to keep her pulse from spiking with expectation when the pair followed Sean toward them.

"Krista, Master Dax requires your butt in the playroom. Sandie, Zach's waiting for you below as well." Sean delivered the message with a wink as he held his hand out for Alessa. Krista and Sandie didn't balk at the summons; instead they jumped up and high-tailed it to the stairs with eager steps.

Paige didn't flush when Master Sean pulled Alessa up and bent his head to draw one turgid nipple into his mouth. Instead, she found herself turned on by the open display, Alessa's gasp of pleasure from his bite and the caring reflected in her Dom's pewter eyes. She didn't want to know what that said about her, or her chances of moving on without regrets after today. Luckily, Troy and Trevor didn't give her time to think about that potential problem.

Trevor whipped off his polo shirt before drawing her up and against his thick chest, the sprinkling of curly hair tickling her sensitive tips. "We can't have you looking like someone's left you out, sugar." He dipped his head and took her mouth with coaxing pressure, just the opposite of Troy's more demanding lips.

Paige basked in the warm pleasure of skin against skin and her heated response to the panties as Trevor's tongue explored her mouth with leisurely strokes. He kissed her much like the way he took command of her body, using a soft yet still dominant approach to get his way. She liked that about him.

Hands went to her waist as Troy moved closer behind her. A groan rumbled from deep in her throat when her shorts dropped to her bare feet and he left her standing in the black panties. His bare chest pressed against her back, sandwiching her between them for the first time. Now she could tell her new friends about the heady experience they'd asked about earlier.

Trevor released her all too soon, but she didn't complain when he spun her about and Troy took over, his mouth covering hers with harder, more forceful possession that elicited a thrill as arousing as the one she experienced under Trevor's control. She relished his more demanding approach in reeling her in as much as she craved the underlying cajoling behind Trevor's dominance.

"Tell me, Paige," Trevor whispered in her ear as the panty vibrations increased to more powerful than before. "How much did you inflate the butt plug?"

"Not… much, *freaking dipshiot!*" she ended on a gasped shudder when the pulsations against her crotch drove her headlong toward an orgasm without warning. A click and they stopped as Troy lifted his head and reached up to cup her breasts while his devious brother found the small attached pump inside her panties and expanded the torture device.

"Not yet, Paige." Troy slid his hand into her panties and found her slick folds. "Nice and wet, just as we'd thought, Trev." Bucking her hips against his hand, she cursed aloud when he pinched her labia then pulled back with a one-word admonishment. "Behave."

"What if I don't want to?" Paige returned in frustration. If this was all she'd get from these two, she wanted a lot, and wanted it now. "It's your fault for turning on these panties during the reception." They each moved back a step and Trevor stepped around her enough for her eyes to follow both men's hands sliding to their waists. *Oh shit.* Why hadn't she noticed the floggers the two were sporting when they'd come back on deck?

"Still determined to give us a hard time, aren't you?" Trevor didn't sound like he minded. Hooking his foot behind one of the front legs of the chaise, he slid it over to the side, right under the cuffed chain he pulled out from the eave of the center cover.

"I can only hope," Paige quipped, aiming her gaze toward their crotches. Anything to take her mind off what they planned to do with those wicked looking leather strands as Troy led her to the lounge.

"Ha, ha." Flicking off the panties, he stripped them down her legs and instructed, "Kneel in the center."

Goosebumps raced across her skin as Paige complied, despite the internal heat their eyes on her always created. She shivered as they each stood on one side of her and raised her hands to the cuffs, securing her arms above her head before they unclipped the floggers from their waists. The two moved with such coordinated sync, she once again wondered how many had come before her, this time pondering why none had stuck.

Trevor trailed the soft strands over her breasts. "What are you thinking, sugar?"

"I'm wondering what the *addlepated bejeesus* you're going to do with those things. What do you think?"

Troy joined in, tickling her buttocks by trailing the leather strips across her globes in a light caress that forced her to suck in a breath against the riotous sensations they conjured up. She didn't know whether to sigh with relief or insist on more.

They shared one of those long, poignant looks that irritated the heck out of her and put her even more on edge as Troy said, "No you weren't." Drawing his arm back, he swatted her ass, leaving behind strips of red-hot, stinging pleasure. "Care to try again?"

Paige narrowed her eyes at him. Her body may submit to their every whim, but she'd be damned if they'd pull her private thoughts from her without giving an ounce in return. "No. Some things are… personal, not meant for sharing without getting something in return." *There, take that,* she mused with smug satisfaction when her comment appeared to startle them both.

"*Mmm,*" Trevor hummed, trailing the flogger down her waist and between her spread thighs. Her hips jerked from the unexpected brush of braided leather over such tender skin, her cream increasing as her need rose. "It seems we have our work cut out for us, Troy."

"It'll be tough, but I guess someone has to take her in hand," he replied with mock dissatisfaction.

Before she could articulate a comeback, they snapped the leather strands against her flesh, front and back, up and down her body, keeping up a steady light pace that delivered an array of dizzying sensations spiraling through her. One slash stung the fleshy underside of her breast while another warmed her thighs. Pain lanced her buttocks and tingles of warmth spread over her abdomen with the next, followed by a sharp, heated reprisal on the delicate flesh of her labia. Her pussy swelled, the tight fullness in her anus emphasizing the emptiness of her vagina. Slamming her eyes shut, she rocked her body toward and away from the lashes, never knowing where the next would land, or how hard.

Through the roaring in her head, she barely made out the soft, murmured words from each man, catching only slight phrases such as 'good girl' or 'the perfect response'. Each one, voiced in those deep, rumbling tones, drew her deeper under their spell until she despaired of ever getting free. By the time she heard the floggers fall to the deck and felt their hands soothing the throbbing lines crisscrossing her body, her need burned more painful than any of the strikes they'd delivered.

"Please," she whispered, refusing to open her eyes and face them as she thrust her pelvis into the hand cupped between her legs.

"Since you asked so nicely," Trevor whispered in her ear. She heard zippers being lowered, the rustle of clothing being removed and felt the shift of the lounge when one knelt in front and one behind her. "Open your eyes, Paige."

She complied, looking into the dark depths of Trevor's gaze before she caught sight of his hand wrapped around his jutting cock. With his other hand, he reached up to cup one breast, his eyes remaining on hers, a small smile playing at the corners of his mouth as Troy latched onto her hips from behind.

"Ask and you shall receive." Troy filled her pussy with one smooth thrust, working his sheathed cock past the tightness caused by the butt plug without pausing. Paige gasped, pushing her butt back against his groin, relishing the invasion, the fullness, the dichotomy of riotous sensations whipping through her body.

She couldn't look away from Trevor as his brother fucked her with ruthless intent, driving her to the brink of orgasm with only a few deep plunging, jackhammer invasions. Troy's tight grip on her hips both frustrated and thrilled her when she struggled to join in on the age-old dance of grinding pelvises, but didn't keep her from tightening around his pistoning cock.

"That's it," he rasped as he scraped his teeth down her arched neck. "Squeeze me, Paige, nice and tight. *Fuck*. Just like that," he groaned when she clamped her muscles around him again.

Trevor released her breast, coasted down to her pussy and rooted out her clit to press the inflamed bud against his brother's driving cock. The tight, abrasive rubs tumbled her headlong over the precipice and into blissful release, her exalted, shaken cry keening in the open air.

Blinking her eyes open, Paige's vision blurred as Troy pulled from her still quivering vagina, rasping over swollen tissues on his retreat and drawing even more full body shudders. She glanced down in time to see Trevor's condom-covered cock pressing between her puffy pussy lips, couldn't look away when they folded around his cockhead as he entered her, hugging his shaft in a loving clutch. A whimper slid past her trembling lips with his slow penetration, filling her where she'd just welcomed his brother. God, that was such a freaking turn-on!

"Lean against me," Troy insisted, pulling her butt onto his hair-roughened thighs. His hands moved to the inside of her thighs and pushed them out until she straddled his thick quads, making more room for Trevor to settle between them.

"Hang on, sugar, time for round two." Trevor thrust with a guttural moan then set up a steady rhythm meant to drive her insane with resuming lust. His hands clutched her thighs, holding tight as he drove into her over and over, discharging shock waves of unbelievable pleasure so intense they darkened her vision and fogged her brain.

Paige writhed between them, her body undulating with the rough fucking, her arms jerking in the restraints and her breathing growing labored as she rode out the storm of pleasure they had unleashed upon her. The bunched muscles of their legs contracted against her softer thighs and buttocks; their heavy breathing warmed her neck; and their busy hands seemed to be everywhere at once, plucking on her nipples, caressing up and down her quaking limbs and quivering stomach.

By the time she came down from the euphoric high and could think straight again, Troy was lowering her into the swirling soothing water of the hot tub, the two of them stepping in and settling at her sides in a comforting show of caring she tried—and failed—not to let affect her heart.

CHAPTER 15

"What's up, bro?" Trevor entered Troy's office Monday morning and took a seat in front of his cluttered desk. They hadn't spoken since returning to their condos after dropping Paige off at her place Saturday night. For Trevor, fucking Paige after enjoying the way she fit in with everyone at Jackson's wedding had sealed his intention to pursue whatever this was between them. Now, the only question left was if his brother felt the same.

Troy waved his hand over the files scattered in front of him. "I've been going over the timeline of our guy's assaults, and the clubs he's hit up. I've been checking deeper into the newest members of each club, have gotten a few eyewitness sightings of all of them after each assault, which means the odds of this asshole returning to the scene of his crime is high. But none of the victims have gone back to the clubs since their attack."

"You can't blame them there. What are you thinking?" Trevor could always tell when Troy was mulling over a possible scenario.

"I'm wondering what he'd do if he returned to a club and discovered his victim hadn't been cowed enough to stay away. I spoke with Damien, and each new male who joined Sanctuary in the last year has been a regular member since, none of them skipping more than a weekend or two without making an appearance."

Trevor pondered what he was saying then narrowed his eyes in speculation. "You're thinking of sending Penny back to Sanctuary as bait. Damien will never go for it, and neither will Paige."

"But Penny might," Troy returned, nonplussed.

Penny wasn't as independent or feisty as Paige, but Trevor had seen the need for closure reflected in her haunted eyes. "Even if she was, Damien still wouldn't allow it." Taking a chance at pushing his brother, he asked bluntly, "Would you, if it was Paige?"

Troy's gut tightened, as if someone had landed a sucker punch. Trevor never did play fair. "Honestly, I don't know. You want to pursue this with her, don't you?"

"Yes, I've always been up front about that." He crossed his arms and leaned back. "She's proven she's submissive, Troy."

"There's more involved here than that." He pointed a finger at Trevor and then a thumb at himself. "You, me and her for a few ménage scenes is all good and well, but you're talking a relationship, one that could lead to something we'll find difficult to walk away from. What then? Polygamy is against the law, the laws you and I swore to uphold and defend."

Trevor tightened his jaw. "Some things, or in this case, some people, are worth crossing lines for. But you're jumping ahead. There's nothing that says we can't enjoy a three-person relationship for as long as we want, or live with whomever we want."

Troy's sigh revealed the frustration they were both feeling. "We'd be opening ourselves up for more heartache. Losing Mom and Dad was hard enough."

Standing, Trevor clasped his hands behind him and paced the compact office, his gaze landing on the last family photo taken of him and Troy with their parents before the accident. It sat next to a framed picture of him, his brother and Ray when the two of them had been in college. Turning to face Troy again, who sat watching him with a calm expression and fire in his eyes, he fisted his hands on his hips and stated, "You were willing to take the risk with Ray."

Troy swore long and hard. There were times he wished he and Trevor didn't know each other so well. "You really want to give a relationship a try?"

"Are you ready to end it with her?" Trevor countered, the simple inquiry hitting Troy in the chest.

"No." Some things, he guessed, were inevitable. Like attractive redheads with cute sayings and a temper who possessed the ability to knock down over twenty years' worth of defenses by just coming apart in their arms. "But we run it by Ray first. I won't keep secrets from him."

"Understood and agreed. Are you honestly considering approaching Penny and Damien about your idea?"

"Yes. Let's go visit Ray this evening, and on our way back, we can stop at Damien's place. I don't want to put off either visit."

Trevor grinned. "Are you more afraid of Ray or Damien?"

"I'm not saying, but you'd be wise to tread carefully with both," he warned.

"You always want to trample on my fun."

Trevor tried to keep from showing Troy how thrilled he was over his brother's willingness to pursue a relationship with Paige. She'd drawn his attention and interest from the moment he'd seen her standing behind Mel's bar and heard her utter one of those ridiculous sayings of hers. His sexual preferences had kept him from pursuing her as she hadn't given off any submissive vibes. The instant, fist-clenching rage that had ripped through him when he'd heard Detective Evans putting her down had been the eye-opening catalyst that prodded him to consider there might be something more he shouldn't pass up. She'd sealed the deal for him when she didn't shy away from the way they'd caged her between them on the dance floor of Sanctuary that first night.

Now that Troy was on board with moving forward, Trevor

looked forward to exploring the possibilities of where the three of them could take their relationship. As he pulled in front of Ray's duplex in the golf course retirement complex their guardian had been enjoying for the past five years, he prayed Ray would give them his blessing. They both cared too much for the man who had refused to give up on two orphaned, out-of-control boys to risk putting a wedge between them, even if it meant ending whatever was between them and Paige before they could see how far it could go.

"I bet he's already out back at the grill," Troy commented as he opened his door.

Trevor took an appreciative sniff as they strolled up the walk. "I can smell barbeque from here. He spent all that time teaching us how to cook and now he refuses to let us pitch in when we come for dinner."

"Maybe he's afraid his lessons didn't stick as much as whatever dish we might bring would." Dry humor laced Troy's voice and the quick look he slanted Trevor's way.

"There is that." Opening the front door, he called out, "Ray!"

"Out back!"

"I was right." Troy led the way through the living room, the display of every award and trophy the two of them had earned in high school and college giving Trevor the usual warm rush. Their guardian had insisted they bring everything of sentimental value from their parents' home to his, making room for each item without complaint. Decades' worth of family photos, both dated and recent, hung on the walls, a tribute to the family they used to have and to the one formed from tragedy. Entering the kitchen, they waved through the screened door.

Tall and on the lean side, Ray Huggins remained in robust shape twenty-three years after he'd scraped them off the streets. Trevor had just turned fifteen, with Troy only a year younger, but the forty-three-year-old detective had never appeared put out over taking them into his bachelor home.

"Grab a beer and join me out here," Ray called out when he spotted them. "It's too nice to eat inside."

"Here." Trevor tossed a bottled brew from the refrigerator to Troy and then followed him out the slider onto the covered patio. The small yard backed onto the ninth hole. Retiring on a golf course was something Ray had planned for years, and they'd both been happy for him when he'd made the move.

"So," Ray said as he placed a plate with grilled fish and potatoes in front of each of them at the table. "What's new with you two?" Grabbing his plate, he settled on a chair and eyed them over a forkful of sea trout he'd caught himself on his last fishing trip to the canal.

Trevor flicked Troy a look, as if to say, 'what a great opening,' but he refused to take the bait. "I have several homicides sitting on my desk, waiting for the perps to walk in and confess. In other words, nothing new." He bit into the juicy fish, shifting his eyes away from Roy's sharply assessing, green-eyed stare.

Ray grunted. "Murder never takes a holiday, does it? You put any of the bastards away this week?" he asked Trevor.

"Two. Easy cases. I don't know why their attorneys bothered, considering what we had on them. Sick fucks, both of them."

"I gotta say, I don't miss dealing with the scum, but I relished the adrenaline rush of taking them down." Ray changed the subject to talking about his recent fishing trip with a group of other retired cops, only one of several he got in every year. He had them chuckling along with him until they were halfway through their second beers. Cocking his head, he asked with his usual, point-blank bluntness, "What's on your minds, boys?" Lifting his brew, he pointed the top toward each of them. "And don't tell me nothing. I can read you two like a book."

Troy looked at Trevor with one raised brow, remaining mute. *I think I'll let big brother break the ice on this one*, he decided, taking the coward's way out.

"Thanks a lot, bro," Trevor mumbled in an aside whisper that earned him a glare from Ray. "Right now, it's too new to say it's 'something,'" he finger-quoted the word, "but we've been seeing this woman..." He stopped there, the small smirk lifting Ray's mouth catching him off guard.

"We've?" Ray asked, his mild tone revealing nothing.

"Yes, we're both... seeing her. And she's been okay with it, so far," Troy added.

Ray paused for dramatic effect before he spoke in a slow drawl, "You two do remember I made it my business to learn everything about you years ago, don't you? What makes you think I stopped when you turned eighteen?"

"What the hell's that supposed to mean?" Troy cast Trevor an uneasy glance but he shrugged, not understanding either what Ray meant.

"I believe your interest in... let's call it *alternative* sex began when you were in college. One more thing you have in common with the gang you've stayed friends with since that summer camp. Did I ever tell you how proud I am of those relationships? All good men, and worthy of your loyalty and friendship for this long."

Troy continued to scowl, but Trevor's half grin mimicked Ray's. "You don't have a problem with it?"

Leaning back in his chair, Ray pushed his plate aside and regarded them both with a steady, solemn gaze. "Your parents raised you boys right long before I came along. I trust you to treat a woman with the respect she deserves. Other than that, what the three of you agree upon regarding your relationship is your business. Can I ask why you are telling me about this one girl when you've never mentioned anyone before?"

Trevor thought about it, but all he could come up with was, "It feels right this time." He shrugged with a rueful grin. "That's all I've got. How about you, Troy?"

"He browbeat me into giving this a try," Troy returned, deadpan.

"Your brother has never succeeded at browbeating you into anything, but not for lack of trying. Look, guys. I say if you think she's worth risking backlash with your peers at work, then go for it. If not, don't jeopardize your careers for a fling." Ray picked up his plate and stood. "Just so you know, any woman you bring into my home will be welcome. Now, come do the dishes before you leave."

"That went well," Trevor stated as he rose.

Troy nodded. "Now all we have to do is pursue Paige without risking our jobs."

"So, WHAT DO YOU THINK?" Nervous butterflies danced in Paige's abdomen as she took a long drink of her double chocolate shake, waiting for Penny's response to her business plans. She'd eaten the whipped cream off the top on her way over to Damien's house. Just a few weeks ago, discontent had her pondering moving on from her housecleaning business, finding something new that would get her out of the ennui plaguing her. After adding three more houses, all in wealthy neighborhoods, to her waiting list this past weekend, she's decided last night to take her sister up on her offer to help her establish a full-fledged business, starting with hiring a few employees. Before that, she'd spent the afternoon at the emergency animal clinic with Teacup, the small poodle pup she was dog-sitting. The poor thing couldn't stop barfing all over the house, which had sent Paige into a full-blown panic. For such a little dog, the amount of bile that had come up had been alarming and ended up with a four-hour ordeal of IV fluids and medications to settle her stomach.

But Paige's work issues hadn't been enough to keep her mind off two certain brothers and the emotions they'd pulled from her on Saturday. After Troy and Trevor had insisted on coming inside and making sure she would be all right alone, she'd spent a restless night wondering where that left her. Then each had called her Sunday, chatted for several minutes and then said goodbye without a hint about where, if anywhere, the three of them would go from here. She'd woken tired and out of sorts this morning and spent the day laboring at two of her largest homes while daydreaming over the mind-boggling euphoria of being fucked by two men she couldn't seem to get out of her system. By the time she arrived home and turned Teacup back over to her owner, she'd needed her sister in the worst way, and not just for her future business plans.

"I think it's a great idea, but you already know that." Penny picked up her own shake while pushing the spreadsheet of her to-do list across the table to Paige. "I agree you should start small, maybe hire a crew of three who can work together and get four houses a day done. Train them as fast as possible to avoid losing anyone on your waiting list. You especially don't want to risk missing out on contracting with these larger homes. Those you can charge a substantial amount more for—and get it. You'll still need to do several places a week, at least for a few months until you're big enough to where you can work office hours out of the house."

"That's my goal, for now, anyway." Paige waved an airy hand and tried to cover her edginess with a light quip. "You know me. I don't stick with anything long-term."

"Are you still talking your job record or record with guys?" Leaning back in her chair, she poked Paige under the table with her foot. "Give. What happened this weekend? And be quick; Damien's due home any time."

Paige frowned. "I thought he was at work."

"He is, but school let out for a half day so he's had all afternoon to get caught up on papers. Now, quit stalling. I want details."

She still couldn't picture her sister's hard-edged Dom as a high school science teacher, but she supposed the man had to work at something. "I fucked them, Penny, one right after the other," Paige blurted, a shiver going through her just from saying it.

Leaning forward with wide eyes, Penny came close to drooling. "Please tell me you loved it. I'll never forgive you if you say otherwise."

The envious awe shining in her eyes thrilled Paige. Whoever

thought she would be one kinky scene up on her sister? Unable to lie, she admitted the truth. "Oh, yeah, I loved it. That's the problem."

"Why would that be a problem? Unless... oh, they said nothing about getting together again, did they? Men," Penny scoffed in derision.

Paige gulped her shake again before saying, "Not a word, which has never bothered me before. Why now, and why them?"

Her evil twin laughed, jumped up and skipped around the table to bend down and hug her. "It's about time!" she squealed before rapping her open hand against the back of Paige's head. "You've not only fallen for one guy, but two. You hussy!"

"I have not!" Her denial came too fast, and even she could hear the lie behind it.

"I see you don't deny being a hussy," Penny tossed over her shoulder as she strode to a trash bin and tossed her empty cup. "I don't know what your hang up is, sis. They're great guys."

"Guys, plural, neither of whom has shown an interest in me other than for sex, and they've gotten that, so now what?"

They both heard cars drive up followed by doors slamming. Penny peeked out of the window over the sink. "Looks like you'll get the chance to ask them yourself in about one minute. Damien's home as well."

Paige hated the sharp claws of jealousy digging into her stomach from the excitement and pleasure reflected in Penny's tone. And when Damien strolled in, his eyes zeroing in on Penny first thing, the pain got sharper. She knew it wasn't envy for her sister's good fortune in finding someone special she felt, but the fact she wanted the same thing for herself. With two men. *God, I'm so fucked, and not in the good way*, she lamented in silence, her pulse spiking when she heard Trevor and Troy's deep voices. Then they entered the house and her heart executed a slow roll in her chest and her body sang with pleasure just from seeing them again. *So fucking fucked.*

"It looks like we get to kill two birds with one visit," Troy drawled, his dark gaze moving over Paige's face before shifting to Damien. "Like I said outside, we have something we want to run by Penny. Odds are, neither you nor Paige will like it."

"Then we'd better all sit down." Damien snatched Penny's hand and led the way into his living room. Sinking down onto a leather recliner, he settled her on his lap, waving a hand toward the matching leather sofa the chair faced. "Have a seat and tell me what brings you here."

Paige allowed Trevor to pull her onto the sofa between him and Troy and tried not to read anything into his tight grip or the way Troy laid a hand on her thigh in a gesture that smacked of possessiveness.

"You have chocolate on your mouth." Trevor swiped a finger over the corner of her lips, his eyes gleaming.

"I just finished a shake." With his mouth so close to hers, Paige found it difficult to think straight.

"Then I'll save the candy bar I brought you for later."

"I'm waiting." Damien's voice cracked with impatience, cutting off their byplay. Paige noticed Penny seemed content to let her new Master push them along.

"I spent a good part of the day tracking the newest members' attendance at the clubs where there have been assaults," Troy stated. "Every one of them has made a return visit since the date of the attack at that club, except for one new member of Sanctuary. Several ceased attending altogether after their second and third visits, at least to the best of each owner's knowledge. Does the name Mitchell Garrison mean anything to you, Penny?"

She shook her head. "Nope, never heard of him."

"If I remember correctly, I approved his membership a few weeks ago and met with him his first night. My assistant manager has been running things since Penny came home with me. Was Dalton sure this guy hasn't been back? It's a big place," Damien questioned with a tight jaw.

"It is," Trevor put in. "As are the other clubs. Which is what makes this theory a long shot, but still worth checking into."

"I can't find anything on Garrison, or several others. That by itself means nothing. I'm aware of that, but damn it, I have to start somewhere." Troy pinned his stormy gaze on Penny. "None of the victims have returned to the clubs. I'm wondering what our perpetrator would do if he saw one of his casualties not cowed by his assault."

A pregnant paused followed Troy's statement before Damien retorted in anger, "Absolutely not."

"No way," Paige added with an emphatic shake of her head.

"Look, I understand, but—"

Damien cut Troy off with a slice of his hand. "No."

Penny laid her hand over his and looked at him with quiet determination. "I want to do this. I *need* to do this."

Paige could see Damien's struggle reflected on his face and knew he would give this to Penny. If she wanted to continue protecting her sister, they left her with no alternative but to come clean about the notes she'd received after being at Sanctuary.

"No, Penny, there's no need. They'd have better luck using me since he's now fixated on me."

Both Trevor and Troy leapt to their feet and glared down at her. "Explain," Troy bit out, his hands fisted on his hips while Trevor crossed his thick arms.

Paige tried getting to her feet, uncomfortable looking up at their glowering faces, but Trevor palmed her shoulder, keeping her in place as he growled, "Talk."

Narrowing her eyes, she returned their angry looks. "Don't browbeat me. It won't work. He left a note on my car after each time I was at the club. They're in my purse."

Damien rose as Troy stomped over to the small entry table where she'd set her purse. The two of them swore as they read the notes and then turned accusing eyes on her. "He threatened you." Troy held up the second note, the one telling her to back off before she ended up worse than her sister. "And you didn't think to tell us?"

Her frustration getting the better of her, Paige shook off Trevor's hand and surged to her feet. "No, I didn't. He didn't leave a clue to his identity and since I wasn't allowed back inside Sanctuary following the auction, there was no point. I haven't heard from him since."

"My God, Paige. He knows where you live," Penny breathed, fear for her sister leaving her visibly shaken.

"I know how to take care of myself."

The three men swore again before Trevor said, "Either Garrison isn't our guy, or Dalton's missed him the two times Paige was there."

"All the more reason why I should go back," Paige insisted. Troy scraped his hand through his hair, his frustrated look telling her he wanted to agree. "You know I'm right."

"Only if I'm there too," Penny stated in a hard tone.

"We'll all be there." Damien included everyone in his statement. "And neither of you will be more than a few feet from one of us."

Trevor hauled Paige against him and tugged her head back with a grip of her short hair. "You won't scene with anybody but us, got it?" He didn't give her a chance to reply, just took possession of her mouth in a way that left her breathless and giddy.

When Troy pressed against her back, pinning her between them and whispered in her ear, "You're ours," she shuddered with sweet pleasure.

It can't be that easy, can it? She'd always been skeptical of anything that appeared too easy, and when that was applied to the new, unorthodox relationship she shared with the brothers, her distrust rose a notch. But she wasn't about to let that keep her from tasting the sugar-coated treat they'd just tempted her with. If it ended up being bad for her, at least she'd have the sweet high to remember them by.

"Okay."

CHAPTER 16

"*N*o one will approach us if they don't lighten up," Penny sighed. With a smile, she accepted the glass of wine Sanctuary's bartender, Master Connor, set in front of her. "Thank you, Sir."

Paige hesitated, hating to address a stranger with such formality. It had taken her weeks to give Troy and Trevor that respect, and they still needed to either remind her or prod her into doing so. But they'd drilled the rules of the club into her and she knew she had to suck it up for the sake of playing her part in catching their culprit. "Thank you, Sir." She smiled and picked up her beer. She tried not to look over to where Troy and Trevor sat at the other end of the bar next to Damien. "I hear you, Penny. Last night was a complete waste of time, and I can't afford to ask for another weekend off from The Precinct." Mel had grudgingly agreed to give her both Friday and Saturday nights off, but warned he might have to call her in if his nephew couldn't fill in for the entire shift.

The club hummed with sexual activity, just as she remembered from her two previous visits. Last night, both she and Penny had turned away several offers to scene, but they'd accepted a few requests to dance. The dim lighting and loud music couldn't disguise the scenes already in play, and Paige found herself hard-pressed to control the urge to join in with her guys. *I have to quit thinking of them as mine*, she chided with a mental shake of her head. How could she allow herself to think of them as hers after just a few short days of their constant presence in her life?

Penny's look turned sly, as if she'd read Paige's mind. "You haven't said much about Troy and Trevor insisting on staying at the house with you this past week. I've got to tell you, sis, from the possessive way those two are eyeing you, there's no denying they're crazy about you. What's it been like, sharing your bed with both men?"

"Crowded," she returned dryly. Her twin always looked on the brighter side of things. Unlike Paige, who would rather dwell on the negatives than risk getting hurt.

"Crowded doesn't sound bad. Damien refuses to switch to a king-size bed because he likes keeping me close."

"Talk about possessive. You do realize neither of us has been in these relationships long enough to even consider shacking up together, yet here we are."

Penny shrugged and sipped her wine, her gaze shifting to Damien and then back to Paige. "What can I say? When it's right, it's right. Why fight it? He makes me happy and gives me what I need. If you can say the same about Troy and Trevor, then don't let the pain of losing Mom and Nana keep you from caring again. You never know what tomorrow will bring."

Paige knew Penny was right, and even with the obstacles a three-way relationship presented, she couldn't deny how much she'd enjoyed sparring with the brothers in the evenings, or the sex that followed. They'd yet to take her in tandem, but each time they inserted the inflatable butt plug, they'd increased the pressure, prepping her for their dual takeover. Waking sandwiched between the two after she'd slipped into sleep with her pulse still racing and her body humming was just as pleasant an experience, one she could get used to real fast.

"First things first." She nodded to the guy approaching them, his eyes on Penny.

"I'm Master Jase. Are you here with a Dom?" he asked Penny.

"No, Sir."

"Then, let's dance."

Paige could hear Penny's reluctance to deny Master Damien in her voice, but she took Jase's hand with ease and a smile. Damien watched the pair with hawk eyes as they maneuvered through the crowd to the dance floor before he slid off his stool and took up a position leaning against the wall closest to the throng of gyrating bodies. The tension in her shoulders eased when Troy and Trevor approached her and she realized they would not leave her sitting there alone for long.

Troy bent down and whispered in her ear, "It would look suspicious if you didn't accept a Dom's offer two nights in a row. Come with us now."

She didn't hesitate to take his hand or follow Trevor over to a chain station. If the perpetrator did show, they had all agreed he wouldn't make a move on either of them inside the club. By getting out on the dance floor and taking part in a scene, she and Penny would draw more attention than sitting at the bar, which was what they wanted. It didn't keep Paige from casting a quick glance across the room to reassure herself Penny was all right before she allowed the guys to pull her tube top off and lift her wrists to the dangling cuffs.

Will I ever get used to the thrill of this, of them? She'd been asking herself that question all week, and as they stripped her multi-colored, calf-length skirt and panties down her body, she tumbled into instant, heated overdrive, doubting she ever would.

"I love the look of you." Trevor coasted his hands down her chest, over her breasts and around her waist to cup her buttocks. "Have I mentioned that?"

"I don't think so." His hard swat covered her right cheek and drew a startled cry along with her scowl. "You... what was that for?"

"For not tacking on Sir, as we have repeatedly instructed." The gleam in Trevor's eyes revealed his enjoyment of delivering those reprimands and squeezing the offended buttock.

"I think she does it on purpose, just to get punished."

Troy smacked her left cheek, the warm throb he'd produced having its usual effect. Her pussy filled with liquid heat, ready and needy for more, and her nipples puckered, drawing their attention, and their mouths. It hadn't taken her long to crave the dual suctions, the simultaneous tugs and nips followed by soothing tongue swipes as much as an addict longed for his next mind-numbing hit. How she would ever return to one lover didn't bear thinking about. The surrounding sounds dimmed with the stroke of their hands over her body, the cupping of her buttocks and squeezing of her thighs, all without letting up on their tortuous attention to her nipples.

"So fucking responsive," Trevor murmured above her damp, throbbing tip before he latched on to the nub again.

"Just like always," Troy agreed before nibbling the fleshy under-side, his teeth sure to leave love bites on her pale flesh.

"Less talk and more action would be nice here, guys," she blew out with a frustrated breath.

A sharp smack landed between her legs, covering her denuded labia and sending stinging pleasure straight up her core. "Damn, *addlepated dipshitiot*!" she exclaimed, her hips jutting forward in a silent plea for a soothing caress.

"She has been a good girl this week." Trevor winked as he palmed her pulsing flesh.

"I haven't forgiven her for keeping those notes from us."

She knew Troy would hold a grudge over that infraction longer than his brother so she gave him her sweetest smile. "Please, *Sir*, if I promise never to do something like that again?"

Troy snorted, his disbelief as obvious as Trevor's. "We know better, baby, but because I'm as eager to move this along as you, I'll let it go. For now."

Paige took what she could get, and when they invaded her pussy and anus with deep, lubed finger plunges, her hips danced a tune to their coordinated thrusts. They sent her pulse on a marathon of calisthenics with the strumming of sensitive nerve endings in both orifices. She thrust her hips forward and back, welcoming their marauding hands and well-aimed dips inside her. Her mind soon blurred with the overflow of sensation, so much so she didn't notice when they rolled on condoms or the sudden shifting of their bodies until Trevor stood in front of her with Troy taking up a position behind.

"Wrap your legs around me, sugar, and hold on tight. We're ready to show you what it means for both of us to take you."

Trevor's face swam before her widening eyes as he slipped between her swollen folds. Gripping her buttocks, he lifted her, and she didn't hesitate to wrap around his waist, locking her ankles together at his lower back. "I... oh, God, I don't know if I can," she gasped on a strangled breath when he spread her cheeks and Troy's cockhead prodded her back hole.

"If we weren't sure you were ready, we wouldn't even try. Trust us and take a deep breath." Troy breached her tight sphincter as Trevor retreated just far enough only his smooth crown remained nestled inside her quivering pussy. Arching her head back, she closed her eyes and rode out the tandem rhythm they set up that robbed her of breath and sanity.

One in, one out, over and over, a tight coil gripping her stomach as sensation built with each strategic thrust. She tried to writhe between them, to build up enough friction to relieve the ache they kept ignoring. Curses fell from her mouth until Trevor stopped them with his lips and she went crazy from the escalating pleasure.

"Now?" Troy growled from behind her.

"Fuck yes, now." Trevor rammed inside her sheath with Troy's withdrawal from her ass and then they began fucking her in earnest, maintaining their steady rhythm of one in, one out as their breathing grew labored and their cocks jerked inside her.

Paige cried out, riding waves of pleasure so intense they darkened her vision and fogged her brain. She tightened her pussy and ass around their pistoning cocks, clutching at their erections in a desperate attempt to hold them inside her until the ecstasy dialed back enough for her to regain her senses. Their deep-throated groans heralded their releases, and the feel of them ejaculating set off another climax that left her shaken.

"Come on, sugar," Trevor panted as he withdrew. "Let's get you down."

Their slow withdrawals left her feeling bereft, but as she slid her legs down and lowered her arms, the sixth sense twins possessed kicked in and turned her blood to ice in her veins. Sudden dread infused her, the kind that made her skin crawl and her stomach drop. Whipping her head toward the dance floor, she croaked one word past the fear clogging her throat. "Penny."

ONE MINUTE, Penny was catching her breath before the next number started, wishing it was Master Damien in front of her looking pleased, and the next a hard arm snaked around her waist from behind, the even harder voice snarling in her ear sending a shockwave of terror through her.

"Agree with me or I'll cut you right here."

Penny froze, unable to breathe when the sharp point of a knife pressed against her lower back. The past few weeks flashed before her eyes; the pleasure she'd reaped from submitting to Damien that she'd begun to believe she would never experience again; the comfort of knowing someone cared enough to give her what she needed; that sense of safety she'd only found with him. *How could I have believed he would let me go without repercussions?* she bemoaned, recognizing the voice whispering in her ear. *Damien won't let him take me.* She had to believe that and repeated that line twice while her ex, Jim Bates, told Master Jace, "Thank you for keeping my sub company until I could get here."

She pleaded with her eyes for Master Jace not to leave, but he didn't know her well enough to decipher the panic slithering under her skin. With a throng of people keeping Damien from getting a close-up look at her, she couldn't rely on him to come forward until Jim tried to usher her outside.

"My pleasure. I didn't know you were waiting for someone, Penny." The censure in Jace's voice didn't hurt her as much as the prick that broke her skin, the sharp pain enough, she knew, to draw a bead of blood.

"She likes to push my buttons. I'll take her in hand for that discrepancy." Jim shifted in front of her, keeping his arm around her waist and the handle of the small knife hidden in his palm as he held her tightly against him.

His nearness caused nausea to churn in her gut, but Penny refused to look away from his disguised face, his features distorted enough she wouldn't have recognized him in the dim lighting, at least not right away. He'd dyed his brown hair black, wore brown contacts to alter his green eyes and had done some creative makeup around his nose and chin. But there was no mistaking the cruel twist to his lips or the coldness in those eyes. Her mind whirling, she thought back over the last year, recalling when Troy mentioned the date of the first attack. Guilt stabbed at her chest as she put two and two together.

"It was you. *You* hurt those women, and me," she accused in a rush of blind disbelief. "How did you manage it, living in South Carolina?"

Jim tried to sway with her to the slow song but she refused to step in tune with him, holding herself rigid despite his scowl. "It was easy enough once they gave me my own office and left me answerable to no one. You know most investigative work can be done through computer research, but not all. It was easy to take off for a few days here and there on the pretext of hunting down leads. But I have no intention of discussing this here, or now. Come with me, sweetheart. We have a lot of catching up to do, starting with your nerve in returning here. Apparently, I didn't hurt you bad enough to keep you from whoring yourself again."

Anger coiled like a snake hissing, ready to let loose with a strike, replacing her fear as she let Jim maneuver her off the dance floor and toward the exit. Once he'd ushered her out from the mass of gyrating bodies, she caught Damien's eye, and all it took was one look at her face to have him straightening with an expression that scared even her. And then all hell broke loose.

Damien kept his pace slow and measured as he approached them, but Troy and Trevor beat him to the rescue when they came up behind them, freeing her from Jim's tight hold by catching him by surprise. Penny stumbled when his arm fell away followed by Jim's sharp cry of pain. She pivoted and saw Troy holding Jim's arm twisted behind his back, the cop's gaze zeroing in on her.

"Penny? Is he…"

"Yes, he's the one. He's also my ex, Jim Bates." She shook from the inside out as she stared at the man she'd wasted a year of her life on before drawing her arm back and slapping his face with as much force as she could muster.

Damien grabbed her arm before she could swing again and didn't hesitate to deliver a double-fisted punch that took Jim to his knees despite Troy's hold on his arm. Paige sidled around Trevor, adding to Jim's woes by snapping, "You fucking asshattery twat-waddle!" before sending a well-aimed knee into his crotch as Troy hauled him up.

Trevor crossed his arms, a small smile kicking up the corners of his mouth, his eyes hard as he stared at Jim and murmured, "That's our girl."

"It looks like you and I get to leave here and go have a nice chat." Troy cuffed Jim, ignoring his blustering threats of reporting police brutality as he ushered him toward the exit. "You guys need to follow me so I can get Penny's statement," he tossed out in passing.

Penny grinned when Trevor snatched Paige and kissed her before he asked Damien, "Would you mind taking Paige home, then driving Penny to the precinct so I can accompany Troy? I plan to prosecute and want to watch the interrogation from the start."

Damien nodded, his arm going around Penny and pulling her close. "We'll be along shortly. I need to get someone to close for me." Penny had never appreciated his tight hold as much and leaned against him while her heartbeat took its time returning to a normal rhythm.

"Damn, that felt good." Paige smiled when Trevor released her to catch up with Troy. "Are you all right?" she asked Penny, looking her over carefully.

"I am now, but maybe you can check my back where he…" Penny gasped when Damien whipped up her top with a curse.

"You're bleeding. Come on. I've got a first-aid kit in my office."

Paige followed them down a short hall and into Damien's office, still shaking from the scare Penny had given her. Thank God the guys had taken one look at her face and moved fast. Jim never heard them come up behind him, and when Troy noticed the knife point, he hadn't hesitated to act. Now, looking at the beaded blood drops on her sister's back, the fear and anger came swooping back. She sucked in a deep breath, reining in both emotions, neither of which would help Penny now.

"Are you sure you're okay?" she asked again, needing the reassurance as she watched Damien dab an antibiotic ointment on the cut.

"Yes, just a little shaky," Penny replied, sinking onto the small sofa across from Damien's desk. "I still can't believe it. It was him, Paige. Jim hurt those girls, and it's tearing me up inside with guilt. I should have—"

"Stop right there," Damien snapped, towering over her and holding her face up to meet the displeasure snapping in his eyes. "He's a sick fuck who took his anger out on helpless women, that's all there was to it. If it hadn't been your break-up, it would've been something else that set him off, or, he would've done a lot worse to you. Not another word."

Penny clammed up, her eyes softening with relief. For the first time, Paige didn't feel uneasy or put out about their relationship. Damien truly cared about her sister, and in light of everything else, she now felt nothing but happiness for her. She still couldn't reconcile with Troy and Trevor's willingness to give a relationship a try, but she'd just witnessed another reminder life was too short to pass up a chance to explore what might be.

Her phone beeped, distracting her from her thoughts, and she pulled it from her purse to read a text from Mel. After replying, she sent a message to the guys then said, "If you don't need me, Mel's in a bind and asked me to come in. I'll catch a cab to the bar. Troy and Trevor can pick me up when they're done at the station."

"You go on, sis. There's nothing for you to do now, but thank you, for everything."

"Hey, that's what sisters are for." Paige narrowed her eyes at Damien. "You take care of her."

"Go, before I turn you over my knees myself," Damien retaliated, his cool tone belying the grin tugging at his lips.

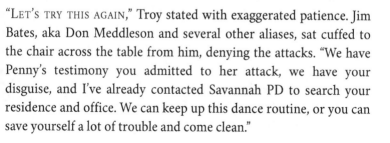

"LET'S TRY THIS AGAIN," Troy stated with exaggerated patience. Jim Bates, aka Don Meddleson and several other aliases, sat cuffed to the chair across the table from him, denying the attacks. "We have Penny's testimony you admitted to her attack, we have your disguise, and I've already contacted Savannah PD to search your residence and office. We can keep up this dance routine, or you can save yourself a lot of trouble and come clean."

"Fuck you. I want a lawyer. No stupid cunt is going to take me down," he sneered.

"No, but a smart woman will. I'll be adding the threats you left for Paige to the charges. I imagine once our handwriting expert matches the writing on those notes you wrote, that'll just be icing on our cake."

Jim frowned in confusion. "What the hell are you talking about? I haven't been near that bitch, let alone threatened her."

Troy's gaze jerked to the two-way mirror, and he wished he could read Trevor's impression. As a DA, he was an expert at seeing through lies. Bates' confusion appeared genuine to him, which had him shifting in his seat with unease. Pulling the two notes from his folder, he slid them across the table. "Are you denying you wrote these and left them on Paige Wilcox's windshield?"

"That's right, asshole, I am." Jim shoved the bagged notes back over to Troy. "I wanted nothing to do with Penny's sister when we were together, and I sure as hell didn't change my mind after we split. Want a sample of my handwriting now? I don't need a lawyer to give you that."

Both Troy and Trevor had received Paige's text about going to the bar to work a few hours. He knew she was safe now, even more so surrounded by cops, so why couldn't he shake the cold knot of fear cramping his abdomen? Pushing back from the table, he grabbed the case folder, saying, "Wait here. Someone will escort you to make your call and then to your cell." Ignoring Jim's foul rebuttal, he sped out of the interrogation room where Trevor was waiting for him with a concerned look.

"Something's not adding up, I feel it too. Let's go."

～

"Take it up with Mel when he gets back, Detective." Paige turned away from Evans' angry, inebriated glower. He had already reached the belligerent, drunk stage when she'd arrived at The Precinct.

She'd done her best to ignore him after serving him a drink that Mel stated would be the last for the night before he'd left to run his nephew home. God, she hoped her boss got back here soon. She wasn't in the mood to put up with this shit.

Evans leaned over the bar and tried to grab her arm, but this time she was too fast for him. "You fucking bitch, who do you think you are to dictate to me?" He slammed his glass on the bar top. "I said pour me another." Several heads turned their way, but, as usual, none of the cops stepped up to interfere. That pissed Paige off as much as Evans' attitude.

"No." She waved her hand, as if shooing away a pesky gnat. "Go back to your table and quit harassing me." Detectives Calhoun and Marshall signaled her from their table, and she took that opportunity to leave Evans blustering alone at the bar. Drawing two beers, she carried them over with a strained smile. "Here you go, guys."

"Thanks, kid." Calhoun cast a resigned look toward Evans who had turned his belligerent, loud rant on his partner. "The commander ordered him into counseling. Let's hope it helps."

Paige thought the cop's attitude had deteriorated enough to require tougher consequences than talk, but knew when to keep her mouth shut. These guys stuck together, no matter what. Troy and Trevor were the only ones she'd ever known to speak up against Mike Evans' behavior.

"Is your sister back on her feet?" Marshall asked, changing the subject, she was sure, on purpose.

"Yes, thanks for asking. And, as of an hour ago, she helped catch the guy who assaulted her and several others."

"That's the best news I've heard all day. Carlson's got to be relieved to put that case to bed." Calhoun raised his glass in a silent toast to success.

I'd like them to put me to bed, she thought with a sigh of longing for the night to end. Paige saw Mel come back in and step behind the bar. "Later, guys," she told the pair before returning to the bar and telling her boss, "Now you're here, I need to haul a load out to the recycle bin."

"Okay. I'll announce last call. Thanks for filling in. Any problems?" Mel sent a pointed glance toward Evans where he had resumed his seat with his partner.

"Nothing I couldn't handle. Be right back."

CHAPTER 17

*P*aige hefted the bag of empty bottles and slipped out the side door Mel had just come in from. The short hall opened out back where the two large trash bins stood off to the side. Lifting one lid, she heaved the empties in, but before she could close it, a hard hand landed on her shoulder and spun her around. She barely had time to blink before a beefy fist came flying toward her face and pain blossomed across her cheek, the punch sending her reeling back against the metal container. Stars filled her vision, shocked surprise and excruciating pain robbing her of a few precious seconds before anger overrode everything else when she recognized the voice cursing a blue streak at her. Stepping to the side, she kicked out and caught Evans behind the knees before he could follow through with another punch.

He stumbled but didn't go down, rounding on her instead with a feral glint in his red-rimmed eyes. "You dare?" he hissed, reaching for her again. "You stupid cunt. You should've heeded my warnings. I'll make you pay for that."

She skipped back again, wondering what he was rambling about and then enlightenment dawned. "*You* left those notes on my car?" she squeaked in surprise.

"I told you you were stupid. Of course I did. Everyone knew about your sister's attack, and with a few clicks on the computer, I learned your address. You've been a fucking thorn in my side long enough."

He lurched toward her, this time grabbing a handful of her skirt as she tried sidestepping him again. With a hard yank, the material ripped, but she still fell toward him while he reached with his other hand toward his holster. Paige cried out and tried to execute another kick aimed at his hand when she spotted Troy and Trevor rushing out the back door. Relief settled her panic but didn't calm her anger.

"Stay out of this, fuckers!" Evans glared at the intruders, as if daring them to intervene. "I'm arresting her sorry ass for assaulting an officer."

That ridiculous statement along with her throbbing face forced a gasped, stuttering response from Paige. "You freaking *douchnozzle moronic imbecile!*" Before she could follow through with another kick, Troy and Trevor dashed forward, barreling into the other cop before he could draw his weapon. They took him down and then hauled him up, pinning him against the dumpster as people filed out of the bar with Mel leading the way.

Taking one look at her face, her boss shouted, "That's it! You're banned from my place, Evans." Striding over to Paige, he stood next to her, crossed his arms and glared at his long-time customers, daring them to argue.

Touched, she laid a shaking hand on his arm, her eyes widening in stunned surprise when Trevor stood at her other side and resumed the same pose and glower. After snapping on cuffs, Troy left Evans standing there and moved to join her and mimic their stances, their show of support in front of their peers making her eyes swim.

Aaron Devri, Evans' partner, stepped forward, holding out a placating hand. "Come on, guys, let's go back inside and I'll spot a round for everyone. Mike's just under a lot of pressure right now. Mike, apologize to Paige..."

"Forget it, Devri," Troy snapped, his turbulent eyes shifting to Paige's swelling face then back to Evans. "You're not getting away with assaulting a woman on my watch." He looked back at the rest of his fellow cops. "Some lines are worth crossing to right a wrong. Evans is done even if it means I end up turning in my resignation."

"And I'll be right with him. Take a stance and do it now."

Paige had never heard Trevor speak in such a cold, controlled tone, never felt his body quake with such suppressed rage. The warmth filling her chest from their support spread throughout her body, dissipating the icy fear Evans' assault and threats had generated. When both Marshall and Calhoun stepped forward in a show of support, the tears blurring her vision fell. One by one, the rest of the men and women she'd befriended in the past year nodded their approval and then turned to go back inside, leaving Evans alone to face his partner and Troy.

"Get these God damned cuffs off me," he demanded of Aaron with the belligerence of someone who didn't know when he was beaten.

With a lingering glance of remorse at Paige, Aaron shook his head. "Sorry, Mike. I'm done standing by you." Without another word, he spun on his heel and followed the others back inside.

"Get him out of here," Mel ordered before giving Paige's shoulder a light squeeze. "Go home and put something on your face and then get some rest."

"I'll call a cab for us, sugar. Troy, meet us at her place when you're done?" Trevor flicked Evans a scathing glance.

"Yeah. This won't take long. Let's go." Disgust laced Troy's voice, but his eyes conveyed sadness for the downfall of a once good cop.

As they walked around to the front parking lot, Paige tossed Evans a bone, wanting to take the pressure off her guys after their public show of support and caring. "If you agree to rehab and counseling, I won't file charges."

"Like hell." Trevor glared at her, pulling her to a halt as they reached Troy's vehicle. "I'm not letting him get away with this." He ran his knuckles over her sore cheek.

Evans showed no remorse for his actions, or acceptance of her generous offer. "Screw that. These charges will never stick, Carlson. I've got fifteen years on you. That'll work in my favor, not yours," he sneered as Troy opened the back door.

"Time will tell, won't it?" Slamming the door, he turned to Paige, cupped her face and drew her up against him to meet his descending mouth. After brushing her cheek with his lips, he settled over her lips in the softest, gentlest kiss he'd ever given her. "Like I said earlier, you're ours. And *no one* touches you like that."

"That's right." Trevor wrapped an arm around her shoulders. "Now, let's go home. It's been a hell of a night."

Paige couldn't agree more.

~

SIX MONTHS LATER

"And you promise this is just a short get together, right?" Paige finished the last of the candy bar Trevor handed her before they'd left home just as Troy pulled into the Gold Star Marina lot.

"For the last time, yes, tonight we're only going out of port far enough we won't disturb anyone else at the marina," Troy growled, his tone impatient, the glance he slid her way indulgent. "Jackson promised the dog to you and he won't renege on it. It's his goal to adopt animals out, not keep them. Hence, the big adoption fundraiser tomorrow."

"I know, I know, but I'm still glad we plan to spend the night at his place. I'll feel better when she's with me." She'd wanted a dog of her own for years, but there was always something keeping her from making that commitment. She'd asked Jackson about getting a dog from his rescue, and when a young lab mix needed a hind leg amputated following a run in with a car, he'd offered her first dibs. Incense at the cruelty of the dog being hit and left to die, she'd jumped at the chance to bring her home as soon as she recovered from surgery, and since the guys had just finished installing a dog door at her house, everything was set.

"She will not be in bed with us," Troy stated as he cut the engine.

"I second that." Trevor grabbed her hand and slid out of the SUV.

"Only if she's scared, or upset." With a teasing grin, Paige snatched Troy's hand and swung both their arms as they strolled up the pier. "I can always sleep in Penny's room on those occasions since she's not planning on returning home."

"Like hell." Troy shook his head as she'd known both he and Trevor would.

Even though they both still owned their condos, they'd been spending most nights at her place, crowding her in her bed. And she loved it—and them—even though none of them had uttered the words aloud. Waking sandwiched between them was something she never tired of, or the creative ways they could come up with to torment her. She shivered just thinking about it and her pussy dampened as they assisted her onto the yacht. Lights shone in welcome from the gathering room; the soft, pulsating music emanating from the closed door matched the rhythm of her heartbeat; the slow rocking of the large vessel felt familiar now after enjoying several excursions on it over the summer months. The trip to the small private island near Bimini had been her favorite. They didn't fuck her together often, instead preferring one at a time or one taking advantage of her delight in giving fellatio while the other used her pussy or ass, but getting double fucked in the ocean rivaled anything else to date.

"Then you may have to give a little at first. I refuse to let Coco fret. She's been through enough trauma already," she insisted. It wouldn't do to let either man think he could run roughshod over her wishes. Unless it came to sex. Then, she would gladly reap the rewards of giving them free rein over her.

Zach lifted his hand from inside the helm, Sean seated next to him. "You're the last on board," he called out. "I'll get us underway. The others are in the gathering room, like you asked."

Trevor nodded. "Thanks. How was the honeymoon, Sean?"

"We had a great time. Alessa's decided we should move to the UK just for the cooler weather and so we can live in a quaint cottage."

"You told her no, didn't you?" Troy asked, frowning.

"She wasn't serious, but yes. No worries. Florida is home for both of us."

Sean and Alessa's return from their trip last week had prompted this party the night before Jackson's big annual fundraiser. Their wedding had been a lovely event, and Paige couldn't recall seeing Alessa so elated. All the gang of seven's wives had embraced her with open arms and offered friendly advice when she'd needed it. They'd even welcomed Penny into their close-knit group. Her sister had enjoyed the two evenings they'd spent hanging out with the girls, but still preferred her new Master to socializing with others. Now that Jim was serving time for three counts of assault and one of attempted murder for his attack on Penny, her twin was free to bask in Damien's growing devotion to her. Since Paige now enjoyed being the center of such focused, caring attention herself, she couldn't begrudge Penny an ounce of her newfound happiness.

"Why do you want everyone in here?" she asked as Trevor held the door to the enclosed recreation room open. The brothers exchanged one of those secretive looks again, which pinged her inner radar. They were up to something.

"Our friends are interested in hearing about Jim's sentence. They've also asked about Evans, and now we can tell them he's passed the department's mandatory rehab stay and his counselor has signed off for him to retire with his full pension. From what Devri has said, Mike has come to terms with his divorce, and with his responsibility for bringing it about. That's a bitter pill to swallow after thirty years, but still no excuse for his behavior. I say good riddance." Troy refused to cut the fellow cop any slack. Trevor handled his continued displeasure with the man by remaining silent about him.

Their whispered conversations and sidelong glances this past week had drawn her suspicions, and even with that explanation, she doubted that was all that was going on. Since she always ended up enjoying their surprises, she didn't question them further. Sandie and Alessa waved at her from across the room where they stood at the tucked away corner bar. The big yacht slid smoothly away from the wharf as they padded over to the curved sofa to join Krista, Hope and Julie, sitting with their guys. Stars shone from the ink-black sky through the arched porthole windows, winking as they glided out into open water. Paige kicked off her sandals when they reached the seating and shoved them aside, enjoying the feel of the thick plush carpet under her bare feet.

"Is Coco in your house tonight?" she asked Jackson, needing reassurance the cute, chocolate lab she'd only seen a short video of was waiting for her. She didn't notice the way Trevor rolled his eyes as he sat on a wide leather chair facing the sofa and pulled her onto his lap.

Troy shook his head, perching on the arm and swinging one leg in a relaxed, casual pose. "Tell her you haven't promised the mutt to someone else so she'll quit harping about it, would you? She's driving us nuts."

"It's your fault for making me wait until tomorrow to pick her up. I wanted to get her last weekend," Paige argued.

"It's too long a drive to make two weekends in a row." Troy yanked on her hair, hard. "Now hush about it."

Jackson chuckled. "She's fine, Paige. And yes, she's in the house keeping Betty company and likely making a mess on my wood floors."

"She's so sweet, Paige. Feel free to bring her with you whenever you come visit. She and Betty get along great." Julie smiled.

"She's not a small horse like the beast you gave Krista, is she?" Dax's long-suffering sigh didn't match the twinkle in his green eyes as he glanced down at Krista perched on his lap.

"At least you've managed to keep your dog out of the bed." Miles' scowl at Hope would have worried Paige if she hadn't come to know the hard-edged Dom and seen first-hand how he turned to putty in his wife's hands. Hope ignored his disgruntled remark, her soft lips curving in a smile that shone in her blue eyes when she looked at her scarred husband.

"I love Max. He's a sweetie. But Jackson assured me Coco wouldn't get much bigger." Paige leaned against Trevor's wide chest and tried not to squirm when he reached around to pull on her nipples as Troy drew his hand up her thigh and slipped under her skirt. She was braless under the plain white camisole top, and the instant pucker of her nipples was noticeable pressing against the thin material. She'd gotten used to this small group, and being naked around them, so she relaxed and basked in the pleasure of one man's touch and the other man's embrace while the conversation picked up without her.

No one noticed when the yacht slowed to an idling bob until Sean and Zach joined them. By then, Miles had Hope strung up between the center poles and Dax was settling Krista in the meshed fucking swing. Julie sat on her heels between Jackson's spread knees, her head tilted back so her long, black hair brushed against the top of her bare buttocks. Both Sean and Zach's appreciative gazes ran over the women before landing on Paige, as if they'd planned their dual appraisal of her nakedness. She didn't understand their nods to Trevor and Troy; they'd seen her naked plenty of times. Then Trevor reached down to spread her thighs over his legs and Troy knelt between them, his eyes traveling from her slick, gaping pussy to her face before he dipped his head to take a slow lick up her seam.

"Tell me, Paige," Trevor whispered in her ear as he plucked at her distended nipples. "Do you like us living with you?"

"Yes," she gasped as Troy suckled her clit, just enough to evoke a contraction and leave her aching for more when he moved back. "You... you know I do."

"And do you like having both of us in your bed every night?" Troy's words blew in a warm breath over her swollen labia.

"Of course. Why?" She shook with need, but a small part of her wondered, and worried, about the sudden questioning.

Ignoring her inquiry, Troy dipped his head again, this time stabbing inside her with his tongue as he inserted two lubed fingers into her rectum. Paige quaked with longing, the heat encompassing her entire crotch spreading throughout her entire body and eliciting the first spasms of an impending orgasm. *Will I ever get used to the pleasure of their dual assault?* Arousal turned to frustration when Troy pulled back again, but as soon as his hands went to his waist to free his cock and Trevor shifted beneath her to do the same, she forgave them for making her wait.

Paige took quick notice of the way everyone in the room paused what they were doing, all eyes turned on her and the brothers. It was one thing to play openly with other couples close by also engaging in a scene, and quite another to be the sole focus of everyone's attention. Troy and Trevor snatched her mind off that discomfort by exchanging one of those secretive looks again. Before she could demand an answer, Troy rose over her, drawing her legs over his shoulders as he pushed through her wet folds the same time as Trevor prodded her anus with the smooth head of his cock. Shock waves rippled throughout her system as they pronounced together, "I love you, Paige. Marry us."

"What?" she gasped, looking in stunned disbelief from Troy looming above her to Trevor, who leaned his head sideways to nuzzle her neck. "How... how can I do that?"

"Legally, you'll only marry one of us, but we're asking you to bind yourself to both of us here," Trevor placed his palm over her heart, "where it matters most. Answer us, Paige."

Never in a million years could she have pictured herself in such a position six months ago when she'd been lamenting over the disinterest of both Carlson brothers. Now, with them handing her everything she desired on a gold platter, happiness danced a jig around her heart, leaving nothing to think about. "Yes, yes, yes... I love you both too," she chanted, the sweeping euphoria of their dual penetration fogging her mind against the round of applause and congratulatory calls resonating around the room.

The entire gang of seven had finally settled down, each with the one person who could erase the traumas of their childhoods and complete them, giving them the future they never knew they'd been searching for.

The End

BJ WANE

I live in the Midwest with my husband and our two dogs, a Poodle/Pyrenees mix and an Irish Water Spaniel. I love dogs, spending time with my daughter, babysitting her two dogs, reading and working puzzles. We have traveled extensively throughout the states, Canada and just once overseas, but I much prefer being a homebody. I worked for a while writing articles for a local magazine but soon found my interest in writing for myself peaking. My first book was strictly spanking erotica, but I slowly evolved to writing erotic romance with an emphasis on spanking. I love hearing from readers and can be reached here: bjwane@cox.net.

Recent accolades include: 5 star, Top Pick review from The Romance Reviews for *Blindsided*, 5 star review from Long & Short Reviews for Hannah & The Dom Next Door, which was also voted Erotic Romance of the Month on LASR, and my most recent title, Her Master At Last, took two spots on top 100 lists in BDSM erotica and Romantic erotica in less than a week!

Visit her Facebook page
https://www.facebook.com/bj.wane
Visit her blog here
bjwane.blogspot.com

Don't miss these exciting titles by BJ Wane and Blushing Books!

Single Titles
Claiming Mia

Cowboy Doms Series
Submitting to the Rancher, Book 1

Virginia Bluebloods Series
Blindsided, Book 1
Bind Me To You, Book 2
Surrender To Me, Book 3
Blackmailed, Book 4
Bound By Two, Book 5
Determined to Master: Complete Series

Murder On Magnolia Island:
The Complete Trilogy
Logan - Book 1
Hunter - Book 2
Ryder - Book 3

Miami Masters
Bound and Saved - Book One
Master Me, Please - Book Two
Mastering Her Fear - Book Three
Bound to Submit - Book Four
His to Master and Own - Book Five
Theirs to Master - Book Six

Masters of the Castle
Witness Protection Program
(Controlling Carlie)

Connect with BJ Wane
bjwane.blogspot.com

CPSIA information can be obtained
at www.ICGtesting.com
Printed in the USA
LVHW022308090919
630430LV00021B/1471

9 781612 589015